SEASO[N]

Jon Cleary, an A[ustralian author] read throughout t[he world, has written] many novels including such famous [titles] as *The Sundowners* and *The High Commissioner*.

Born in 1917, Jon Cleary left school at fifteen to become a commercial artist and film cartoonist – even a laundryman and bushworker. Then his first novel won second prize in Australia's biggest literary contest and launched him on his successful writing career.

Seven of his books have been filmed, and his novel *Peter's Pence* was awarded the American Edgar Allan Poe Prize as the best crime novel of 1974.

Jon Cleary's most recent novels have been *The Phoenix Tree*, *The City of Fading Light*, *Dragons at the Party*, *Now and Then, Amen*, *Babylon South* and *Murder Song*. He lives in Sydney and travels the world researching his novels with his wife Joy.

Available in Fontana by the same author

The Sundowners
The Beaufort Sisters
The Phoenix Tree
High Road to China
The High Commissioner
The City of Fading Light
Dragons at the Party
Helga's Web
Ransom
Now and Then, Amen
Babylon South

JON CLEARY

Season of Doubt

FONTANA/Collins

To Richard Ollard

First published by William Collins Sons & Co. Ltd 1968
First issued by Fontana Paperbacks 1970
Reissued October 1990

Copyright © Sundowner Productions Pty Ltd 1968

Printed and bound in Great Britain by
William Collins Sons & Co. Ltd, Glasgow

CONDITIONS OF SALE

This book is sold subject to the condition
that it shall not, by way of trade or otherwise,
be lent, re-sold, hired out or otherwise circulated
without the publisher's prior consent in any form of
binding or cover other than that in which it is
published and without a similar condition
including this condition being imposed
on the subsequent purchaser

CHAPTER 1

"You could help us kill Nasser."

I shook my head, trying not to show any reaction. "That would hardly come under the heading of American aid."

Fahad's smile was like the wink of a wall-eyed man: it said nothing but what you read into it. "But what better aid could you give us, Mr. Tancred? Especially now, when he is such a thorn under your saddle. I have heard that you Americans have helped other countries get rid of their leaders. We know there are some in Egypt who would be glad to see him go. You would be doing them—and us— a favour." Again the smile, almost like an involuntary tic of his lips: "And yourselves, too."

I refused the bait. Kim Roosevelt in Iran and Jack Peurifoy in Guatemala had done their jobs, but they were safe now: Roosevelt retired and Peurifoy dead. It was those of us still in the Foreign Service who were taunted with the embarrassing questions. I looked out the window at the grey-green deadpan sea. Far out there was a rent in the overcast sky and a pillar of sunlight leaned threateningly over a ship as it steamed slowly in towards Beirut. I tried to remember what ships were due in to-day, but couldn't. I had never had the sort of mind that could remember routine details when a really big problem crowded in. That was why I always made sure I had a good secretary.

I looked back at Fahad, wondering what sort of secretaries they had down in the mountains of the Yemen. We had been sitting here now for half an hour and so far Fahad had not got to the point of his visit; he had spent a year at Oxford and another year at Harvard, but neither university had been able to cure him of the Arab addiction to circumlocution. I'm a Yale man myself, but I think even we would have failed. He had just made a very pointed suggestion, but I knew that was only part of the circumlocution: he knew as well as I did what my answer would be.

"My official title here is First Secretary. But you know

I'm the chief of the Economic Section—otherwise you wouldn't have made your appointment with me, but with someone else. I guess—and it is just surmise, nothing else —" God Almighty, I thought, I'm talking like *them* now, an Arab from South Carolina. "I guess there *are* First Secretaries of embassies, not necessarily American embassies, who get themselves involved in dirty deals. But not Economic Secretaries. If you want to get rid of President Nasser, you've come to the wrong office."

He smiled. "Which office should I have gone to?"

Bluntly I said, 'What do you really want?'

He smiled again, this time more frankly. He was not offended by my blunt question; that was part of the bargaining and bargaining was another Arab enjoyment. He rubbed a finger along his long nose and sat back in his chair. He was not a handsome man and the contradiction in his clothes didn't help him. He was Brooks Brothers and J. Press as far as the neck: cordovan shoes, gaberdine suit, button-down shirt, striped tie; but on his head he wore a white turban wound round a gold-embroidered cylindrical hat. This had been happening for the last twenty or thirty years with the younger Arabs; they came west, found Savile Row or Madison Avenue and all at once wanted to throw away their own comfortable, colourful robes for what passes as plumage with us Western males. Some of them went all the way, even buying a Lock, Cavanagh or Stetson hat. Fahad hadn't gone that far. He was a *sayyid*, one of the Yemeni aristocrats, descended in direct line from the Prophet himself, and his embroidered hat was his badge of rank. He could not let anyone forget that, even me, an Unbeliever.

"We want planes, Mr. Tancred. As many as you can give us, but at least fifty. And some light artillery, the sort you are using in Vietnam. We think it should be ideal for use in our mountains."

"*Sayyid* Fahad Aziz, I have to admire your bravado in coming in here. We don't even recognise the Imam any longer—"

"That was a mistake, Mr. Tancred, as you will come to see in the future—possibly the *very near* future. The Republican dogs won't last as soon as Nasser has to withdraw his troops."

"Aren't you taking a risk moving around Beirut at a time like this?"

"Possibly, but only from the odd fanatic. And Beirut does not have as many of those as other Arab cities. I am here only for two days and I do not move from my hotel unless I have to. Such as to come here, for instance —" He smiled again. "In my car downstairs I have a chauffeur and two very good bodyguards. The risk is not very much, Mr. Tancred. You forget we have been fighting for almost six years. Longer even than you Americans have been fighting in Vietnam.'

They never allow us to forget Vietnam. But I had to forget it; life was complicated enough here. "How could we sell you arms when we still diplomatically recognise the Republicans?"

"There are ways and means, Mr. Tancred. Private dealers who will buy the arms from your government—"

"We don't sell arms to private dealers. Not new stuff."

"We don't want the latest equipment. In our war we are grateful for anything that is not hopelessly antiquated. Planes, for instance. We'd settle for some of your F-86K Sabre jets."

"You can buy those from someone else besides us. The Germans had some." I shouldn't have given him such advice, but I wanted to get him out of my hair.

"We have already examined that source, Mr. Tancred. Those planes have already been sold. The other available sources have also dried up. So that is why we have to come to the original fountainhead, as it were."

I shook my head. "I'm sorry. You heard the announcement last night—"

"What announcement, Mr Tancred?"

"I'd forgotten. You wouldn't have heard it on the radio here in Beirut. The only time we Americans have got a mention it has been to abuse us."

"You should listen to Cairo Radio, Mr. Tancred." The smile again was bland: it could have been malicious or sympathetic. "The radio here is polite in comparison. But the Lebanese have to play their cards carefully. They never like to offend anyone with money, and the Americans still have more money than anyone else. This business with Israel may be over in a week, then the Lebanese will have to go back to their trading, making their money where they can."

I let the crack about the Lebanese pass. No one is as contemptuous of other Arabs as Arabs themselves; even the Arab solidarity of the last few days had all the solidarity of a gelatine house. The picture of King Hussein and Nasser embracing each other in Cairo had been as incongruous as a picture of Bobby Kennedy and Goldwater kissing each other in Arizona; Looking Glass Land was turning up in the most unexpected corners of the globe. Except, perhaps, here in Beirut. The Lebanese, possibly because half of them are Christians, are the most practical of the Arabs. Christianity, among other things, has taught people to recognise on which side their bread is buttered.

"What was the announcement, Mr Tancred?"

"Just that we are not taking sides. If it got out that we were supplying arms to anyone, *anyone* at all, here in the Middle East, someone else would make propaganda out of it."

"My dear Mr. Tancred—" The smile was now trying to be persuasive. "We royalists in the Yemen, the supporters of our wise and beloved Imam, we have our own war. We are not concerned in the least with what goes on between Israel and her neighbours."

"You should be. If war breaks out, Egypt might have to withdraw the forty or fifty thousand troops she has in the Yemen helping your enemies. If that happens, you don't need any extra planes or artillery. You can use the money for other purposes."

"Such as?"

He was baiting me again, so that he could tell me, with a smile, to mind my own business. I tried a smile of my own, one that I felt was sitting on my face like the side effect of a stroke. "I am too humble, Fahad Aziz, to advise a wise man like yourself."

"You are sounding more like an Arab every day, Mr. Tancred."

"I accept the compliment," I said, and wondered what Rubenfeld and Markovitch back in Washington would think of me. Or Ambassador Goldberg at the United Nations, doing his best to be a neutral Jew.

I got up, walked to the window, trying politely to tell

him that the meeting was going on too long. It had taken me some time to appreciate the drawn-out Arab social courtesies: a year in Cairo, six months in Amman, six months now in Beirut. In a way they reminded me of the South, the Old South that my mother was always trying to revive: people coming to our house in Charleston, expecially those from the North, must often have wondered if Mother wasn't a little out of her head with her ante-bellum memories, memories that were not her own but which she had borrowed from my great-grandmother. But Mother would not have made a hit with Fahad. For all the button-down shirt, he was an old-style Muslim when it came to women. Mother, like most American women, had no old-world charm when it came to comment on *purdah*.

Fahad stood up, came and stood beside me. He was preparing to leave, but he was going in his own good time. He looked down into the street at the party of German tourists just alighting from their bus. "They are everywhere now, aren't they, the Germans? They could not make it here to Beirut during the war. But here they are now and they don't have to worry about their welcome. Look!"

A dozen or more young men had been standing just along from where the bus had pulled up, lethargically waving their posters and chanting slogans with the boredom of two hours of not having anything new to say. Now abruptly they came to life, moved down towards the bus, brandishing their posters, shaking hands with the Germans and inviting them to tell the Yanks to go home. The Germans looked embarrassed, sneaking glances across at our embassy; then they escaped into the curio stores and the pickets went back to their almost languid demonstrating. I knew from reports that had come in this morning that the demonstrations in other Arab cities were more than just token gestures such as this one.

As if he had read my mind Fahad said, "If the situation gets worse, the demonstrations will get worse. You Americans are going to lose anyway, Mr. Tancred. Why not sell us what we want?"

There was a tap on the door and Janet Ponder came in to put some letters on my desk. The letters were only an excuse; she had guessed the meeting was going on too long for my liking. "You haven't forgotten your lunch appointment, Mr. Tancred?"

I looked at my watch, though I knew I still had three-quarters of an hour. I thanked her, she winked at me behind Fahad's back and went to the door. "Oh, a Mr. Barrington-Briggs called. He said he'd call later."

"Briggs?"

"The way he said it, it sounded hyphenated. He might have been English, but it was hard to tell."

She went out, and for a moment I wondered who Barrington-Briggs might be. I knew two or three Briggs, but none of them had sported a hyphen; that probably meant he was English. But the only English Briggs I had known was lost somewhere in the past and he had never been the sort to suggest that there might be a hyphen somewhere in his name.

"A very pretty girl," said Fahad. "Did you choose her yourself, Mr. Tancred?"

If I said yes, he would get the wrong idea: the Foreign Service hadn't yet got around to the idea of its secretarial pool being run on the lines of a harem. "No, Secretary of State Rusk chooses them for us. It's one of the privileges of his office."

"Privileges?" He wasn't sure whether I was fooling or not. The Arabs have a good sense of humour, but there are touchy areas and even after two years I was still feeling my way through them.

"*Sayyid* Fahad Aziz." It was time to become formal again. "If you will give me a list of what you want——"

"I have it here, Mr. Tancred," he said, and with that infuriating smile produced an envelope from his pocket. I had guessed two minutes after he had entered my office that he had some sort of paper he wanted to present to me, but I had to wait all this time before custom would allow me to ask him for it. I don't know how long we Americans are going to last in the Middle East, but chances are it won't be as long as the British have. We don't have their patience. We can be as hypocritical as they, but we don't disguise it as well.

I took the envelope, not opening it, because that would only prolong the discussion. "I shall discuss it this afternoon with the Ambassador. Then, of course, it has to go back to Washington. It will take time. And, of course, the decision is not mine."

"Of course, Mr. Tancred. But we know that it is your wise recommendations that influence the final decisions. Good morning. I always enjoy visits to your office, Mr. Tancred. Your wit and wisdom make business a pleasure." I inclined my head, wondering what gems of wit and wisdom I'd allowed to escape; I didn't have such a store of either that I could afford to squander them. I held open the door for him. He paused and gave me the smile again. "Remember, Mr. Tancred, you are not the only store in the *suq.*"

Arab proverbs and sayings: there is one for every conceivable goddam situation or occasion. But I couldn't let him get away with the last word; after all, since we didn't diplomatically recognise his side, I didn't have to be diplomatically polite all the time. "You forget, *Sayyid* Fahad Aziz. *You* have no other store you can go to. Not now."

I closed the door after him more sharply than was necessary, returned to the window and looked out. The pickets were still there, chanting in that zombie-like rhythm that takes over all demonstrators when they find they are getting no reaction from the picketed. One of the young men saw me at the window and held up a large poster of Nasser, waving it at me threateningly as if Nasser's picture was enough to have me quaking.

"You Americans will never understand how much the Arabs admire Nasser," Lucille had said. "No, more than admire. *Love* him. They've been waiting years for a popular hero and now they've got one, someone who tells the imperialists where to get off, even if sometimes he hurts the Arabs and himself in the process."

"You think *I'm* an imperialist?" I had asked.

"You are, more than you think you are. You all are, you Americans, the British, the French. Even the Russians, though good Arabs aren't supposed to say that."

Perhaps Lucille was right: perhaps I was more of an imperialist than I thought myself. Lucille was only half-Arab. Her mother had been French, and the French, especially French women, have a pragmatic objectivity about them that allows them to recognise the truth about others. They may not always recognise the truth about themselves, but that is another matter.

Seeing me at the window the chanters had stepped up their rhythm and their volume. I turned back to my desk, picked up the letters Janet had brought in, glanced at them without taking in what they said. The hum of the air-conditioning unit in the window kept out most of the outside sounds, but the demonstrators were shouting now, working themselves up into a hysterical anger. The next step could be the throwing of stones.

I could feel the back of my neck beginning to prickle as I waited for the first sound of breaking glass. My office was on one of the higher floors and it would have taken someone with a rifle arm like that of Willie Mays to have put a stone through my window. But after a few minutes the shouting died away and still no stones had been thrown. Then I realised that the prickling at the back of my neck had been with me all the time, that it had begun when Nasser had made his move down on the Gulf of Aqaba. The dry air of the Middle East, always static with trouble, had begun to build up a charge that might blow us all to eternity.

It had been difficult to keep track of the train of events that had led up to what the newspapers, with their talent for the doom-filled, circulation-catching phrase, had been describing as the brink of World War Three. It seemed to have been a succession of large blunders brought on by small irritations. There had been the massive Israeli retaliation blows for the terrorist attacks by the Syrians. Then Nasser had started mobilising, claiming Israel was planning an all-out invasion of Syria, something none of our military experts expected at all; if Israel was going to attack she would have to attack on all fronts at once and that would mean taking on Syria, Jordan, Egypt and all the committed Arab nations behind them. And finally there had been U Thant's inexplicably sudden surrender to Nasser's demand that the United Nations force should be withdrawn from the Israeli-Egypt border. We knew that Nasser had the legal right to demand the withdrawal, since the force was on Egyptian territory, but reports had come in that Nasser hadn't really expected U Thant to do what he was asked so quickly. It was hard to tell who had been calling whose bluff; but privately, if not officially, I thought it was U Thant who had blundered. Officially we were saying nothing, trying to be, for better or worse, as neutral as it was possible to be in our situation. With so many millions of dollars tied up in oil in the Middle East, with something like four million Jewish voters at home, neutrality was, to some people, almost an act of aggression.

Janet came back into the room, a crease of concern between the dark brows that were just a little too thick for the rest of her smooth pretty face. Janet came from Nebraska, had come all this way looking for adventure, but I had the feeling that if something really adventurous happened to her, she would be too frightened to enjoy it. She was a good secretary, but she was not a heroine.

"Do you think they are likely to get dangerous? I mean, try to storm the building or something?"

"I've just counted them, Janet. There are only fifteen of them down there. You need more than that for a storming."

"Well, it's not nice listening to them." She smiled at herself, trying to keep her courage up. "You don't get this sort of thing in Lincoln, Nebraska."

"You mean, *Yanks Go Home*? That's the sheltered life you Nebraskans lead. Has your Arab boy friend been telling you to go home, too?"

She blushed. "That's been off for over a month. I wrote and told my mother and she wasn't happy at all. She couldn't sort of see an Ay-rab son-in-law in Lincoln, Nebraska."

"Who's the lucky guy now?"

"Oh, I don't know he's so lucky." Her modesty was not a coy pose; that was part of her charm. "He's a Swiss. He's with Swissair."

"Just the man for you now. You couldn't have picked a better one. A guy who's really neutral, and with his own airline, in case you need a quick getaway."

"You're pulling my leg again."

"Heaven forbid, Miss Ponder. You know how they are about things like that back home in Foggy Bottom."

"I never worked in Washington, you know that. What a terrible name for a place! Foggy Bottom."

"Your mother wouldn't like that in Lincoln, Nebraska. Well, I'm going to lunch. I'll be at the St. Georges."

"Be careful, Mr. Tancred, won't you?" Her concern for me was touching. She held me in much higher regard than I deserved. She was given to hero-worship; she had a ladder of heroes, all elected for reasons that bore no relation to each other: Bobby Kennedy, General Westmoreland, the Duke of Edinburgh, Paul Newman. And, believe it or not, me. Why couldn't I have fallen in love with a nice simple American girl like her?

"Yes, Janet. I'll be careful."

2

I went out through the back of the embassy, through the parking lot and when I came into the street I was out of sight of the demonstrators. I didn't take my car, because a Mustang with CD plates on it would almost surely stamp me as an American government representative. To-day I was a little too weary to have to show the flag.

The walk to the St. Georges from the embassy is not far, anyway. One or two people standing in doorways stared at me as I passed them, but none of them made any comment. I knew they had recognised me as an American and had probably guessed that I came from the embassy, but it is a curious fact that nationals seem to resent a foreigner less when he is on foot than when he is in a car. Detroit has a lot to answer for.

The threat of war hadn't put the brakes on Beirut's traffic. The cars were still taking the corners with a squeal of tyres; horns were blasting as drivers tried to force a Mercedes through a space hardly big enough for a Mini-Minor. I once heard a Western-educated Arab, returning to Cairo after five years, say that he thought every Arab had Allah as a co-driver and most of the driving was left to Allah. I edged closer to the wall, on the narrow sidewalk, as three Mercedes swept by me nose to tail, all of them bent on nailing some pedestrian, Arab or American, it didn't matter. The Germans never managed to get even close to Beirut during World War Two, but they have taken over its streets now. Two out of every three cars seem to be Mercedes.

I was early for my lunch appointment, so I went out on to the terrace of the St. Georges, sat down at one of the shaded tables and ordered a drink. I hoped that Fahad was not staying at the St. Georges. Officially I would feel no embarrassment, but personally I knew I would feel uncomfortable if he should look out of his window and see me lunching with his enemy, the agent for the Yemeni Republic. I have not yet developed the thick skin that all good diplomats should have and I doubt now that, at thirty-six, I ever shall.

The terrace was crowded. There were still some tourists, even Americans, but it was evident that they no longer looked on this as a vacation. Near me four Middle Western matrons were discussing whether they should take a risk and go to Baalbek ("I mean, we've come all this way, it'll be a pity to miss it") or try and catch the Pan Am plane going out this afternoon ("I mean, what if we should be *interned* or something?"). I should have turned to them and advised them to catch the plane, but all at once I didn't want other people's problems. If they didn't have the sense to go to our Consul at the embassy and ask his advice, the hell with them. I turned away from them, trying not to be recognised as an American (avoiding recognition by Arabs *and* Americans? I was trying to carry my neutrality too far). And looked up into the dark grinning face of Caradoc Briggs.

"Briggsy! What the hell—— It was you who called this morning! *Barrington*-Briggs? I never knew you were hyphenated."

"Don't make it sound so sexual, chum." He sat down, grinning across at me, the same old Briggs who didn't appear to have changed at all in almost fifteen years. "No, it's the old family name. It happens in England quite a lot. Two old families marry, merge their names. Something to do with entail, all that legal jazz."

A memory came back out of all those long hours in the Korean prisoner-of-war camp when there had been nothing to do but talk. "You're still a liar, Doc. Your mother's name was Evans. I can remember you telling me how Welsh she was, how you got the name of Caradoc——"

He grinned more broadly, still an unabashed as ever at being found out in a lie. "It's the job. I'm a sort of salesman. The best salesman in England always have double-barrelled names. It suggests there might be an old school tie hidden in your wardrobe."

"What are you selling?"

"Girls."

"You need a double-barrelled name and an old school tie for that?'

"Not that sort of girl. Dancers, singers, entertainers. I'm here to try and sell an act or two to the Casino."

"Now!"

"You've changed, Paul. You never used to talk in exclamation marks all the time. Is that the way they're talking in Washington these days? No wonder you're all so hysterical."

"Watch it."

"I'm pulling your leg." He waved to the waiter, ordered a drink, then turned back to me. He looked at me critically, then shook his head. "You haven't changed that much. A bit more worried looking, but then you always were a worrying bugger, weren't you? You married or anything?"

"No," I said, but he had noticed my hesitation.

"You mean, no you're not married, but there's something going for you. Where? Here or in the States?"

"Here."

"American or a local girl?"

"You're still as inquisitive as ever. She's French-Arab."

"I could say something with an exclamation mark. It's not the right time for that sort of alliance, is it?"

"Let's skip it, Doc." It was my turn to look at him critically. And now I noticed there were changes. He had put on weight, had the beginning of middle-age spread round his waist, and he moved with less of the nervous energy that had been so much a part of him in Korea. But something else about him had changed, and I wasn't sure what it was. "What about you? You married?"

He shook his head, and for a moment his dark, blunt-featured face had a familiar look. I had seen it there when some of the gook guards in the compound in the hills east of Pyong-yang had done an about-face, rebuffed him and sent him back to be just one of the rest of us, the four or five hundred of us imprisoned there on that bare dusty slope above the Taedong River. He had been the camp scrounger and none of us had ever resented his friendly relations with the gooks; we knew it was a means to an end and a good many of us had benefited from it. I had been one of them myself.

I remembered the night seven of us, including Caradoc Briggs, had tried to break out of the camp. It had been a black night with no moon or stars, cold as an ice-hung cave; the memory of it made me shiver even now in the bright Beirut sun. It is no easy task to move cautiously and silently when you are half frozen; your limbs feel like lengths of metal and all your joints are rusted. But somehow we got through the wire and had made it almost to the river below the camp when the guards opened fire on us. Five men died at once; I was hit in the leg. Only Briggs was unhurt.

He had picked me up, slung me across his shoulder and started stumbling among the rocks as the gooks, carrying flashlights and shouting to each other in their high, schoolboy voices, had come plunging down the hill. I had beat with my hand on Briggs' back and finally he had halted, lowered me gently to the ground and sunk on his knees beside me.

"It's no use, Doc——"

"I know, chum." His breath was coming in great tearing gasps; the effort of carrying me had exhausted him and the cold air must have been like needles of ice in his lungs. "The bastards are too close——"

"Leave me, Doc. They'll pick me up——"

I felt rather than saw him shake his head. He pressed my shoulder, then I heard him moving clumsily away among the rocks. I said good-bye silently to him, never expecting to see him again.

When the gooks, none too gently, carried me back to the compound, Briggs was there with the rest of the prisoners to greet me. I had never asked him how he had got back through the wire without being discovered, nor why he had come back. I was just glad to see him.

Prisoners got no medical treatment in that camp and we were left to look after ourselves. It was Briggs who had miraculously produced some sulfa drugs, keeping up the supply till my wound was healed. He had looked after us all, providing us with the occasional extra rations, the jacket or greatcoat for those who had arrived in camp without any protection against the bitter Korean winter, and once, a bigger miracle to us than the turning of water into wine, he had come into our hut with a bottle of Scotch. Nobody ever asked where he got these things and he never told us. He was on first-name terms with a lot of the gooks and once he had been seen shaking hands with the compound commandant. Somewhere amongst those North Koreans were his contacts and we were prepared to let him use them without questions from us. But occasionally, somehow or other, he would put a foot wrong and then he would be treated just like the rest of us. And then I would see that expression on his face, the closing up as of a fist. He hated those gooks, but I never did find out whether he hated them because of what they were, our enemies, or because he had had to pander to them and then they had turned on him. It had always been difficult to tell how his pride worked.

"No," he said, still grim-looking. "That once was enough. I told you about her."

I shook my head. "No, Doc. You told me about a dozen dames you had lived with. Actresses, snake-charmers, I think there was also a duchess. But never any wife, Doc."

The grim look went out of his face "A duchess, eh? Did I tell you that? Christ, I spun some beauts, didn't I? No, there was no duchess. She was just put in to keep you jokers amused. You needed entertaining, you know. You were a miserable lot of buggers." He had his own way of pronouncing certain words, a mixture of Welsh lilt and what an Englishman in that camp had told me were Mancunian vowels. He could almost make *bugger* sound poetic, some feat considering its original connotation. "No, the wife was one of my major mistakes. And I've made some beauts."

We sat in silence for a while, both of us staring out across the harbour. A speedboat came slicing across the water, whipping its double-forked tail of water-skiers. It swung by below the terrace, sceams of delight coming up from the two bikini-clad girls on the skis: *someone* wasn't letting their day be spoiled by the threat of war.

"What's the name of that ship?" Briggs said abruptly.

The ship I had seen earlier from my office was just coming into the roads, sliding in on the far side of the Russian freighter that had arrived yesterday with what we had learned was supposed to be a cargo of sewing machines.

There are more sewing machines delivered to Middle East ports than the whole of the New York garment trade could have used in its entire history. I wondered what this new arrival would have brought.

"Hell, I don't know. I can't read that far."

"You're the Economic joker at your embassy. I thought you'd have all these ships tabbed as soon as they hove in sight."

"It's flying the Liberian flag, that's all I can tell. What's your interest in her, anyway? You got a cargo of girls on her?"

He looked out at the ship for a moment, then looked back at me. "I use planes. An old flying man, would he use ships?"

"Have you done any flying? I mean, since——"

"Since I got out of the RAF?" The waiter had brought his drink and Briggs sat sipping it for a moment. "Not much. I did a bit of ferrying, but that was all I was good for. I tried for a job with BOAC, but they didn't want to know me. Three prangs as a fighter pilot didn't qualify me for putting a Boeing down at Heathrow. They thought I might make once or twice safely enough, but they liked their pilots to last a bit longer than that. They were very nice to an old war hero, gave me a plastic cover for my DFC ribbon. But that was as far as they were prepared to go."

"You're starting to sound Welsh."

"What do you mean?"

"Sorry for yourself."

He laughed, a loud bark, and the Middle Western widows at the next table jumped as if they had been shot at. "Christ, no. The Welsh never felt sorry for themselves. We get a bit low sometimes, down in the dumps. But then we get drunk, start a fight with someone, preferably an Englishman, and then everything's all right." He sat up straight, almost spilling his drink; some of the old nervous energy began to crackle in him again. "There's no need for me to feel sorry for myself. I'm sitting on top of the bloody world. Haven't you noticed the signs of affluence? Look at that suit. Italian silk, cost me Christ knows how much. I'm sounding vulgar, I know, but I'm just trying to show you. I'm all right, chum. I'm a long bloody way from feeling sorry for myself."

There was nothing to do but nod agreement; you don't

get anywhere disagreeing with a man's assessment of himself. "How long are you going to be in Beirut?"

He shrugged. "The point is, how long are *you* going to be here?"

There was a stir among the drinkers on the terrace and I turned to look across to the waterfront promenade. Beyond it the Hotel Phoenicia reared up, all glass and concrete lacework, the plastic-Byzantine style of achirtecture that is mushrooming everywhere hotels are being built in the Middle East. The Phoenicia is American-run and when it was opened there was a great welcome to it in the Beirut newspapers. It looked now as if the farewell was about to start.

A crowd of demonstrators was moving along the waterfront, waving posters and shouting, their voices coming across the water in what seemed to be one long shriek of protest. They turned up the slight slope that led up to the entrance of the hotel, then abruptly stopped, those at the back pushing forward so that the crowd now spread out right across the road. I wondered what had made them pull up, then I saw the red berets, like dark poppies, beyond the moving field of heads. Squad 16, the riot police, were out. That meant the government knew trouble was coming.

The Middle Western widows were already moving quickly off the terrace; Baalbek was forgotten and they were headed back to the antiquities of Kansas City. Others began to follow them, and I recognised some of them, the Armenian merchants who were going to have to choose sides within the next day or so. I felt sorry for them. In this present dispute there was a lot of talk about the persecution of Jews and the plight of Arab refugees, but the Armenians could have sung their own sad songs. They had felt the blows of Assyrians, Medes, Persians, Greeks, Romans, Turks, Huns, Russians and Arabs; they could perhaps make a claim to being the world's oldest minority. If they weren't, then they certainly knew as much as anyone the pressures that can be put on a minority. The last Armenian disappeared into the hotel and it never entered my head to think of them as cowardly. They were doing their best to be neutral and I envied them their lack of influence.

"We'll stay till we're told to go," I said. "By the Lebanese government, not by mobs in the street."

One or two of the people on the terrace who knew me looked across to see how I was reacting to the demonstration. I hid my feelings as best I could. It would be wrong, too arrogant, to make a show of unconcern; but it would be just as wrong to show that I was worried. We Americans are still learning how to use the chameleon mask of diplomacy.

The demonstrators were still shouting, but their protest had lost its edge; they hadn't expected to be turned back by their own police, especially the tough cops of Squad 16. They were not practised demonstrators, not like their counterparts in Cairo and Damascus and Baghdad. I could see one or two men running around on the outskirts of the crowd, trying to whip up some sort of anger: they would be the professional organisers. But they were having no success; Billy Graham's cheerleaders could have done no worse. The demonstrators were prepared to hate Americans, but they weren't prepared to get their heads cracked as part of the deal. The crowd had already begun to back down the slope, spreading out along the promenade. Some of them looked across the water at the St. Georges and shouted at us on the terrace, but they made no move to come around to the hotel. The St. Georges has no American money in it and was built long before we Americans started to have any influence in the Lebanon. During the summer more than half its guests might be Americans, but the Lebanese don't think of it as an American hotel. The shouters were probably Communists who were just working off their frustration by indulging in a bit of class hatred. The cost of a drink here on the terrace would have bought a square meal for a family of four down in the *suq*.

The police had moved down the slope, moving with the quick jerky stride that seems to be the occupational affliction of all riot police. The demonstrators let out one final shout of defiance, then broke and ran. The tension went out of those on the terrace and everyone went back to his drinking.

I looked back at Briggs, and somehow sensed he had been watching me all the time instead of the demonstrators. His face was closed up again, but not this time with anger or hatred. There was no time to put a name to the expression on his face because as soon as he saw me looking at him his face broke open again in a twisted grin. "We're in the same boat."

"What do you mean?"

The grin remained on his face, the sort of grin that accompanies a *double-entendre*, except that what he had said had no dirty meaning: "British or American, for the next few weeks or months we're going to be the jokers least likely to succeed around here. No matter what happens between the Yids and the Wogs, we're going to get some of the blame."

"I'd be careful about that Yids and Wogs bit."

"Didn't you notice I lowered my voice when I said it? Some of my best friends are Wogs, but I'd never call them that to their face. Bad for business."

"Years ago you used to be a socialist. Now you sound just like an old-fashioned capitalist imperialist."

"That socialist bit was my old man's influence. By inclination I'm a bloody capitalist. I'm all for sharing the wealth—after I've had my cut. As for being an imperialist——" He shook his head. "No. You jokers can have all that now. There's no future in it."

Then Husain al-Qataba appeared, threading his way through the tables with lumbering dignity. Yemenis tend to run to leanness, like most mountain people, but Husain had been in Beirut now for almost three years. The Western-style living had got to him, turning him from a mountain hawk into a fat waddling plains turkey. Yesterday when I had seen him he had been wearing Western clothes, but to-day he was all Arab. He wore a white head-dress held down by two black coils and a black-bordered white cloak over a white robe. A chain of yellow worry-beads hung like dried berries from his hand. All he was lacking was a camel.

I introduced him to Briggs and the latter surprised me with the elaborate formality of his greeting. He might call them Wogs behind their backs, but it seemed that he could teach me something about Arab courtesies. I wondered where he had learned them. Then he looked at me. "How about dinner to-night? I may have to leave to-morrow."

As Briggs went away across the terrace Husain looked after him. "What does your friend sell, Mr. Tancred? I recognise a salesman."

"Girls. Dancers and singers."

"It is the wrong time to be selling them. Perhaps he should come back later, after the Arab victory."

"Victory? Is there going to be a war?"

He lowered his bulk on to a chair, ordered a lemonade and began to run the worry-beads slowly through his fingers. All but his hands had gone to fat; he still had the fine slender fingers that you find in the Arab of pure blood. "Who knows, Mr. Tancred? That is up to the Jews."

"How will it affect your war?"

"We are winning that." Winning it with poison gas, I thought, which suggested some sort of desperation. But I said nothing: after all, *these* were the people we officially recognised as the government of the Yemen.

I turned my head to tell the waiter we should soon want our table in the dining-room. And saw Briggs moving off with Fahad Aziz, both of them talking and nodding to each other like old friends.

This might be the wrong time, but it seemed there was still a market for girls in the Middle East. *But in the mountains of the Yemen?*

CHAPTER 2

I can't remember whether it was Shakespeare, Goethe or a ticket agent on the Atlantic Coast Line Railroad who said, No man knows his destination. But as a kid growing up in South Carolina in the Thirties I had no idea that some day, by my own choice, I would finish up on the other side of the world in a region completely alien to my heritage, torn by doubt and conscience and yet still unable to bring myself to retreat to the isolation that was the shell protecting my father and mother. Even when I was sent north to school at Groton, knowing that I would then be going to Yale, I still had no other idea but to return to Charleston and continue the life that had been that of the Tancreds and the Beaudines for almost two centuries. America was in the war by then and at thirteen I believed that World War Two was going to be the war to end all wars. And of course we were going to win it and it would be over long before I would be old enough to fight in it.

I missed the second war to end all wars, but I made the next. At the end of my first year at Yale I enlisted to fight in Korea, in Truman's War, as my mother called it. She hated the thought of her only child going off to fight for a lot of Orientals she had never heard of before 1950. My father was disappointed I was interrupting my law studies, yet at the same time quietly delighted to know he had bred a soldier. He had had a week's fighting at Belleau, was wounded and sent home; he was not one of the boring reminiscing veterans you find around so many Legion posts, but he had lived secretly on that week's memory ever since. I say secretly, because he never openly talked about it; but a man over the years gives himself away piece by piece, especially to his children. The Tancreds had always been much lesser folk than the Beaudines, and though my father's and mother's marriage had been a genuine love match, Dad had always been aware of the fact that the rest of the Beaudines thought Mother had married beneath her. Somehow that week at Belleau Wood when he had been wounded and had won a decoration had proved himself to himself if not to the Beaudines. *They* had never made any other war but the War between the States and none of them had distinguished himself in that. In fact one Beaudine held the Confederacy record for the greatest number of miles covered in retreat on one day. It was said that every time he shouted "Forward!", his horse automatically headed for New Orleans. The Tancreds, my father and I, had done better than that.

I'm not sure when I began to think of going into the Foreign Service. It could have been in those long months spent in the prison camp after I had been shot down. Or it could have been in those weeks spent in Charleston when I was repatriated home. Whenever it was, at the end of my final year in law school I told my parents I was not coming back to Charleston. By then my father was a US District Judge and his law firm was being run by two dyed-in-the-skin segregationists with whom I knew I could never work in harmony. I had become a liberal and an internationalist, something my father did his best to understand and something my mother never understood and could hardly bring herself to forgive. I took the road to Washington, but with no idea of what destination lay beyond it.

"I still think it bloody incredible, you and me being here," Briggs was saying now. "All those years being out of touch, then I fly in here, I'm at the St. Georges and someone mentions your name——"

"Who was that? Fahad Aziz?"

He looked sideways at me without turning his head. For a moment I thought he was going to give me another one of his lies, but then he said, "Yes, it was him."

"How come my name came up in the conversation? You're supposed to be selling dancing girls. Economic Secretaries don't go in for that sort of commerce." It was my turn to look sideways: "You're not going to tell me you're trying to sell some chorus girls to perform down there in those Yemeni mountains?"

"I met old Fahad five or six years ago, before the war down there started. When I was doing some air ferrying. I flew in a plane his government had bought."

"Sorry if I sounded suspicious. But right now, the way things are——"

We were driving from the embassy along the Avenue de Paris and round towards the Corniche de Chouran. The demonstrators had given up and gone home from picketing the embassy and now in the late evening it didn't seem like a wilful provocation to be driving along the promenade in an American car with CD plates. A breeze blew in from the sea, taking some of the heat and tension out of the air; and up on our left the American University, the college that Daniel Bliss had started a century ago to improve the lot of the Arab people, stood as tranquil as ever among its cypresses. An old man plodded along on the sidewalk, six chairs strapped to his back; in the fading light he looked like a man carrying his own curious form of torture rack. The lights had been switched on in the cafés and bars down along the waterfront, and the amplifiers there were blaring out a song. That was the one jarring note in the peace of the evening. A week ago they had all been playing American or British numbers: The Beatles, The Beach Boys, Sinatra. This evening it was the husky-voiced Um Kalthoum, Egypt's number one singer, belting out the latest top of the Arab hit parade.

"What's that song?" Briggs asked. "I've been hearing it all day."

"It's a propaganda song. All about the army of the

Arabs, how they're going to take Palestine in flaming battle."

"I wonder what sort of songs they're playing in Tel Aviv?"

I pulled the car in before my garage, tooted the horn and at once Ahmed appeared out of the shadows of the tall oleanders that stood at either side of the steps leading up to the house. He swung up the garage door and I drove the car in. We got out and I introduced Ahmed to Briggs. The latter put out a friendly hand and the boy shyly shook it. He was small for his age, fifteen, and he had none of the cheeky confidence of the usual Arab street urchin. He was a Kurd, one of a large family that lived in the refugee village of shacks out along the banks of the Beirut River. I had never seen his parents, but once a week he went home like a dutiful son to pay his respects to them. He had only one eye and his face was thickly veiled with pockmarks and he was a constant reminder to me of the poverty still to be found behind the expensive façade of the city. He slept in the garage and I paid him a small weekly wage to clean the car and run messages for me. What I paid him is something I'll keep to myself. I suffered from the dilemma of all Americans living abroad: to pay what one considered a decent wage by home standards or to settle for local conditions. Just let me say that Ahmed seemed satisfied.

"Pretty big house," Briggs said as we began to climb up the steps leading from the street. "For one man, I mean."

"I've got only the bottom floor. The landlord lives on the two upper floors. He's a diamond merchant here in town, one of the biggest." I didn't look at him as I said, "His daughter is the girl I told you about."

He shook his head. "Too close to home, chum.'

We had reached the top of the steps, a rather long climb that had Briggs puffing a little. Here we were now in the small patio that led to the front door. The garden, a small forest of thick shrubs, loomed up on either side, lush with dark shadows. I heard a voice hiss in Arabic, "That's him!", then the three figures hurled themselves out of the shrubbery.

I saw the flash of the knife and I ducked and, in an instinctive movement, went in low at the man nearest me. I hit him with my briefcase, a State weapon, and he grunted as he closed with me. I could smell the sweat on him, and when I hit him again he belched in my face: it was like being coughed at by a camel. I wasn't frightened by what was happening; perhaps subconsciously I had been expecting it all day. In some strange way I almost welcomed the attack: it enabled me to work off some of my frustrated anger. I went after him, hitting him again, this time with my fist, sending him down; then I turned and went back to help Briggs. But he seemed in little need of help. He was indulging himself in what looked like a very advanced class of judo. He had already sent one man flying and was dealing with the second man, chopping at him with savage blows that threatened to knock the man's head off his shoulders. I pulled up, and that moment of relaxing almost cost me my life.

The man behind me came up off the ground. I heard him move, but I was only half-way round to meet him when his knife came down in a fierce stab. I felt something hit my shoulder, but it wasn't the knife, it was Briggs' arm as he pushed me out of the way. The knife went into his arm and I heard his gasp, "You bastard!"

Then the man was picked up and flung, literally, across the patio. He hit the top step screaming, then he was rolling down the steps, over and over like some crazy acrobat who had got into an exercise he couldn't control. He hit the landing half-way down the steps, lay for a moment, then picked himself up and went staggering down the street. I turned as I heard movement behind me, but we were not being attacked again. The other two men had plunged through the shrubbery, then I heard them scrambling over the wall into the garden next door. Briggs made to move after them, but I grabbed his jacket.

"Let 'em go. We'd never catch them. How's your arm?"

Before Briggs could reply I heard the car drive away from the bottom of the steps. I looked down and saw the silhouettes of Lucille and her father against the glow from the street lamp. We stood there in the patio till they had come up, puffing from the exertion of the climb.

"I'll have to have one of those little funiculars installed." Naami Zaid drew a deep breath, then smiled at both of us. "Someone came out into the street just as we drove up. He looked as if he had fallen down the steps. Was he a friend?"

"Not exactly."

I introduced Briggs, but he didn't put out his hand to take Zaid's. "I think I'd better not. I've had a little accident."

Lucille had said nothing, but I had felt her looking at us closely. The twilight here in the patio was very dim now, but it was enough to show that both Briggs and I were dusty and dishevelled. Now she crossed quickly to the porch, switched on the light and came back to us. "What's been happening?"

I mentally shrugged. I had hoped to keep the incident to ourselves, but Briggs had given it away. I led the way into my apartment, explaining as we went what had happened. Lucille, familiar with the apartment, went straight to the bathroom to get hot water, a towel and whatever was needed to dress Briggs' wound. I helped him out of his jacket and was shocked to see how bloody his forearm was. He blinked a little when he saw himself how bad it was, and when I looked up into his face I saw he had gone pale beneath his tan.

"I don't think I'd say no to a short snort."

Zaid looked round, crossed to the bottles on the side table against the wall, and came back with a stiff whisky. He handed it to Briggs and the latter downed it as if it were water. Then Lucille came back, cut the sleeve out of Briggs' shirt and began to sponge his arm.

"This needs some stitches in it." She looked at me. "Paul, you'd better phone Dr. Jafet."

I was about to pick up the phone when Zaid said, "I don't think Dr. Jafet would want to come here to-night, Paul."

I knew what he meant, but I couldn't keep the bitterness out of my voice. I was beginning to have a delayed reaction to the thugs' attempt to kill me. "I thought medical men were supposed to be neutral."

Zaid raised his hands in a gesture of resignation. He was big for an Arab, as tall and heavily built as Briggs, but he had the quick, expressive gestures you usually find in small men. Though not facially alike, he and Briggs had a certain similarity. "Don't blame Dr. Jafet, Paul. Ninety-nine per cent of his patients would be Arabs. He could lose them all if it were known that he came here to-night. I'll take

Mr. Briggs to Jafet's surgery. No one needs to know that you were involved at all."

Briggs started to protest that he didn't want to put anyone to any bother, but Zaid had already taken the phone from me and was calling his chauffeur to come back to the house. All at once I had the feeling of being helpless in my own home, trapped by my nationality. Anger started to boil up in me, but it was anger that had no target. I wasn't angry at Zaid or Briggs or Lucille; or even at the thugs who had tried to kill me. It was the sort of anger that suddenly attacks a man when he finds himself in a situation that he can't control.

Lucille knew me well enough to recognise my symptoms. She said, "Don't be difficult, Paul. Father is only trying to help."

Embarrassed, I looked at Briggs. "I'm sorry, Doc. I bring you here, get you cut up like this——"

"Forget it. We're in this together. We're both foreigners here." He grinned at Zaid and Lucille. "It's something us British and Americans find hard to swallow. That in someone else's country we're the foreigners."

Lucille had bound his arm with a small towel through which the blood was already beginning to soak. I picked up his jacket, put it over his shoulders and pressed his good arm. "Okay. And thanks."

"What for?"

"You saved my life. If you hadn't put your arm in the way, that knife would have gone right through me."

I heard Lucille behind me suck in her breath, and suddenly the anger went out of me. I looked at her and for a moment both of us were careless of how much of our love we showed to her father and Briggs. It was the one thing about which I could not be neutral.

Briggs said, "I'll be back, Paul."

Then he and Zaid left, and I turned back to Lucille. She still stood with the basin of hot water in her hands, as she had been standing when she had heard me thank Briggs for saving my life.

"I'd die if you died," she said.

I shook my head gently. Her passion at times astonished me, it was in such contrast to the cool pragmatism that was her usual approach to life. She had inherited what I guessed was her mother's smallness of frame; the only hint of her father was in the dark eyes and the blue-black hair. She carried herself well, with her head held high on her long beautiful neck, so that she looked taller than she was. She had an unhurried, dignified walk and this, allied to the almost arrogant way she held her head, gave her a look of cool elegance that suggested the austere indifference of a professional mannequin. Then the soft husky voice, so unlike the harsh voices of so many Arab women, could break the image as it did now. It was the soft vibrant sound of all the emotion that was pent up in her.

"Don't talk like that, darling. No one is going to die."

She took the basin back to the bathroom and I followed her to the door. "*Someone* is going to die," she said. "All this past week isn't leading up to some sort of peaceful anticlimax."

"Do you think there is going to be a war?"

"You're the diplomat. You're the one who is supposed to have the answer to that."

She was like most women: she got angry with a man when he tried to play down some danger in which he had been involved. I don't think men do this to appear casually heroic; they do it because they want to minimise the effect on someone they care for. But of course I'm speaking as a man: maybe women *want* to be shocked and worried by what their men have been through. Love is much more of a total involvement for them than it is for us.

"You'd better wash up while I make some coffee."

"You're talking like a wife." I smiled, trying to make it sound like banter, trying to get her to relax.

But she didn't answer that, went out to the kitchen and left me alone in the bathroom. I started to feel angry again myself; lovers are like children. I took my time, had a shower, went into the bedroom and put on fresh clothes. I looked in the mirror at the confused man who was Paul Victor Tancred. He looked an average man in height, build and looks; the sort of man third from the left in the third row of all class photographs, the one nobody ever notices unless he is pointed out. My mother calls me (even at thirty-six) her *handsome* son, but that in a way is only a defiant statement of her own good looks; I look more like my father who has only become handsome in his old age, as some men do. At fifty-five or sixty I may be handsome, but that's an age when looks should be the last concern of any intelligent man. If he hasn't developed by then something deeper and better than that to attract women, then his life has been a wasteland. Lucille used to say that it was my eyes that first attracted her; to her they had a look of sympathy and conscience. Some women might look for more, but that, anyway, was what made Lucille look at me twice. Her mistake, which she hadn't yet realised, was to think that conscience was only a strength. It could also be a weakness.

I went out into the living-room prepared for more acrimony; but she handed me my coffee with a smile. I put the cup down on the table, took her in my arms and kissed her. She kissed me back, fiercely, bruising my lips; then she slid out of my arms, went round the low table and sat down in a chair opposite me. She put her hand to her mouth, looked up at me and smiled again.

"Why couldn't we have met in some nice peaceful city?"

"Such as?" I began to drink my coffee. It was Turkish coffee, thick and sweet. It is treasonable, I know, but I prefer it to that national myth, the good American cup of coffee.

"Oh, I don't know. Paris, perhaps."

"I don't think Americans feel peaceful, or anyway comfortable, anywhere these days. Not even in American cities."

"Was that why those men were trying to kill you tonight? Because you are an American?" She had stopped smiling, but there was no bitterness now.

"I can't think of any other reason. They weren't muggers looking for a quick way of earning a buck." I remembered the hissed "That's him!"; any ordinary thugs wouldn't have been so careful about identifying their victim. I said, with what must have sounded something like petulance, "It's a pretty poor reason. We're not supposed to be at war with you yet."

"With whom?" Her voice was just a little sharp, and I realised my mistake.

"Sorry. I mean the Arabs, your father's people. I never know where to place you."

She relented. "I'm never sure, myself."

She got up and began to move about the apartment. It was better furnished than the usual rented apartment in

Beirut, but it hadn't been when I first moved in. Lucille had added the extras——"our own apartment is *over*-furnished. Mother was always buying stuff, but could never throw anything away." Her mother must have had a liking for things Arabic; I was surrounded by ornate brass, intricately-worked woodwork, patterned carpets; at times I felt I was the sultan of a mini-seraglio. But I never said a word of criticism to Lucille. She had adored her mother and three years after her death still missed her. Marie Zaid had been the widow of a Vichy French officer who had been killed in the Syrian campaign in 1941; she had stayed on in Beirut and a year later had married Naami Zaid. She must have been a remarkable woman because she was still a real presence to her husband and her daughter.

Lucille stopped in the middle of the room, turned and faced me. For the first time I was then aware of *her* confusion; the past week had had its effect on her, too. I was suddenly ashamed of my preoccupation with myself; government officials too often think that international crises concern only themselves. Even the threat of war can cause casualties among people in the streets.

"What will happen to us, Paul? You and me?"

"We'll be all right," I said, but in my own ears my voice gave no hint of hope. Love is no armour when you have no faith in yourself.

2

"Four stitches," said Briggs. "I'll give that bugger what-for if ever I catch up with him."

"You won't see him again."

"Do you think *you* will?"

I shrugged. "I don't know. Maybe. What I don't get is why *me*? I'm not that important at the embassy. If they want to make some sort of gesture, why not the Ambassador?"

"That could have been too big a gesture. At this stage, anyway. If they kill a minor diplomat—I'm not being personal—if they kill someone like you, it makes the headlines but it doesn't mean the breaking off of diplomatic relations. Nasser is playing for headlines just now." He sipped his whisky, then sat turning the glass nervously in his big hand. His left arm was in a sling and the temporary inconvenience seemed to irritate him almost as much as if he were bound by a strait-jacket. "You know, you're not *that* unimportant. You are the joker who handles the arms deals. If the Arabs thought you were selling to the Israelis——"

"I don't do any direct selling here in Beirut. I'm the guy they come to when they want to do a bit of underhand buying. If it's a direct above-the-board deal, they talk to the guy at our embassy in their own capital. That goes for the Israelis or any of the Arabs." I sipped my own whisky. "In any case, we're not the *big* arms suppliers in the Middle East. The Russians, the French and you British sell more than we do. The Russians have sold four times the amount of arms that we have."

"The Wogs think you're on the Jews' side."

"We can't win. The French have practically had a monopoly on supplying the Israeli air force, but who's abusing the French these days? Not the Arabs. We've given twelve times more military aid to the Arabs than we've given to the Israelis, but whose friend does Nasser say we are? Not his."

Zaid had brought Briggs back from the doctor's, then he and Lucille had left and gone upstairs to their apartment. Zaid had been circumspectly polite about everything; he had asked no questions, but had been content with only what I had told him. He had not asked me if I wanted to call in the police, and on his return he had told me that he had told Dr Jafet that Briggs was *his* guest. Jafet had not asked how Briggs had been wounded; he was the sort of doctor who knew when and when not to question his wealthy clients. Zaid had offered to drive Briggs back to his hotel, but I had insisted I should do that.

"I owe him at least that," I had said. "And anyway we want to talk. We haven't seen each other in fifteen years."

Zaid had raised an eyebrow. "Then you must be almost strangers to each other after such a long time."

"Not exactly," Briggs had said. "There are just a few gaps to fill in, that's all."

When Lucille and her father had left, Briggs said, "I can see why you got yourself involved. She's a beauty."

"Two weeks ago I was thinking about asking her to marry me. But now——"

"Why did you wait so long? How long have you known her?"

"Six months."

"I'd have asked her at the end of the first week." Then he had grinned. "That's my trouble, of course. Too bloody hasty."

I'm diffident about prying too much into another man's private life, but Briggs had always intrigued me. So I said, "Is that what happened with your wife?"

He took the drink I poured for him, sat down on the couch and lay back among Madame Zaid's silken cushions. He idly flipped through the folded newspapers lying on the table beside him, the delaying action of a man who wants to exchange confidences but doesn't quite know how to start. He had the gift of gab, but not when it came to telling the truth.

"*The Guardian*, eh, you read that? That used to be one of my bibles, once. When it was the *Manchester Guardian*. I went to Manchester Grammar School. That's a school for bright kids. When I got in there, my old dad nearly had a hernia from delight and pride." He drank from his glass, then looked down at the amber liquid in it. "In a way I'm glad he and the old lady died before they saw how I wasted my chance there. They were both killed in an air raid."

"What happened? Did you leave school?"

"No. I went to live with my married sister and she made me finish school. My dad had always wanted me to go to university, then go in for politics. But I didn't care about anything after he and Mum were killed. I couldn't have stomached three or four years of university. I left Manchester when I was eighteen, went down to London. That was the end of the war. I had a dozen jobs in the next twelve months. Then I became a layabout, living off the dole. I registered as an actor down at the labour exchange. You turned up once a week, told 'em you hadn't made it that week as Laurence Olivier's replacement, and they handed you a couple of quid. I grew a beard, used to sit in a dingy café in Earl's Court Road and recite poetry to anyone who'd listen to me. Christ, I was a beatnik 'way back there in 1947. These other buggers are late-comers."

"What happened then?"

"Ah, that was when I began to act hasty. Have moments of aberration. Do something, then wonder the next morning —why, for Christ's sake? That was how I went into the RAF. Walked by the recruiting office one day. Next day, beardless and brainless, I was on my way to officers' training school."

"It wasn't as quick as that. Getting a commission, I mean."

He grinned. "No, not quite. That was after I got married. I needed the extra cash." He took another drink, sat staring at his glass again. "I woke up one morning, found I was married to the dumbest bird in all bloody England. Size thirty-eight tits, size one brain. She thought a lay preacher was the public relations man for a brothel. Everything with her was sex. I'm all for it myself, but you don't want to talk about it at breakfast, dinner and tea."

"You still married to her?"

He shook his head. "That was why I applied for that exchange posting to the US Air Force, to get away from her. Even Korea was preferable to her. It worked. I knew if I was out of her bed even for a week-end, she'd find someone else. She did. She wrote to me while I was in that camp with you, told me she'd met a joker who was really virile, and did I want a divorce?" He sat in silence for a while, and I felt ashamed at how much I had begun to demolish him with my original question.

"You sound well rid of her."

He looked up. "Oh, I don't blame her. I blame myself, getting myself involved with her in the first place. I let her spoil me for marriage. I think now I'd like to be married, you know, a decent marriage, with a wife you could talk to and kids."

"It's not too late."

"Yes, it is. I'm a romantic, it's the Welsh in me. I could get someone now, but it wouldn't be the way I want it. I live in Chelsea. I walk along the King's Road and I look at all the birds in their mini-skirts and I want to cry. I'm too old by fifteen years. Not too old for the sex bit. Just too old to be starting life all over again."

He said nothing for a while, just sat staring at *The Guardian* on the side table, as if it were some relic of his lost years. It was then that he looked at his arm in its sling and said, "Four stitches. I'll give that bugger what-for if ever I catch up with him."

A little later I drove him back to his hotel. As we pulled up in front of the Phoenicia I noticed the policemen standing on either side of the entrance. There were four of them, not riot squad men but they were big and tough-looking enough to frighten off any demonstrators who might have any ideas about charging the hotel. I instinctively looked back, but there were no demonstrators on the other side of the road, only a group of taxi drivers. There would be no demonstration from them, not till the last paying fare had departed.

We went up in the escalator to the main lobby. It was full of departing guests, all talking in soft urgent voices to each other; there seemed to be a sense of shame to them, as if they all felt they should remain to man the Phoenicia's barricades. These were the first refugees: if war broke out there would be thousands more, but none as well-heeled and as organised as this group. They sat on their Mark Cross or Harrods luggage and waited for Pan Am, BOAC and Air France to call for them. A pretty, dark-haired woman in an embroidered cashmere suit walked nervously up and down, a mink coat in a plastic bag over her arm. She looked at Briggs and me as we passed close by her and her eyes opened wide in shock as she saw Briggs' arm in its sling.

'Don't worry, love,' said Briggs, pausing just a moment. "It's only a case of drinker's elbow."

She blinked, but before she could reply we had moved on across to the elevators and were being taken up to the restaurant on the top floor. Driving in in the car it had suddenly occurred to us that we had had no dinner and that we were both very hungry. The elevator doors opened and the boy, a plump, too-unctuous fourteen-year-old, said, "Have a very pleasant dinner, sirs."

"He'll make it as manager here one day," said Briggs. "The best hotel manager is the joker who can turn a blind eye to the world outside."

"Still, the kid is right. I *am* going to enjoy my dinner."

We were passing through the bar into the dining-room when a woman's voice said, "Caradoc Briggs! I might have known you'd be here."

I saw the tightness in Briggs' face even before he stopped and turned to greet the woman. She sat at a table with a man I knew slightly, one of the Secretaries from the Greek embassy. It was hard to tell how old she was: she could have been twenty-five or thirty-five: her natural face had been lost years ago under a permanent mask of make-up. The first impression was one of brittle hardness, she was the sort of girl you found in bars all over the world, as much part of the furniture as the bottles on the shelf, the never-empty ashtrays and the switched-on smile of the bartender. Then you noticed her eyes, as I did, and thought again. Her eyes were beautiful, with long lashes that were her own, and a look of sympathy for a world that hadn't treated her with as much warmth as she had hoped for. This girl, you felt, would suffer from what is sometimes the worst sort of heart trouble: a kind heart.

"Sandra." Briggs bent down and kissed the girl on the cheek. I had expected him to be boisterous towards her, it would have fitted the image of both of them, but he was almost politely formal. "Paul Tancred, Sandra Holden. Miss Holden and I are old friends. She is a dancer."

"Not any more, Doc. I'm too old for high kicks these days. I'm a showgirl now. You know, beads, feathers and a big smile. What on earth have you done to your arm?"

"A little accident. It's nothing." He had joked with the woman downstairs in the cashmere suit, the stranger; but with this girl, the old friend, he was stiff and uncomfortable. 'Well, Mr. Tancred and I are late for dinner. I'll give you a ring."

He nodded to the Greek and went to move on, but Sandra Holden put a hand on his good arm. "I'm not going to let you get away like that, Doc. You don't know where to get me. I'm not in the book. I have my number ——" She fumbled in her handbag, while Briggs, the Greek and I stood awkwardly by with that mixture of amusement and exasperation that men wear on their faces when women go treasure-hunting in their handbags. Briggs looked impatient and, I'm sure, would have moved on, but the girl was still holding on to his arm. "Oh damn, I haven't got it! Andy, you know my number. What is it?"

The Greek, who up till now hadn't opened his mouth,

was glad of the opportunity to be recognised. He gave the number, looking at Briggs and me with that faint air of superiority that suggested that he was at least *that* far ahead of us: he knew her number.

"Oh, I'm sorry, Andy. I forgot to introduce you. This is Mr. Lucasta. He's been telling me all about Athens. I suppose you were over there, too, were you, Doc, when the trouble was on?" She looked at Lucasta. "Mr. Briggs sells aeroplanes and tanks and guns and things. He's a second-hand arms dealer. Isn't that what you call yourself, Doc?"

"Yes," said Briggs. He seemed to relax, as if there was now no urgency to get to our dinner table, and looked at me. "That's what I call myself when I'm telling the truth."

CHAPTER 3

"I've just lost my appetite," I said, closing the menu and handing it back to the maitre d'. "I'll just have an omelette."

"It has been a very bad day, Mr. Tancred. Nobody has been eating. And everybody is leaving. The hotel will be empty soon. Right at the height of the season, too."

"Not completely empty. Mr. Briggs will be staying, I'm sure."

"I'll have a tournedos and a half-bottle of claret." Briggs waited till the man had gone, then he said, "You think I'm a right sort of bastard."

"I could think of another name for you, but though I'm truthful I'm also polite in public."

He flushed a little, but he seemed in better control of himself than I was of myself. "Don't put on the American Puritan act, Paul."

I had contained myself till we had finished the pleasantries with Sandra Holden and the Greek. Then we had come on into the restaurant in a stiff silence that seemed so tangible a separation between us that when the maitre d' came up to us he assumed that we were not together. I was tempted to ask for a table for one, indeed was about to do so; but Briggs must have guessed what was in my mind and abruptly made himself the host.

"Mr. Tancred is with me. We'd like a table for two in a quiet corner."

The man, a veteran of other Middle East hotels and other crises, was not without ironic humour. "Any corner you wish, sir," he said, and led us through the almost empty restaurant.

L'Age d'Or is one of the most sumptuous restaurants in the Middle East and, unlike the restaurants in so many American-managed hotels, its food is excellent. It was the wrong setting in which to tell a long-lost friend to get lost again. I looked out of the tall wide windows at the city below us. There was no official blackout as yet, but the city was darker than usual. Most of the big neon signs on top of the buildings had been switched off and I noticed that out in the harbour the ships there were showing no more than their riding lights.

I looked back at Briggs. "Why the hell didn't you tell me? For Christ's sake, why the theatrical agent bit?"

"You wouldn't have made me welcome if you'd known the truth at the start, would you?" He waited for my answer and at last I reluctantly shook my head. "I'd hoped to be out of here before you found out what I was doing."

"What are you dealing in? Smuggled arms?"

"Look, Paul. I'm in a perfectly legitimate business. There are three of us, partners, we call ourselves Vulcan Sales——"

"I've heard of Vulcan. I never knew you were in it."

"You probably saw my name some time, but never connected it with me. All of us in this game, there's a file on us in Washington. I'm probably filed under Barrington-Briggs, C.W. You Yanks are never quite sure how to file a double-barrelled name."

"Am I allowed to ask what you're doing here now? Are you here hoping to pick up a quick buck?"

"You've developed a nice sour tongue since I saw you last." He was becoming more relaxed; he wasn't calling me Paul any more. "I'm here to collect the balance of payment on a shipment of rifles. The ship sailed from Antwerp two days before the trouble broke out here in the Middle East. It had nothing to do with the current situation."

"Is the ship coming in here to Beirut?"

He hesitated, as if debating how much he should tell me. "It arrived to-day. The *Dobbs Ferry*. The one that was flying the Liberian flag. But that's just between you and me."

"Who's it for?"

He shook his head. "I'm afraid that's none of your business."

"Was it for Fahad Aziz?" But he just shook his head again, and I said, "Does he want to buy something else from you? That girl mentioned you also sold planes and tanks."

"Stay out of this, Paul." He was less relaxed again. "This has nothing to do with you. I'm a British subject. Our embassy will soon be on my neck if they think I'm going to be troublesome."

"They'll think that sure enough, soon as they find out why you're here."

He had turned away as the waiter brought the wine, but he stopped and looked back at me with that side glance that at times could look comical. He wasn't being comical now: "Who's going to tell them?"

I waited till the waiter had gone away. Then: "You sonofabitch."

He grinned. "My old mum wouldn't like that." Then his face tightened, closed up like a fist. For a moment I thought he was going to start a fight right there in the restaurant; then he looked down at his arm in the sling, shrugged and sat back in his chair. "Look, Paul. I'm not asking any favours. I know you have your job to do. But don't start treating me like I was some bloody criminal or something. My business is legitimate. Governments, your government included, are bloody glad to make use of us. They get stuck with, say, fifty obsolete aircraft, what are they going to do with them? There's too much money wrapped up in them for them to be junked. But if your government sells them to one country, there's sure to be another country that bellyaches about it. That's where we come in. You sell them to us, or someone like us, and we find a buyer and make a profit for ourselves. Your government gets some of its money back on the planes, the buyer is happy to pay our margin of profit because it relieves him of any obligation to your government, and the country that might have bellyached accepts the situation because it knows that the next time *it* might be the buyer."

I had no argument, for I knew that he was telling me the truth. But I couldn't help saying bitterly: "Some profit. I read about your outfit. You bought some F-86 Sabres from the Germans and sold them in South America. You made something like three million dollars on the deal."

"I keep telling you, chum, it's all legitimate. You Yanks are the apostles of free enterprise, you shouldn't be complaining. What's the difference between your government selling arms and us private jokers doing the same?"

"We do it because we have to, for political reasons. You *jokers* do it just for the money."

"Oh Christ!" He looked at me almost pityingly. "They've really brainwashed you, haven't they? All you foreign policy people are the same. Our Foreign Office is just as bad. There's a double standard you jokers use that's aimed to keep the rest of us out in the cold."

"That's not true." My voice was lame.

"It is, you know. Look, who's to blame for outfits like ours? What was an F-86 worth when it was new? Eighty to eighty-five thousand quid. About two hundred and twenty-five thousand bucks. They become obsolete and what price does your government put on them? Roughly forty-five thousand dollars. Or anyway that's what the Germans priced them at. There were half a dozen buyers for that particular lot of planes. But for political reasons—your phrase, cock—neither the Germans nor your government wanted a direct deal with any of the buyers. We got the tip that if we wanted to be the middlemen, we'd be welcome. We stepped in, took the lot at forty-five thousand dollars a plane. Then we went out and sold to the highest bidder."

"What did you get?"

"One hundred and fifty thousand dollars a plane. And they were glad to pay it."

"I'm in the wrong business."

"No, you're not. You'd be no good in my business. You have a conscience."

"Haven't you?"

"If I have, it hasn't been tested yet."

"How long are you going to be here in Beirut?"

"I don't know." The waiter put our food down in front

of us. Briggs waited till he had gone, then he looked at me from under his thick dark brows. "That may be a matter of conscience."

I began to eat my omelette, which through no fault of the chef tasted like wet paper pulp. The rest of the meal was as tasteless: the cheese, the coffee and the brandy that Briggs almost forced on me. Good brandy is one of the few things for which I have acquired an educated taste, one of the few things my father ever taught me. But this cognac could have been a non-vintage Coke for all the effect it had on me.

The waiter brought the check. I reached for it, but Briggs clamped his hand down on it. "Your turn next time."

"How do you know there's going to be a next time?"

He grinned. "I wish you wouldn't be so bloody-minded, Paul. I didn't choose to be on this side of the fence against you. What I'm trying to sell, ten thousand rifles, adds up to bugger-all besides what all your pious governments have given the Arabs and Israelis."

"It's the timing I'm objecting to——"

"What's the good of me trying to flog these rifles when no one wants them? Now's the time when we make our killing——" He stopped. "Sorry. That's not the right choice of word. But when trouble isn't brewing, when everything is nice and peaceful all round the world—and that's bloody rare, I'll admit—you know what I'm reduced to doing? Flogging Crimean War pieces to museums and collectors."

"My heart bleeds for you."

"We also sell about a quarter of a million guns a year, rifles and pistols, to peace-loving American citizens. Did you know that one American family in five owns a lethal weapon? And one in four of those is a two-gun family? Don't start throwing stones, Paul—the glass in your house is too thin." He signed the check, reached into his pocket, then smiled broadly. "Forgot the bloody thing again. My wallet, always leaving it lying around. Lend me some cash, will you, cock? I want to tip the maitre d'."

"Add it to the check."

"No, I like the personal touch. I may be gone from here to-morrow, but I'd like this bloke to remember me. You never know when I'll be back this way again."

I held out my wallet. "Take what you like."

"I'll see you get it back first thing to-morrow."

"Forget it. Treat it as a bribe for you to get out of town and stay out."

"I'd like to oblige, Paul," he said soberly. "But I don't think you could meet my price."

2

I drove home through the soft early summer night. The air, warm and humid, reminded me of the other home outside Charleston; it reminded me, too, of Charlene. My mother never neglected to mention her in her letters, even though Charlene was now the wife of another man and the mother of his three children. She had been my wife for six months and never had two people been more unsuited; the one thing that had saved us from bitterness towards each other was that we both realised how incompatible we were. It was my mother who had been bitter. Charlene's family was even older than the Beaudines and the Tancreds. Charleston is the most aristocratic of all American cities; it might be the last place in America where money still doesn't count. It has families who are as much part of its fabric as the forts that figured in the War of Independence and the War between the States: the Hugers, the Ravenels, and Charlene's family. The Beaudines were almost as grand, but not quite: to have married into Charlene's family would have at last meant reaching the top. I suddenly began to laugh, laughing at a weak joke as a man does when he himself is weak from physical and mental exhaustion. If I had remained married to Charlene long enough, maybe my mother would have suggested that we hyphenate *our* names.

I tooted the horn as I drew up and Ahmed, rubbing sleep out of his eyes, came out of the garage. "I'm sorry, Ahmed," I said in my rough Arabic. "I shouldn't have waked you up."

"It is all right, Mr. Tancred, sir. You do not ask much of me."

I haven't asked much of anyone since I came here, I thought, *except friendship*. Americanism had become something of a disease in this part of the world; and not only here. Maybe we should walk down the streets with a wooden clapperbell, like the old time lepers.

"Has anyone come here for me, Ahmed?" Only when I had said it, did I realise I had never asked him this question before. I was getting jumpy.

"No, Mr. Tancred, sir." Then he half-turned and nodded across the road. "That car, sir, has been there a long time. Perhaps they are friends waiting for you to come home."

But even as I turned to look across the road the car, a light-coloured Volkswagen, started up and drove quickly along the sea-front, heading up towards the cafés and bars on the point above the Pigeons' Grotto. If they stopped there, they would be at home. In the cafés and bars there you found most of the plotters of Beirut. Some of them had lately begun to move up to the cafés along the Rue Hamra, where there were more symbols of affluence to spice their revolutionary hatred; but the journeyman plotters, the boys who did the dirty work like gun-smuggling or organising demonstrations, still hung out at Pigeon Point. I might drive along to Pigeon Point, find the Volkswagen, but I would never find the men who had been in it. They would be lost among a hundred others like them in the bars where the atmosphere of intrigue was thicker than the Turkish coffee with which every plotter seemed to stoke himself.

Ahmed looked at me and said gravely, "I have been afraid for you, sir."

I was touched by his concern. First Janet Ponder, now Ahmed: I was building up debts all along the line. But how long would it take to win over the whole of Beirut? "I'll take care, Ahmed."

"May God protect you, sir." He ran his hand over the dust on the fender. "Shall I wash the car now, sir?"

"Leave it till the morning. Do it early." *Before anyone else is up to see you washing an American's car.* But I didn't say that.

"I shall wash it before the sun comes up, Mr. Tancred. Before I go to visit my parents."

"They must be proud of you as a son, Ahmed."

He smiled shyly, and responded in the formal Arabic way to a compliment. "May God forgive me, sir. They are good people who have had a very bad time. But we pray things will get better."

"We all do that, Ahmed," I said, and made up my

mind to double his wages next week. The hell with the idea that the natives mustn't be spoiled.

I drove my car into the garage, said good night to Ahmed and slowly climbed the steps to the house. I walked in the middle of the steps, trying to look to both sides of me at once; the oleanders whispered among themselves in the slight breeze coming in from the sea, and I could feel the back of my neck beginning to prickle again. The shadows could have held an army of assassins.

I reached the door of my apartment safely. I was sweating and breathing heavily, as if I had just run a dozen miles through Indian territory. I had trouble fitting my key into the lock; I tried twice and missed each time. Then abruptly the door swung back and Lucille stood there.

She saw at once how nervous I was, but she said nothing. She went ahead of me into the living-room, poured me a stiff drink and sat and watched while I took the first long swallow. Then at last she said, not accusingly but sympathetically, "You're afraid, aren't you?"

I took another sip of the whisky: a man doesn't like being asked such a question by a woman. "I don't know whether I'm afraid or just worried. Maybe it amounts to the same thing."

"Do you think those men this evening were after you?"

"Who else?" Then my thinking, which had slowed down, abruptly quickened: "You mean they might have been after Briggs?"

"It is possible. What does he do?"

"He's some sort of theatrical agent." I don't know why I lied to her. Maybe I had some idea that the fewer people knew about my problem, the less complicated it would be. And in any event I didn't want *her* worried or afraid.

Then she said, "I'm thinking of leaving here, Paul."

I almost spilled my drink in my surprise. Driving home, while thinking about Charlene, I had also been thinking about Lucille. It had occurred to me that she had become the one constant thing in my life here in Beirut. My work certainly was not: I knew I had only to make one good-sized mistake and I'd be on the first plane home to Washington. And now suddenly I was in danger of losing Lucille.

"Why, for God's sake?"

"There is going to be war."

'You mean you've got the word in the last couple of hours?" My sarcasm was clumsy, but I had had too many upsets to-night to be thinking clearly. I saw her face stiffen and awkwardly I tried to smooth things over: "Darling, even if there is a war, Beirut won't be touched. Militarily, it won't mean a thing to the Israelis. And the Arabs won't want to operate from here. It'll remain what it's always been, a sort of Middle East Lisbon." She looked blank and I explained: "Lisbon was the market place for spies and double-dealing during World War Two. Beirut is just like it."

"I'm not afraid of bombs. It's just that——" She bit her lip. "I don't feel at home here any more."

"Where would you go?"

"Paris." Then she looked at me and said quietly, "Couldn't you ask for a transfer?"

"To Paris? I'm still too junior for a post like that."

"Anywhere, then. Anywhere but an Arab country."

"What have you got against the Arabs?"

She didn't reply at once. She got up, moved across to the record player and put on an L.P. Dave Brubeck was yearning for the Swanee River. It wasn't appropriate; but she *could* have put on Irving Berlin's *Over There* or a Sousa march. Only I don't have those records. I like my musical patriotism muted. She stood in front of the record player and said, "I have nothing against them. But they're beginning to have something against me. Some of them, anyway. At school to-day——" She stopped and bit her lip again. I couldn't remember ever having seen her so troubled.

"What happened?" She had graduated from the American University with an arts degree and now worked there as a counsellor.

"There was a demonstration up there to-day. They had to call the police in, they used fire hoses to break them up. Afterwards——" She twisted her mouth, looked down at her dress as if she expected to see something there: "One of the students came into my office after the police had gone, told me they had expected more support from the Arabs on the staff. Then he spat at me."

"The bastard! Who was it? Did you report it?"

She shrugged. Now she had told me what had happened to her, she seemed suddenly more relaxed. "What was the use? Spittle doesn't hurt. It could have been a stone." She looked across at me. "That's what it might be next time."

Brubeck was down among the old folks, far far away; but all the world was sad and weary: "I could ask for a transfer home," I said. "To Washington, I mean. But I really don't want to go. Not yet."

"Why not, Paul? What good are you doing here?"

She didn't have to say that; but she didn't seem to think she had said anything wrong. "Maybe no good at all right now. I'm trying to take a long view." Which was not easy, considering the department I was working for. The long view has never been one of State's more constant accomplishments.

I got up, took her in my arms. We had been lovers long enough for us not to feel that every embrace had to have sex in it. I kissed her softly on the cheek. "I can't go just now, darling. I don't know what the hell I can contribute to what's going on now, but there must be *something*. I don't think I'm a guy who's going to save the world, I'm not trying to be a Crusader——"

She smiled. "This would be the wrong time for a Crusader, wouldn't it? The last thing the Jews and the Arabs want is an interfering Christian. You have an unfortunate name, haven't you? It's a wonder someone hasn't said anything."

It was only after I had begun my preparatory studies of Middle East history before being posted to Cairo that I had discovered that I had the same name as the Crusader governor of Antioch. It had amused me and pleased my mother: could the Tancreds of South Carolina go back that far? Only when I had gone deeper into Middle East history had I also discovered that the Crusaders were mostly knights in very tarnished armour; and none of them, least of all the governor of Antioch, would have drawn many votes from either Arab or Jew. Tancred, the knight from Charleston, South Carolina, had done his best not to be associated with that Tancred from Normandy.

"Someone has to interfere. Maybe not me, but *someone*."

"Isn't that the trouble with Americans? You're always interfering?"

"I'm holding you in my arms, and you're telling me, Yank Go Home——"

She smiled again, kissed me and put her arms round my neck. "No, I'm not, my darling. Or if I'm telling you to go home, it's only you I mean. You as just you, not as an American. I know what you're trying to tell me, that someone has got to do something about pulling the world together——" She kissed me again, smiled again: "But do you really think it could be you to do it?"

"I'm not that conceited. At least I hope I'm not. But maybe a dozen men like me, or a couple of dozen, if we can just do the right thing at the right time in the right places——" Behind me Brubeck had begun to play *The Lonesome Road*: he was laughing at me. "Not just here. Beirut, Cairo, Baghdad, Tel Aviv. I don't know, a dozen places. Anywhere where we can get people, including our own people, to take the long view."

"And what *is* the long view?"

And there she had me. "Don't ask me to define it. I'm still groping my way out of my own myopia. One of the things I know it needs is compromise. And that's a dirty word in Washington. Or it is in international relations. It's a perfectly good American word when it comes to domestic deals." I kissed her again, less gently this time, "Do you want to go to Paris right away?"

She shook her head. "Let's go to bed. There's no compromise there."

I grinned. "I thought that was where all compromise began?"

She was in no mood for joking. "Not between you and me."

Then there was a ring at the front door. I looked at her. "Your father?"

"No. Unless something's wrong——"

Naami Zaid was very broad-minded as Arab fathers go; perhaps it had been the influence of his French wife, though Lucille had told me that French *mothers* were not necessarily broad-minded. Anyhow, he must have known that Lucille and I had been lovers from the first month after we had met, and he had been most discreet in his acceptance of it. If it was he now, he had never before come knocking on my door at a moment that might have been inopportune.

But when I opened the door, cautiously, because the old prickle had suddenly returned to the back of my neck, it was not Zaid who stood there. I had to look twice to recognise him, because I had never seen him out of uniform before: it was Captain Hacobian.

"I am sorry to disturb you so late, Mr. Tancred." There was no unctuousness about Vahan Hacobian; he spoke politely but firmly. He was an Armenian in a police force that did not employ too many of his race; he had risen to captain on ability and strength of character. He did special work for the Sûreté and I had met him once or twice at receptions. We were not friends, but we were friendly, which is the most that a foreign diplomat and a local policeman can expect to be.

I ushered him into the living-room, puzzled as to why he was calling on me so late. And the back of my neck was still prickling. Lucille had disappeared. I looked at the bedroom and saw that its door was closed. Beirut is a city that has as much professional sin as any city in the world, but its respectable lovers are required to be as circumspect as those in, well, say Charleston, South Carolina.

Hacobian got straight to the point. "How well do you know the man you dined with to-night, Mr. Tancred? I'm talking about Mr. Barrington-Briggs."

I played for time, still trying to get my mind out of low gear, by offering him a drink. He hesitated, then asked for Scotch. He stood in the centre of the room looking casually about him while I poured the drink; there was an air of authority and purpose about him that began to make me feel uneasy. I knew I could plead diplomatic immunity if things got too sticky; but no diplomat likes trouble. Diplomacy, in essence, is the very avoidance of trouble.

He took the drink, raised the glass to me, then sat down when I nodded to a chair. He was a tall slim man with dark grey curly hair and heavily-lidded eyes; he was remarkably handsome, but he seemed completely unaware of his looks. To-night he looked weary and there was an undercoat of grey pallor in his tanned face. I had always thought him an inscrutable man, but now he looked as exposed as an innocent schoolboy. He had his troubles, too. All at once I began to feel a little less uneasy.

"What about Briggs?" I couldn't get out *Barrington-Briggs*: it was as if that was another man altogether, one I didn't know. Though to-night had proved I really didn't know Briggs, either.

"Has he been trying to sell you any arms, Mr. Tancred?"

I had to smile at his question; and suddenly he smiled, too. The tension went out of the room and we both settled back in our chairs. "That must be the first time *that* question has ever been put. The United States *buying* arms?"

His smile, too, was remarkably handsome: it lit up the whole of his face, was not just an expression of teeth. "I had to broach the subject somehow. Mr. Barrington-Briggs has a shipment of rifles, ten thousand of them, on a ship in the harbour right now."

"I know that. I found it out only at dinner to-night. But he didn't say what he was going to do with them."

"He is, as you Americans say, stuck with them. They are in packing cases marked *Sewing Machines*——" He saw the smile flicker round the edge of my mouth and he nodded. "They never show any imagination, do they?"

"I thought Briggs would have done better than that."

"How did you meet him?"

I told him; then asked, "Who was meant to take the rifles?"

"The Kurds."

"The ones here in Beirut?" The Kurds, among whom were Ahmed's family, are refugees from Turkey, Iraq and Iran. They live in tin-and-cardboard shacks on the banks of the river just north of the city, every shack surmounted by the new universal talisman, the TV antenna, and they dream of going back to the homeland that no longer exists. They look south, envy the Jews their Israel, and mourn their own Diaspora.

Hacobian nodded. "They are always planning trouble. These rifles were supposed to go through to Damascus and they'd have been distributed from there. But now they know we know what are in the cases, and so they don't want them."

"What are you going to do—confiscate them?" Brubeck had come to the end of *Camptown Races*. I got up, turned off the record player, then stood leaning against the book-

50

case. I glanced towards the bedroom door. Lucille would be getting impatient; women don't like to be kept waiting, least of all in bed.

"We can't. The cases are marked *In Transit*, so it's up to the Syrian Customs people—if the cases ever get that far. You know what it is like here, Mr. Tancred. We have to turn a blind eye to so much that goes through here. That's why and how we make our money. This is virtually an open port. We can only crack down when the stuff is being unloaded here. We have told the Syrians about the rifles, and they will certainly grab them if the cases ever get across their border. But now the captain of the ship can't find anyone to sign for the cases. So they aren't going to be unloaded."

"How does Briggs come into this? I mean, how did you find out about him?"

"He's been watched ever since he arrived. This isn't his first visit to Beirut."

"Did you have two of your men watching my place to-night? In a light-coloured Volkswagen?"

He had finished his drink. He put his glass down carefully on one of Mrs. Zaid's brass tables and stood up. He was soberly dressed in a black suit, white shirt and black tie: he looked like one of the Swiss bankers who flew in here every so often to deliver account statements to those oil sheiks who had no confidence in their own Arab banks. "When was that?"

"Half an hour, maybe forty-five minutes ago. Briggs wasn't with me. I left him at the Phoenicia."

"Then they weren't my men."

"What about earlier in the evening?"

"You mean when Mr. Barrington-Briggs went to Dr. Jafet's with Mr. Zaid? Yes, they were watching your place then."

"Do you know why he went to Dr. Jafet's?"

"Yes, he had a knife wound. What happened, Mr Tancred?"

I sighed. So much for all our secrecy in not having Jafet come here. I told Hacobian all that had happened, then said, "Your men might have been able to prevent what happened. Or aren't they supposed to interfere with assassinations? Is that only a minor offence compared to gun-running?"

He shook his head sympathetically. "You are tired, Mr. Tancred. American sarcasm is never very subtle, but especially at midnight." I started to protest, but he held up a gently admonishing hand. "Don't be offended, Mr. Tancred. I wasn't offended by *your* remark. You and I are a minority in this city. We should be friends." He said almost plaintively, except that his dignity would never allow him to sound plaintive: "Armenians are very happy in America, aren't they?"

"As happy as most people, I guess. There are a lot of them in California."

"Perhaps I shall go there when I retire. I have read the stories of William Saroyan. Are Armenians really as happy as that in America?"

"No one is as happy as Saroyan would like them to be. But what about Briggs? What do you want me to do about him?"

"Stay away from him, Mr. Tancred." The dream of happy Armenians in California went out of his face; the weariness came back. "He doesn't want those ten thousand rifles returned to him, so he is trying hard to find a buyer for them. He may also be trying to sell something else. Planes, or tanks. There are plenty of buyers around just now." He smiled. "You see, Mr. Tancred, I'm not anti-American. The less America has to do with this war, the better it will be for her in the long run."

"You think there is going to be a war?"

"The *mullahs* are already calling for a *jehad*, a holy war. It can't be far off." He moved towards the front door, opened it. "Mr. Barrington-Briggs may be one of the first casualties. I should hate it if you were also hurt, Mr. Tancred."

"Have you any idea who it was who jumped us to-night?"

He shook his head. "A man who deals in arms never has any friends, Mr. Tancred, only enemies. There could be a dozen people wanting to get rid of Mr. Barrington-Briggs. People who don't want to buy from him and want to make sure that no one else buys from him. Good night, Mr. Tancred." He stopped, turned back and smiled. "Did you know you have the name of a Crusader?"

I nodded, sure now that we were friends. "Keep it to

yourself, Captain. Now isn't the time to be digging up ancient history."

"It's only ancient history to Americans. It is very recent history to the Arabs. The Middle Ages was only yesterday to them. That is their trouble. They still don't quite belong to to-day." He smiled that beautiful smile. "Keep *that* to yourself, Mr. Tancred. Now isn't the time for me to be having such thoughts."

"Good night, Captain. Come again."

"I shall be glad to. And if you see Mr. Barrington-Briggs —Do you have any influence with him?"

"None at all."

"A pity. It would have been better if you could have persuaded him to leave Beirut. Now I shall have to do it. Life isn't easy for a policeman anywhere, but particularly in Beirut. There are so many toes that can be trodden on."

He crossed the patio and went down the steps to the street, his black suit making him just another shadow among the shadows of the oleanders. I closed the door, went back into the living-room as Lucille came out of the bedroom. There was no need to tell her why Hacobian had called. She had heard it all through the bedroom door.

"So they were after your friend Mr. Briggs? A theatrical agent. Why did you lie to me?"

"Would it have mattered if you hadn't found out the truth about him?"

"Yes. If something had happened to you because of him, I'd have wanted to know the truth of it. If you had died, I'd never have understood why it should have been because of some shifty theatrical agent. It would have all been so stupid and sordid."

"For Christ's sake, stop talking of me dying!"

She stroked my cheek, like a mother comforting a child. "You're exhausted, darling. Go to bed."

"Are you coming?"

Then we heard footsteps going up the stairs that led to the Zaid apartment; they were heavy footsteps, easily recognisable as those of her father. "It's too late now. Love is patient, but sex isn't." She smiled. "Where did I get that from?"

"You probably read it in one of those paperback books they sell to tourists down in the *suq*. The Arabs write more crap about love and sex——"

She was right: I was exhausted, irritable and acting like a sonofabitch. But she didn't get angy with me. She kissed me on the lips, coolly and softly, the mixture of forgiveness and surrender, the kiss of true love. "Good night, darling. To-morrow night will be better."

She went out, closing the front door quietly behind her, then I heard her going up the stairs. She had never stayed the night with me. She respected her father enough not to face him with that much rebellion. Naami Zaid was an Arab who belonged to to-day, but it was not so long since he himself had escaped from the rigid conventions of yesterday. Lucille, the half-Arab, knew the sensitivity of Arab pride.

I put out the light in the living-room and went into bed. Sixty miles to the south, Arab and Jew were just beginning their long night, staring into the darkness of each other's land across the border that was like a charged wire between them. Still farther south Jew and Egyptian, who is not truly Arab, faced each other across another border. And in Washington, Moscow, London and a dozen other capitals men sat waiting for the flash that war had begun.

I was all at once too tired to care. A man has just so much compassion to spare for the world. After a while he reaches the bedrock of selfishness. I fell into bed and dreamed of going fishing with my father, catching large-mouth bass that we cooked in 1870 cognac above a camp fire on the banks of a river called—*Jordan*?

CHAPTER 4

"In a word, the word is neutrality." The Ambassador was a man who spent his life coining aphorisms, most of them on a par with wooden nickels. Tom Bredgar looked like an advertising type who had had an attack of social conscience, who had come into government but had brought with him the looks and attitude of a Madison Avenue man. With his crew-cut iron-grey hair, his thick-rimmed glasses and his beaked nose he looked like a savage owl, one who had grown up in the barns of Manhattan and knew that in that town no one, least of all a sucker, was entitled to an even break. Yet the truth of him was that he had never lived or worked in New York, had never been in an advertising agency in his life. He had been born and brought up on a ranch in Wyoming and had been a Foreign Service career man ever since he had left the University of Wyoming. Despite the slick outward appearance, the conceit with word-playing, underneath there was still a simple man who believed in principles, honest friendship and the desire to look for the best in man, not the worst.

"The latest from Washington," he said, "is that we must not only *be* neutral, we must *look* neutral." Then he sighed. "It is not going to be easy for us, especially since Washington doesn't seem to know what a netural look is."

"Personally, I think we should come out on the side of Israel," said Joe Oxford. "At least there we're dealing with a country that knows its own mind. With the Ay-rabs, there are too many of them for us to be able to please them all."

Oxford was the Military Attaché. He was a big man, all bone and muscle, and always looked too big for his clothes. Janet Ponder had suggested that he deliberately bought his clothes a size too small—— "He just wants to show off his muscles. He's like those girls who buy small sweaters to show off their big bosoms." Ever since then I had a mental image of Oxford as the only Army tackle with a big bosom. He had gone to West Point, played for Army against Navy, been on the verge of All-American nomination, served in Vietnam and now, with that marvellous talent government sometimes shows for inappropriate posting, he was here in Beirut, unable to speak a word of Arabic, still calling them Ay-rabs and almost giving himself a hernia trying to restrain his contempt of them.

We were all in the conference room next to the Ambassador's office. There was always a morning meeting and until recently they had been mostly dull and over in twenty minutes or half an hour. But for the past three weeks they had sometimes gone on for two or three hours; and the atmosphere at times had been sharp and acrimonious as the backroom atmosphere at a political convention. Had anyone had the room bugged he must have sometimes wondered if we were all Americans and all supposed to be working for the same purpose.

"Besides," Joe Oxford went on, expanding his wide chest so that I thought we were all going to be mown down by exploding shirt buttons, "the Israelis are goddam tops as soldiers. If there's gonna be a war, my money'd be on them."

"This happens to be a situation that a war isn't going to solve," said Ben Criska, and looked across at me. "That right, Paul?"

Ben Criska is an anonymous-looking man, the sort who fades from your memory as soon as you have left him: he is like a visiting-card, a name and nothing more. His visiting-card said he was an advisory officer from the Department of Agriculture, but everyone in the embassy, even the porters down in the lobby, knew he was from the CIA. It was a joke that Criska shared: in Beirut, where spying is every man's hobby, no government espionage man had a chance of going unrecognised. Criska didn't mind. The important thing was that his agents and contacts were not recognised.

"It's not going to solve anything for us," I said, and looked at the Ambassador. "I think Washington is right, sir. But it has to be a positive neutrality, if there is such a thing. The Arabs don't read a fact as a fact. They read whatever they want into it. If we just stand on the sideline with our arms folded, and there's a war and they get beaten, they won't say we were neutral. They'll say we were on the Israeli side because we didn't step in to help the Arabs whack hell out of them."

"Seems to me you're too inclined to pander to the Ay-rabs," said Oxford. "Once we start making allowance for this emotionalism, how long we gonna have to go on doing it?"

Several other heads around the table nodded, the same men who always looked at me with hostility every time I put any point of view for the Arabs. I did not help myself when my viewpoint was often muddled, but it was not easy to be clear-sighted about a people whose every action and utterance was just as likely to contradict the one just made. I was not anti-Israel, as these men around the table had more than once implied, but I did not think all the legal and moral rights were on the side of Israel. And if that latter viewpoint was going to be the one of our government, then we might just as well pack up and move out of the Middle East right now.

"What's the latest on the Russians?" Bill Lebow is a First Secretary like myself. He had got as far as he would go, and he knew it; he would never sit at the head of a table as Tom Bredgar was. He had failed because he had never had any other beliefs than those of his immediate boss; he had gone through life naked, putting on other men's creeds like a uniform. He had worked for Hearst and believed in America First, for Luce and believed in Republicanism, for the Rockefeller Foundation and believed in humanitarianism. For the last ten years he had worked for the government and had been lost for something to believe in. He had a negative sort of honesty, and I both liked and felt sorry for him.

"Washington is still in touch with them on the Hot Line." Bredgar took off his glasses and polished them. Without them he suddenly looked weary and older; his face was a calendar of every day and night of the past three weeks. "We're supposed to be co-operating on this, but somehow I've got the feeling the Russians are still one jump ahead of us." He suddenly smiled, taking all the exhaustion and fierceness out of his face. "I wonder who says to who, Don't call us, we'll call you?"

We all laughed, and some of the tension went out of the room. Business went on for another fifteen minutes, then the meeting broke up. Bredgar called me back as I was about to leave the room. He stood up, walked to the window and stood there waiting till he and I were alone.

"You think I'm sometimes a little facetious, don't you, Paul?" He stood there smiling at me while I wondered how I was supposed to answer that one. Then he waved a hand, telling me to relax. "Don't worry. I'm not going to put any black mark against your record. I know I deal out more corn than I should, pretty poor corn, too. But Christ," he said explosively, "someone has to do it. There's so little sense of humour around here. I sometimes wonder if I'm running a funeral parlour. When you first came here, Paul, you had a sense of humour. Whatever happened to it?"

"I've sometimes wondered that myself, sir." I wondered if I should tell him about the attack last night. But if I did, he might insist on reporting it to the police and that would mean a 24-hour guard squatting on my doorstep. That, I did not want; it would somehow be the final surrender of my freedom from commitment. Also, as Lucille had remarked, maybe the attack had been meant for Briggs, not me.

"Are you letting Joe Oxford and the other guys get you down?"

He'd asked the question, so obviously he expected an answer. "Could be, sir. It may be that they're right and I don't want to admit it. I know my arguments at times have about as much force as a fistful of Jell-O. But I'm not convinced everything is as clear-cut as they like to make out."

"If it's any consolation, I have the same fuzzy outlook as you. I just wish I could get rid of the feeling that the Russians know more than they're telling us." He took off his glasses, polished them again. He did it automatically, a habit of his when he was faced with a problem that defeated him. He narrowed his eyes, squinting out at the featureless sea, empty as a blue desert. "It's this being powerless to anything that gets me down, Paul. They think they have it tough out in Saigon, but at least out there they know who the enemy is. Here in the Arab countries, every ambassador like myself is hamstrung. There isn't any enemy, only a race of people too suspicious to welcome friendship."

"Can you blame them, sir? We've broken enough promises to them."

He nodded morosely. "I know. But whoever got anywhere in international politics by admitting his mistakes?"

When I got out into the corridor Ben Criska was waiting for me by the elevator. "Paul, have you heard anything about a guy named Barrington-Briggs, an Englishman?"

I felt myself stiffen, but Criska didn't seem to be accusing me. "I've met him. Why?"

"One of my contacts called me this morning, said this Barrington-Briggs was trying to get rid of some arms. How come he came to see you? Was he after your customer list?" He grinned at his small joke, and I knew then he didn't connect me seriously with Briggs.

"Something like that. I advised him to try Sears Roebuck. They have a pretty fair-sized mailing list."

"Well, if he comes by again, buzz me, will you? I'll drop down to your office. I'd like to look him over."

When I got down to my outer office Janet Ponder and Ruth Hacker were standing at the window looking down at the pickets in the street.

"It's not that they're *doing* anything," Janet said. "Maybe that would be better. It's the *waiting* for them to do something, you know what I mean?"

"Is there any talk of evacuating us, Mr. Tancred?" Ruth Hacker was a small neat woman who always looked as if she had just been delivered from the dry cleaners; I had the feeling that if you put out a hand to touch her, you would be prevented by an invisible plastic bag. She was in her mid-thirties and had lived in Beirut for five or six years. No one knew why she had come to Beirut nor did she ever offer any information about what she had done back in the States. Her personal history, too, seemed to have been dry cleaned.

I said irritably, "Don't be ridiculous! There's no need to get hysterical because of a few demonstrators——"

"I'm not hysterical, Mr. Tancred," she said coolly. "I have no more urge to leave Beirut than you have. Nor am I frightened by the people here."

"I'm sorry, Ruth." I could feel Janet looking at me with disappointment; I had just fallen down several rungs in her ladder of hero-worship. "I've just had a rough session upstairs. I shouldn't have said that."

Janet smiled, forgiving me at once. Ruth Hacker smiled, too, but it was a dry-cleaned smile: it didn't mean a thing. "We're all a little edgy, Mr. Tancred." She sat down at her typewriter, began to insert the number of carbons that Washington insisted upon. She did it without getting her fingers smudged or showing any annoyance as most of the other girls did; she was always cold and correct in her attitude towards Washington's addiction to multiplication. She was cold and correct to me, too, but she had put me in my place as neatly as if she had been Secretary Rusk himself.

Janet, not an insensitive girl, came to my rescue. "You should take the week-end off, go up into the mountains.

There may be some more trouble for you in your office. Mr. Grimsby-Orr is waiting in there for you."

I made a face. "Are we fighting the British now?"

But when I went into my inner office Grimsby-Orr bounced out of his chair with a wide smile and a handshake that almost crushed my fingers. He was my opposite number at the British Embassy and he was anything but the languid type that, somehow, has become the stock image of the Foreign Office man. He was short, stocky, red-haired and as thickly-freckled as a ten-day-old pear; he seethed with energy and I always thought of him as in the middle of a squash rackets rally. He added to that picture with a trick he had of occasionally stopping talking to look down at his hand, as if suddenly wondering where his racket had gone.

"I've forgotten my manners, dropping in on you like this." He spoke in a quick staccato way, like a man with one eye on a train that was about to pull out, and I was always expecting him to go dashing off in mid-sentence. "But you chaps are always so damned busy now, one has to take chances."

"Aren't you fellers busy?"

He grinned, dropped back into his chair: I almost expected him to bounce out again like a rubber ball. "We're just observing. I'm afraid this kettle of fish is all yours and the Russians'."

"Don't look so pleased about it."

The grin disappeared from his face. All the bounce went out of him; he seemed to sag in his chair. "I'm not pleased, Paul, far from it. One doesn't like being told by old friends that one is no longer wanted."

He was only forty, but he belonged to another era. He was one of a dying breed of men, the Arab-loving Englishmen such as Doughty, Cox, Lawrence; he had accompanied Thesiger on one of his treks across southern Arabia; he spoke Arabic fluently, and he understood the Arabs better perhaps than they understood themselves. Like the others before him, he was, unfortunately, not understood by the politicians of his own government.

I didn't want to rub salt into his wounds, so I shuffled the papers on my desk and made a pretence of being short of time. "What did you want to see me about, Guy?"

He blinked, as if he had been interrupted from some

brief reverie. He did the trick of looking down at his racket hand, then he looked up at me. He seemed to swell, the bounce coming back into him. "Captain Hacobian called on me this morning. While I was having breakfast. Most unusual. That's an American business habit, isn't it, meeting over breakfast? Terrible for the digestion."

"We spread dyspepsia powder on our toast instead of marmalade. It solves the problem."

"I must try it, if Hacobian calls for breakfast again. Though I don't think he will. At least I hope not. We have enough on our plate without worrying about what some of the nationals are getting up to on their own account." I had already guessed why he was here, but I waited for him to go on: "Chap named Barrington-Briggs. I gather you knew him?"

"Not very well. I used to know him—*well* I mean—but that was years ago, when we were in Korea."

"You know he's an arms dealer now?"

I nodded. "That was something I only discovered last night."

"He's made several trips here before. Three, to be exact, the last one in September last year."

"Whom did he sell to that time?"

"That we don't know. You know what this town is like. Deals go on here every minute of the day, but who ever knows who the buyers and sellers are? So long as the actual goods don't come through here, we can't do any checking."

"How do you know about his previous trips then?"

"Hacobian seems to know everything. Well, nearly everything." He looked down at his hand again, then back at me. "He doesn't know whom Barrington-Briggs is dealing with now. Do you?"

"Guy, I'm as much in the dark about Briggs as you are. More, maybe. Why all the concern? So he's got ten thousand rifles he wants to unload. But you know as well as I do, if this current situation blows up into a war, small arms won't amount to more than a bladderful of piss on a forest fire."

"I like that." He grinned. "Is that something from the American classics?"

"None of your bloody British superiority. Come on, what else is Briggs trying to sell? If war breaks out,

61

the buyers, whoever they are, will be wanting planes and tanks."

"That's what he has, evidently. Planes and tanks."

"Where the hell did he get them?"

"From you. The United States." He didn't smirk, but I knew he wouldn't. He was not the sort of Englishman who took delight in our mistakes. "He did a deal some time ago, selling planes to South America that he had bought from the Germans."

"I knew about that one."

"Well, evidently one or two of the NATO countries have some more obsolete, or semi-obsolete, planes and tanks. Your government okayed further deals beyond that German one. Barrington-Briggs and his partners took them up—one of his partners is an American, that was why your government okayed the deals." He nodded when he saw the look on my face. "I know. We do the same thing. We think so long as we give the okay to only our own nationals, that makes it all right morally. What happens after the initial deal doesn't concern us."

"So what has Briggs to sell?"

"We're not sure of the figures, but something like a hundred Starfighters and a hundred and fifty tanks. Shermans, and a few of our Centurions. They're all a few years out of date, but if this war breaks out, anything will be welcome. Evidently he can deliver at once, with spare parts into the bargain."

"Who do you think the buyers are? The Egyptians, the Jordanians, the Iraqis?"

He shrugged. "We just don't know. It could even be the Israelis, though I don't think so. All their stuff is very up-to-date. They have Mirage and Mystère aircraft, some pretty decent tanks, Centurions, some of the latest Shermans and some French AMX's. Anyhow, can't think who would be acting for them now. Their fellow was fished out of the sea off the Pigeons' Grotto a fortnight ago. Had had his throat cut. Hacobian told me that this morning."

"He didn't tell me."

"Why should he? He's like everyone else here, thinks all Americans are on the Israelis' side. He only told me because he knows my past record."

"Are you against the Israelis?"

He shook his head, looked down at his hand again:

he was racket-less in a game that was deadly serious, winner-take-all. "I'm not against anyone, Paul. Except perhaps some of the politicians in both our governments. We've been bumbling here in the Middle East for years till I don't think anyone trusts us any more, Arab or Jew. You seem to be following our example. Washington seems to have left your foreign policy in this area to your oil companies."

I knew this was partly true. Washington, to the disgust and sometimes the anger of all of us trying to do a job here in the area, had for too long looked upon the Middle East as something of a backwater. For six months, up till only a month or two ago, there had been no Assistant Secretary of State for Near Eastern and South Asian affairs; evidently someone in Washington hadn't thought it urgent that the position be filled. For three months, up till last week, we had had no ambassador in Cairo, only a chargé-d'affaires who, we guessed, was just as frustrated and ignored as the rest of us.

"I'm afraid that's been most of your trouble all along, Paul. Washington has never seemed to have a foreign policy, only an attitude. It's very depressing. Frightening, too. Because whether you like it or not, you chaps are the ones who'll have to take over from us here. If you don't, the Russians will. Most people are inclined to dismiss the Middle East, think of it as just a lot of sand, flies and camel-dung. But it's still the hub of the world. Whoever rules it, can rule the Mediterranean. By projection, that means he can rule all of Southern Europe. Napoleon knew that a hundred and fifty years ago. The situation hasn't changed much since. I really do think it's about time Washington pulled its finger out." He grinned again. "That's one of *our* classic sayings. One of our leading aphorists, the Duke of Edinburgh."

I was not in the mood for a lecture, no matter how right I might think he was. I shuffled the papers on my desk again. "What about Briggs?"

Grimsby-Orr stood up, flexing his knees, as if sitting in a chair for ten minutes was too much for a man as athletic as he was. "I'm trying to be helpful, Paul," he said quietly, his words not rushing out now. He had sensed my irritation at his remarks on Washington. "If we can get on to Barrington-Briggs, we'll have him out of here before he can even pack a bag. If he comes to see you again, get on the blower to me at once. He could be an embarrassment to both of us, a damned bad one. We don't want him around if we can possibly get rid of him. Agreed?"

"Agreed," I said, and tried to sound more agreeable. I liked Grimsby-Orr and I knew he felt the tragedy of what might happen here more than I did. After all he had lived most of his adult life here and he loved the region and its people. No decent man, and Grimsby-Orr was all of that, gets pleasure out of the stupidity of his friends. "Where's Briggs now?"

"That's more of the trouble. He checked out of the Phoenicia late last night, somehow managed to get past the men Hacobian had on his tail. He didn't go out on any of the planes last night and he doesn't stand a chance of getting out this morning—Hacobian has at least a dozen men out at the airport. So he's in hiding somewhere. That must mean he has a deal cooking. We have to stop him, Paul. If he sells those planes and tanks, nobody is going to query who did the actual deal. They'll be recognised as American and British and that will be enough. If they go to the Arabs, the Israelis will accuse you of taking sides and you'll have every Jewish voter in America howling for President Johnson's blood. If by chance they should go to the Israelis, then you can guess whose blood the Arabs will be howling for. Not just howling, but probably taking it. What's your blood group, just in case?"

"I don't think it would be the same as yours. Yours would be too cold."

He shook his head, grinning, and gave me the vice-like handshake. "A myth. Some of the hottest-blooded men in history have been Englishmen. We must be responsible for two-thirds of the half-caste population of the world."

"Tell me something. How long has your name been hyphenated?"

"You're thinking about Barrington-Briggs? Yes, I know his is bogus. As for mine—well, that in a way was due to the hot blood of an Englishman. An ancestor of mine, a Hugo Grimsby, got a girl in the family way, girl named Elizabeth Orr. Her father was very much against the affair, especially since he couldn't stand the Grimsbys. In the end he had to agree to the marriage, but he wasn't going to have his daughter just a plain Orr." He grinned suddenly. "It's a family joke. We go in for puns."

"I'll tell it to our chief. He'll appreciate it."

"Do that. He'll probably be glad of a laugh just now. Anyway, that's how I came to be a Grimsby-Orr." He stopped with his hand on the door leading to the outer office. "Now we have to catch that other bastard, Barrington-Briggs. Cheerio, Paul."

2

Rue Hamra is the Bond Street of Beirut, its Rue du Faubourg-St.-Honoré. You couldn't call it the city's Fifth Avenue; Beirut is too densely packed to be able to afford wide streets in its centre. I didn't know the city in the days before it became a boom town, but some of the old-timers claim it was the most beautiful city in the Middle East. Now most of the old red-roofed villas, with their arched bay windows, have been knocked down and replaced by the jerry-built concrete boxes that are supposed to be the less developed countries' compliment to the twentieth century. America has been blamed for a lot, but I don't think we should take the blame for all the sins of our imitators. I'm one American who would have preferred the old Beirut, even though I have seen no more than just traces of it. Rue Hamra does not belong to the rest.

Lucille and I sat at a table outside the café-bar on the corner of Rue Hamra and Rue Jeanne d'Arc. Neither of us had much appetite for lunch and each of us had settled for a sandwich and a lemonade. I would have preferred a Coke, but something had stopped me asking for it: I was being ridiculously un-American. At the next table to us were four young Swedish tourists: huge, neutral and each of them with two bottles of Coke in front of him. Goddam them, I thought, and hated and envied them for their non-involvement.

Lucille saw me looking at them and smiled. "You might just as well have had your Coke. Nobody would take you for anything but an American."

"Was that what attracted you in the first place? That I was an American?"

Her dark hair fell down over her brow as she shook her head, and she raised a hand to push it back: there are some gestures that women do that make them amongst the most graceful of animals. "*Mon chéri*," she said, being French and feminine and loving, "that was the last thing I thought of. Only silly young girls fall in love with a man's nationality. When I was at school in France, the girls there were all in love with Americans. But they thought every American was Marlon Brando."

I put my hand on hers and said, "I love you."

She raised her glass to drink from it, but then she paused and looked at me over the rim of it. "Why don't we leave Beirut then?"

"What about your father?" It was a hedging sort of question; I had the feeling that Naami Zaid would be well able to look after himself. "All his clients are in this part of the world. Diamond merchants aren't like fellers who own delicatessens, they can't start up business anywhere at all and get customers right off the bat."

"Papa has made enough money to be able to retire." She always used the informal French *Papa* instead of the formal *Father*, which an Arab girl of her class would normally use. There was little, if any, of the Arab style in her speech: she never went in for rhetoric and only occasionally did she sound formal, and the latter of course could have been the French in her as much as the Arab. "If I told him I wanted to leave Beirut, I think he would."

"Was there another demonstration up at the university this morning? Has someone else been insulting you again?"

She shook her head and again her hair fell down over her brow. She let it hang and it seemed to accentuate the despondency that dulled her face. "It's not just that, Paul. It's——" She made a gesture, of hopelessness or frustration, it was hard to tell which. "If war breaks out, it might be difficult for us to leave. They might refuse us exit permits or whatever they use in wartime."

"Why would they do that? This isn't a military country. They won't call up women. Or your father. He's too old."

"I'm tired of having to take sides."

"Don't you think I am, too?" My voice was a little sharper than I had intended.

She looked at me, but said nothing. Besides us the four Swedish young men laughed at some joke, safe in their neutrality. Big and tanned, they looked so healthy and invulnerable to illness, disease and even bombs that I suddenly hated them. But then reason came back: why hate people for their wisdom? The Swedes are not cowards: they just know when to mind their own business. I looked away from them, past the waiter in his purple jacket moving with sinuous grace between the tables. Why purple? I wondered. It was a colour for mourning; but then I remembered it was also a favourite colour of homosexuals and, from what I read, of the hippies back home. I looked at the face of the mourning, hippie, homosexual waiter; but he just looked bored and fed-up with his job. He went across to a group of four men sitting at an end table, began to take their order with that superior air of the young waiter who was doing the customers a favour while he filled in time till something better came up. *Watch yourself son*, I thought, *those guys have cut the throats of more important people than part-time waiters.*

"Who are those men?" Lucille asked.

"Syrians. They used to belong to the Baathist party but something went wrong and they found themselves out in the cold. The grey-haired one was a Cabinet Minister. They meet here every day and do their plotting for the next revolution. They've had about fourteen or fifteen coups in the last twenty years. It must be time for another one."

She smiled, and I knew the tension had gone out of the atmosphere between us. "Don't sound so smug. I know one or two democracies that might benefit from a coup."

"Careful. I wouldn't want J. Edgar Hoover to know I'm in love with an agitator."

She pressed my hand, still smiling, agitating me a great deal. Then she looked across at the Syrians again and said, "Who's the girl with them?"

The purple-coated waiter had moved on and now I saw the girl on the other side of the grey-haired ex-Minister. He turned to her, and said something and everyone at the table laughed; Sandra Holden seemed to be on easy terms with everyone around the Mediterranean. I looked for the Greek, Lucasta, but maybe he was just the man who picked up her dinner tab: there was no sign of him. Then, suddenly alert and no longer just bloody-minded, I wondered where Briggs was. Maybe Sandra knew.

"Her name is Sandra Holden. She's a showgirl. When she leaves, I'll be following her. So would you like to be a nice understanding girl, eat up your sandwich and get lost?"

"Am I allowed to ask why? Am I being, what do you call it, brushed off?" But she was finishing of her sandwich and wiping her fingers on her napkin.

"I have to find Briggs, he's checked out of his hotel and no one knows where he is. Maybe Sandra does. She's an old friend of his."

Lucille looked across at her. "She looks like an old friend to a lot of men."

I grinned at her. "That makes me safe then. There's too much competition."

She didn't smile back. "Don't get too involved, darling. I don't mean with her. With everything."

"I can't opt out now." I looked at her steadily thinking: *I am involved with everything. With you, with the Arabs, the Israelis; any man capable of love and conscience can't avoid involvement.* "But I promise to be careful. Is that enough?"

"It's not enough, but it will have to do." She stood up, pressing my hand but not kissing me; in public the Arab in her was always uppermost. "I'll see you this evening. And if you catch up with Mr. Briggs, just tell him to go home."

"Why?"

"That way I think you will be safer."

I smiled at her concern for me and watched her go down Rue Jeanne d'Arc, back to the university and the students who kept spittle in their mouths for uninvolved counsellors.

Then I sat back in my chair and waited for Sandra Holden to lead me to Briggs. I had no evidence at all that she knew where he was, yet I could not have been more confident. Maybe it was the confidence born of despair; you know things can't get any worse, so they must get better. How much better things would be when I found Briggs, I did not know; but at least with him out of the Lebanon one more complication would have been disposed of. That would leave us only ninety-nine to deal with.

The men she was with all had their heads together; she sat back from them, leafing through a copy of the London *Daily Express*. She was either foolish or brave reading that newspaper: it was all for blowing Nasser to

Kingdom Come: to read it sometimes, you would have thought it was in favour of the return of Farouk. Then the ex-Minister looked at her, flicked the newspaper with a finger and the other men laughed; Sandra Holden smiled, shrugged and went on reading. I knew then that the British belligerency was no longer taken seriously by the Arab revolutionaries, and I wondered how long it would be before they would be laughing at us. I was glad Grimsby-Orr was not with me. He would not have been angry, but distressed, and I don't like to see my friends distressed.

A German mini-skirted tourist went by, beautiful, healthy and careless; and the revolutionaries forgot their plotting, looked up and became just plain men. They stared after her with that expression that tortures the faces of all Muslim men when they see an emancipated Western woman, especially one as brazen as the German girl: lust battles with disapproval.

Then Sandra Holden and the ex-Minister stood up, went through all the formalities of an Arab farewell, hands clashing together like silent cymbals. The other three men sat down again, going back to their plotting and their girl-watching, and Sandra Holden and her grey-haired friend went off down Rue Hamra. I followed them, feeling slightly ridiculous; my sense of risibility would have been the despair of Ben Criska; he would never have used me as one of his agents. We passed a movie house, with people queueing up for their escapism, to get away from all the talk of approaching war: the programme was a double feature, *Seven Pistols for McGregor* and *Murderers' Row*. It seemed an ideal show for an arms dealer like Briggs and a revolutionary like the ex-Minister.

The girl and the man crossed the street and turned up a side street. I crossed behind them, jumping hastily on to the sidewalk to avoid being run down by a Mercedes doing about twenty-five miles an hour in reverse. Beirut's narrow streets are mostly one-way, but the local drivers take one-way to mean that the car's front has to be facing in a certain direction; it has nothing to do with the direction in which the car is moving. Reverse gear gets more used in Beirut than in any six other cities in the world.

Sandra Holden and the ex-Minister disappeared into a new block of apartments. Being an amateur at this trailing game I almost blundered in after them; I pulled up just in time outside the glass entrance doors and saw them waiting in the foyer for the elevator. Then the elevator doors opened, they got in, the doors closed and I quickly entered the foyer. The indicator beside the elevator doors stopped at 11. Then I went across to the mail-boxes and checked the names of the tenants on the eleventh floor. Sandra Holden lived in 1104.

I waited half an hour in a bar across the street for the ex-Minister to emerge from the block of apartments. At last he came out, moving off quickly down the street with the air of a man intent on business. He did not look like a man who had just come out from a quick assignation. I am no expert on how a man looks after such a date, but I should think the last air he would wear would be a business-like one. He would wear that going *into* the deal. The ex-Minister hadn't gone up to Sandra Holden's apartment for any sex.

Two minutes after the ex-Minister had left I pressed the bell beside the door of Apartment 1104. Briggs, his arm now out of its sling, opened the door. His face tightened for a moment in the familiar expression, then it broke open in a wide smile. "Hello, chum. Playing private eye now?"

"I'm practising, just in case I have to look around for another job. You could put me out of work. Are you going to ask me in?"

He opened the door wider and I went into a large livingroom that opened out on to a long narrow balcony. Sandra Holden, in a bikini, lay on a canvas lounge out there. She waved to me, and I followed Briggs out on to the balcony. As we went out I passed a coffee table on which were two coffee cups and some papers with figures scrawled on them; I guessed that was where Briggs and the ex-Minister had talked their business while Sandra Holden took the sun. I was fast learning to be a detective.

"I saw you in the café on the Rue Hamra," Sandra Holden said, rubbing another skin of oil on herself. She was a light golden tan that went beautifully with her golden hair; she was what I guessed they called a Golden Girl in the show business advertisements. But I could see the untanned skin beneath the edges of her minute brassière and I wondered how she disguised her piebald complexion when she wore just her beads and feathers. "A very nice-looking girl you were with."

"My fiancée." I looked at Briggs. "You've been expecting me then?"

He nodded, "Sort of. I don't under-rate your intelligence. If you were looking for me and you saw Sandra——" He gestured, moving the arm with the stitches in it just a little carefully.

"How did you know I would be looking for you?"

"I didn't know for sure. But I gather everyone else is. The police, some chap named Grimsby-Orr from our embassy. I guessed you'd have to be in the act, too." He sighed. "You used to be such an easy-going bloke once, never interfering, always minding your own business."

"I was young and selfish in those days. Now I'm dedicated to seeing my friends don't get themselves into trouble."

"We're still friends? After last night?" He sounded surprised, as if he never expected any such thing as friendship to survive. Oh Christ, I thought, here I go again betrayed by the American's national disease, the urge for friendship. How much more invulnerable were the self-contained British and French.

I said lamely, "I was never able to hold a grudge. I'm very weak in the grudge-holding muscle."

Sandra giggled. "That sounds terribly vulgar. I think we could all do with a drink."

She got up and went into the living-room, walking with the careless coyless grace of a girl who had spent probably more than half of her life walking half-naked in front of men. Briggs looked after her and nodded his head appreciatively. "She's a good girl, that. If things get sticky here, I hope she gets out in time."

"Why don't you take her out with you?"

"I could do worse, a bloody sight worse." He put on dark glasses and beneath them his face looked suddenly sober; no, more than that. Sad. The dark glasses hid the lively eyes and he looked like a different Briggs. There was a blue-black stubble of beard on his jaw and in the harsh light thrown up from the concrete floor of the balcony the lines round his mouth looked like deep scars. Then he looked at me and said in a business-like voice, "What do you want, Paul?"

"I want you out of town. Now. To-day. I'm telling you this for your own good." *And mine*, I thought, *or anyway for the good of America and Britain*. But I didn't say that: patriotic speeches curdle my tongue. I was always embarrassed at embassy Fourth of July celebrations, retreating unpatriotically to the men's room when the speeches were to be made. I think if I had been given warning I'd have probably gone to the men's room when Patrick Henry shouted, "Give me liberty or give me death!" I'm a silent patriot, the type who survives only for his own lifetime but never for history.

"What's going to happen?"

"Either Captain Hacobian, of the police——"

"I know him. We met the first time I came here."

"When was that?" It didn't really matter in the present context, but I felt I wanted to know. I was filling in the blank fifteen years, searching back through the empty years to find the Briggs who had, in an indirect way, saved my life and that of countless other Americans in that prison camp outside Pyongyang.

"I came here in '58, when the rebellion was on. I thought I might get back into flying, be a mercenary—I wasn't in the arms business then. But your Marines scotched that when they landed here. You Yanks are always getting in my way in this part of the world. Captain Hacobian drove me out to the airport when I left the country." He smiled beneath the dark glasses, but somehow it wasn't a cheerful smile. "He didn't do it as a sort of friendly gesture."

"How's he been the other times you've been here?"

"Polite would be the best I could say for him."

"Grimsby-Orr, the guy at your embassy, also wants you out of the country."

"Grimsby-Orr and the embassy can get stuffed," he said without any heat. "Our governments, for the last twenty years, no, more than that, for the last fifty years, they've buggered things up here with the Arabs. What they think doesn't matter a bugger to me now."

"You know, if I reported all this to Grimsby-Orr he could stop you from buying any more British arms."

"You wouldn't report it, Paul." Sandra came out on to the balcony, bringing a tray with three drinks on it. He took a glass and raised it to me. "I salute you. You're too nice a bloke to be mixed up in something as dirty as international politics. You still think in personal terms, which is a terrible affliction for a diplomat. I read you like a book, chum. A good book, one I enjoy and I'll treasure. But you're not a book I'd read on how to survive in the skulduggery that passes for diplomatic relations. End of speech." He grinned, a cheerful friendly smile this time, raised his glass again and drank from it.

"Does that mean you don't think he's a very good diplomat?" Sandra asked, lying back on her lounge and balancing her glass on the coaster of her navel.

"Is that what I mean, Paul?"

I shrugged, sat down and put on my own dark glasses. Sandra was wearing hers, and the three of us sat and looked at each other like expressionless skulls. "Try and get him to leave the country, Sandra."

She shook her head. "I never try to make up a man's mind for him, Paul. A girl who does that always finishes up with the dirty end of the stick. If you'll forgive the expression." She half-giggled, then stopped. "Sorry. I'm always thinking people read a double meaning into what I say. Comes of being on the same bill with so many second-rate comedians."

Briggs said, "I'll be gone in a few days, Paul. You'll just have to sweat it out till then. I can't afford to leave sooner."

"What's holding you?"

The dark glasses stared at me for a long moment, then he turned his head and nodded out across the city down towards the harbour. "What's out there. Those rifles. I just can't dump all that business."

"How much are they worth?"

"At the going price, about eighty-five thousand quid. A quarter of a million dollars. There's ten thousand of them."

"Eight pounds ten a rifle. Twenty-five bucks. How much did you pay for them?"

"I wouldn't tell this to anyone else. Three quid. Eight and a half dollars."

"That's quite a profit."

"I could do much better elsewhere. Down around Aden, for instance, they're offering anything up to a hundred quid a rifle."

"Why aren't you selling them down there?"

"I have a morality of some sort about this game." His face was set beneath the dark glasses. "I don't sell stuff that's likely to be used against our own boys."

"I'm in the wrong business," said Sandra, trying to lighten the atmosphere. "Is there an opening for lady arms dealers?"

"I thought you were in the business?" I said. "You brought your Syrian friend here."

"Don't be nasty, Paul—do you mind if I call you Paul? No, you're wrong. I'm not Doc's errand girl, if that's what you mean. I did him a favour to-day, that was all."

"Lay off Sandra," Briggs said amiably. "She's not in this at all."

I looked back at him. "Are those rifles all that's holding you here?"

"What else?"

I plunged: "What about the Starfighters and the tanks?"

The dark glasses stared at me, then at last he said, "Don't worry about those, Paul. You're anticipating too much."

I backed down. "If we bought the rifles from you, would you get out of town?"

He sucked his bottom lip, as if considering the offer. "A quarter of a million dollars would be nothing to you chaps, would it?"

"I'd have to get the Ambassador to okay it, but I think I can swing it. All I want, Doc, is for you to get the hell out of here and not complicate things any further."

Briggs looked at Sandra and she said, "Take it, Doc. And I might go with you. That's if you want me to, I mean," she added, and sounded surprisingly modest and unsophisticated.

"I'll think about it."

"Are you talking to me or Sandra?" I said.

He grinned at each of us. "Both. How soon could you deliver the money?"

"Cut it out, Doc. It's not going to be that sort of transaction. I'll try and get you a cheque this afternoon, but it won't be payable on a bank here. You'll have to get out of the country to cash it, Switzerland maybe. We'd see you to a plane here and have someone from another of our embassies meet you wherever you're going to cash the the cheque."

"You wouldn't trust me? I thought we were still friends?"

"I'm not doing this as a friendly act. I'm acting in my official capacity. I can't go handing over a quarter of a million dollars of government money to a friend."

"I thought it happened all the time in the States." Then he grinned again; he was as relaxed as if he were discussing no more than a deal over a small plot of land. "I'm pulling your leg. See if your Ambassador will okay the money."

Sandra said, "If you get the money, Paul, I'll guarantee he'll get out of Beirut."

Briggs looked at her, smiling; but it was impossible to tell if the smile was in the eyes behind the dark glasses. "Don't you start anticipating, love. We're a long way from any guarantees yet." A jet went overhead, climbing as it headed out to sea, taking with it the last of the tourist refugees. It was the Pan Am plane bound for New York, for America and what passed for peace there: we had heard this morning of more riots in the cities. Briggs was right: there were no guarantees anywhere. He looked back at me. "Who knows, war may break out before you even get back to your embassy."

"Then I guess you'll really be in business."

"Don't sound so bitter, chum. You Yanks are the apostles of private enterprise. You can't blame me if I got the message."

"You're a sonofabitch, Doc. I don't know why I bother."

He put his hand on my shoulder, began to usher me through the living-room towards the front door. "I'm only a sonofabitch in business, Paul. If you and I had met again in, well, anywhere but here. Paris, Rome, London. If we'd met there, you'd have thought I was the greatest bloke on earth and I'd have thought the same about you. Geography has buggered everything for us. Geography and politics. If it weren't for those two, you and I would be the best of friends."

"Who wouldn't?" I said.

CHAPTER 5

"Personally, I think it's blackmail," said Bill Lebow.

"It's not blackmail. He didn't put up the proposition. I did."

"Well, it still doesn't seem right to me." But Lebow wasn't adamant in his objections and I hadn't expected him to be. He had made his gesture and now he sat back, glad that the decision wasn't his.

"What do you think, Ben?" the Ambassador said.

Criska was quietly emphatic. "Pay it. Get him out of town as fast as we can. I'd even pay him for the Starfighters and the tanks, if it came to the pinch. You sure pick some beauts for friends, Paul." But he said it without rancour.

Bredgar looked at Joe Oxford. "What's your assessment, Joe?"

"The rifles won't amount to much if a real war blows up." Oxford ran a finger round inside his collar, easing the strangulation on his bull neck. "Neither will the tanks and planes, militarily speaking, that is. But it's like you say, sir. Politically it could be bad. But I'm like Bill. It just sticks in my craw that we gotta pay this damned profiteer good American money to get out of here." He ran his finger round his collar again, easing his craw this time.

Bredgar took off his glasses, sat back and polished them. He had just come back from lunch with the Turkish Ambassador; he had had *Kadin Budu*, spiced meatballs, and they kept repeating on him. He put his hand to his mouth now, belched quietly, and smiled. "Sorry, gentlemen. The wages of diplomacy. Yes, well, it looks as if it's worth paying off this feller. How soon do you want him out of here, Paul?"

"The quicker the better, sir. To-day if possible."

He nodded, put his glasses back on. Unlike Bill Lebow he was not afraid of decisions; instead he relished them. We had all been kept powerless and impotent for the past few weeks by Washington's indecision; now he could do something constructive. "Then there isn't time to check with Washington," he said, and you could almost read the satisfaction in his face. "I'll authorise the deal. But I'll need a long memo from you, Paul, explaining why we've had to do it. You can back him up, Ben. How do we pay the money?"

"I think the best arrangement would be an authorisation to draw on our embassy's account in Berne. We can contact them, explain the situation and have them draw a cheque, debiting it against us. That will mean Briggs has to go to Switzerland to collect it."

"Don't you trust him?" Oxford said.

I wished it had not been he who asked the question; but I had to tell the truth: "Right now I don't think I'd trust anyone."

"It's the only way," said the Ambassador, and belched again.

Fifteen minutes later I left the Ambassador's office with an authorisation to pay Briggs two hundred and fifty thousand dollars; the cynical part of my mind thought that at last I was paying off the debt of those sulfa drugs years ago. Ben Criska was waiting in the hall and rode down in the elevator with me. He looked tired, a man of intrigue who knew that the days of intrigue were nearly over. When war broke out he would be able to take a vacation, at least till the opening hostilities were over and the war had settled down into what, for want of a better name, we call a way of life.

"I think you should warn your friend, Paul. Tell him everyone here in town, every embassy or party or agent who's interested in buying arms, has got him tabbed. He's playing a dangerous game. If he reneges on this deal, sticks around, he's likely to finish up in the local morgue. Everyone is playing for keeps now."

"I know," I said, and wondered where the men were who had been playing for keeps last night when they had attacked me and Briggs.

The elevator reached the ground floor, the doors opened and we stepped out into the foyer. Criska looked out through the front doors, past the rather shabby garden. "You better go out the back way. The Rover Boys are back."

The demonstrators were marching up and down out in the streets, not listlessly as they had been yesterday but with purpose and a good deal of noise. There were many more of them, perhaps a couple of hundred, and someone had organized them. This was no rabble, but a disciplined company. The professionals had moved.

"I wonder what my old man would think of this," Criska said, and smiled wryly. "He once spent three months picketing United States Steel. My mother would pack his lunch-pail every day and off he'd go, just like to a regular job. Then she'd go out and scrub floors to keep the rest of us in food. My old man ever since has been on the side of pickets, no matter what."

"What side has your mother been on?"

His smile widened. "She'd bowl that lot over with a fire hose."

It took me only ten minutes to walk up through the back streets to Sandra Holden's apartment building. Outside the entrance a young boy stopped me and offered me a roll of lottery tickets; I hesitated, then stopped and bought a couple. I had the feeling that my luck was going to change for the better.

Sandra Holden, dressed now in a pale green sleeveless dress, opened the door of 1104. "That didn't take long. Have you got it already?"

"American efficiency." I followed her into the apartment, closing the door behind me. "Where's Doc?"

"Your guess is as good as mine." She stood behind a deep lounge chair, her fingers picking nervously at the material. She had evidently just finished doing her nails; the bottle of polish stood on the coffee table. I noticed that the papers with Briggs' scribbled figures on them had gone. 'I'm sorry, Paul. I'm afraid he's done the dirty on you."

I swore under my breath, too angry to feel let down. "What happened?"

"About ten minutes after you left he got a phone call. I don't know who it was, he answered the phone. He just came out, kissed me good-bye and said to tell you he hoped he'd meet you in London or Paris or Rome. He also said he was sorry." She looked up, her marvellous eyes shining as if she was pretty close to tears. "I think he meant it, Paul. That he was sorry, I mean."

The anger went out of me and I sat down, feeling weak and empty now. I nodded. "He probably did. But it doesn't help. What about you? Was he sorry for you, too? Did he pull a fast one on you, too?"

She shook her head, came around the chair and sank down into it. I had the feeling she was trying to be brave, but I think she was as empty and let down as I was. "There's never been anything between me and Doc. At least, nothing permanent. I've known him off and on for ten years, but that's the way it's always been. Off and on. Doc is not the one for anything permanent when it comes to relationships."

"What about you?"

She was biting the ends of her fingers, and it was plain now that Briggs' sudden departure *had* upset her. I hoped the polish on her nails was dry. "I think about it. Something permanent, I mean. I'm getting on. For a showgirl, I mean. I'm thirty-four, thirty-five in November. The bosom doesn't stay firm for ever."

"The way you look in your bikini, you've still got a few years yet."

She shook her head. "It's getting to be too much of a struggle. I'd just like to relax, let myself go just even for a month. It's been a long long time now, always keeping an eye on this." She patted her body impersonally, a workwoman and her tool of trade. "I've only ever had one other job. I was a filing clerk in an office in London. I was always getting my fingers pinched in the files and my bottom pinched by the men clerks. So I took dancing lessons and I got a job dancing in a chorus on telly. You didn't have to be very good in those days."

"When did you meet Doc?" I was still filling in the fifteen years, even though he had gone off and it might be another fifteen years before we met again.

"Oh, a long time later. I gave up the dancing lark for a while, I went in for beauty contests. I was in every one they put on. I was running around so fast, I didn't have time to get out of my bathing costume. I was always in the final seven. Once I won second prize, at Aberystwyth, that's in Wales, it was. Then I took stock, as they say. If I couldn't make it as Miss Aberystwyth, then I knew there was no chance of me ever making the big stuff, Miss England, Miss World, all that. That was when I met Doc for the first time. He'd come to Aberystwyth on what he said was a sentimental journey. He'd spent a holiday there when he was a kid. He's very sentimental, did you know that?"

"I hadn't suspected it," I said, and tried not to sound too dry and sardonic. "He's never been sentimental enough to ask you to marry him?"

She smiled ruefully. "He's never taken the bait. I've given up hope. I told him about the nine proposals I've had since I came to Beirut, but all he said was, Choose carefully, love. But I'll have to say yes to someone soon. There's no one so pathetic as an unmarried retired showgirl. It makes a farce of all the years you've been working, as if somehow you've been cheating all that time. You know what I mean?" She stood up, the tears quite plain in her eyes now. 'If you do find him, Paul, tell him I'd like to see him again. Just once."

I looked at her, the beautiful woman who every night out at the Casino du Liban was admired and lusted after by all the men patrons, envied and perhaps even hated by the women. All she had was her beauty and nothing else. A few pounds in the bank, a wardrobe of good clothes, this apartment. I looked around the apartment: she had called it home. Home was three or four rooms, furnished by someone else, nothing of Sandra in it but the *Daily Express* thrown on a chair and the bottle of nail polish on the coffee table. I wondered what was home to Briggs.

"I'll do that."

She opened the door and Captain Hacobian stood there, his finger raised to press the bell. His face showed no surprise at seeing me; he just greeted us both with his beautiful smile. *Here's a man for you, Sandra*, I thought; then I remembered Hacobian had a wife and five children. "I take it, Mr. Tancred, our friend is not here?"

"He was, Captain. But he flew the coop about an hour ago. Miss Holden doesn't think he's coming back."

Hacobian looked carefully at Sandra. There was nothing insulting in his stare: he was being a policeman, not just a man. "I think you had better not leave your apartment, Miss Holden."

"I have to go to work to-night out at the Casino." She bit the ends of her fingers again. "Honestly, Captain, I don't know where Mr. Briggs has gone———"

"She's telling the truth," I said. "Let her go to work

to-night. I'm sure one of your men won't mind keeping an eye on her. Especially in her working costume out at the Casino."

"Don't be dirty, Paul," she said.

"I wasn't. I was trying to be complimentary."

Hacobian considered a moment, then he nodded. "There'll be a man downstairs the rest of the day, Miss Holden. Don't try and avoid him. But don't be too kind to him either. He's a young man and very impressionable." He gave her the brilliant smile again, and I knew then he didn't suspect her of too much complicity in the Briggs affair.

When we got outside the building a policeman was waiting beside the police car. He was young and he did look impressionable; faced by all the bare bosoms out at the Casino to-night he might be ruined for ever as a policeman.

Hacobian gave him his instructions, the young man saluted and went into the foyer, and Hacobian looked after him with the sad look of a father losing a son.

"I should send one of the older men, the ones with fat wives and a dozen kids."

"You mean the older ones are more trustworthy?"

"No. The older ones just deserve a night out among all the beautiful flesh. The young ones get it every night, but the older men have probably forgotten what it looks like."

"Somehow I never thought you'd worry about fringe benefits for your men."

"You don't know me very well, Mr. Tancred. I'm always concerned for everyone's welfare. Shall we go and look for your friend Mr. Briggs?"

"You got any idea where he might be?"

"None at all. But we might try the ship out in the harbour. I'm sure he hasn't flown off without leaving *some* instructions for the captain of the ship."

We drove down through the city. In the centre of town it seemed to be business as usual; no one here was concerned with demonstrating, unless it was sidewalk peddlers demonstrating their "genuine" Parker pens. We pulled up at a traffic light on the corner of the Place des Martyrs and a fat sidewalk salesman darted out at us flashing a bouquet of can-openers in one hand. The police car was a plain black Mercedes, unmarked, and the spiv was leaning on my door, thrusting the can-openers at me, before he saw Hacobian sitting on the far side of me.

"Ah, Captain! Protector of the poor——" He burst into a rhetoric of apology, backing away and up on to the sidewalk. But as we drove on I looked back and saw the handful of can-openers thrust upwards in a universal gesture.

Hacobian had been looking in his rear-vision mirror, but the gesture didn't upset him. He looked at me and smiled. "If war breaks out, I wonder what that man will be selling next week? Do you think your friend Briggs began life that way?"

"According to him, he started as a reciter of poetry."

"Then he must feel at home among the Arabs. They like to think they are the only people who still respect the poet."

"And what about you, an Armenian?"

He smiled again, sadly this time. "We are too busy surviving to listen to the poets. It is that way also with Americans, yes?"

"Yes," I said, and smiled sadly in return.

A customs launch took us out to the *Dobbs Ferry*. It was not a new ship and looked like a renovated Liberty ship; the Liberian maritime flag covers a fleet of sins. We climbed a rickety gangway of steps and a Chinese seaman took us along to the captain, who was sunning himself on a small square of deck outside his cabin.

He was a Dutchman, hairy-chested and big, overweight but still with muscle showing under the fat. He stood up with a grace that was unexpected and shook his hands with both of us. Hacobian explained to him the purpose of our visit.

The Dutchman scratched his chest, leaving a furrow in the thick dark hair. "I haven't seen Mr. Barrington-Briggs, but I got a message from him half an hour ago. I'm to sail as soon as I can." He gestured down at the decks where seamen were loading the last of what looked like cases of beer. "I'll be on my way in an hour or two."

"Is Mr. Briggs going with you?" I asked.

"He didn't say so."

"Where's your next port, Captain?" Hacobian asked.

The Dutchman shrugged. "All I have to do immediately

is get out of territorial waters. I'm to get my sailing orders late to-night or early to-morrow by radio."

I looked at Hacobian, but he didn't return my glance. He just looked straight at the Dutchman and said, "In view of the current situation, Captain, I could get an order to prevent you sailing."

"Captain——" The two men meticulously respected the other's rank; there was no animosity between them. "I know you could and I wouldn't blame you. I'm not in favour of what's in the holds, but I'm not the owner of this ship. Only its master——" He grinned, just a crack in the red rock of his face. "There's a difference."

"Will you get the order?" I said to Hacobian.

Hacobian hesitated, and the Dutchman said, "There's one thing, Captain. Beirut is a port that lives on other people's trade. If you stopped me from sailing and then my orders turned out to be for another Arab port, who would get the blame? From your name I take it you are an Armenian, right, Captain?"

"You are very shrewd, Captain," said Hacobian. "I hope you are not also insulting."

"No, Captain," said the Dutchman. "Just trying to be neutral."

"Forget it," I said to Hacobian. "Maybe Briggs has done the right thing by both of us. Maybe he's decided to cut his losses and get out while the going's good."

"Do you believe that, Mr. Tancred?"

I looked back at Beirut, from this distance somnolent, peaceful and beautiful under the afternoon sun. Clouds had blossomed on the mountains behind, and a slow avalanche of shadow was rolling down to engulf the city. Was Briggs somewhere there packing his bags, doing the right thing by me?

"I don't know, Captain. I don't think anyone, not even Briggs, knows what Briggs is going to do next."

2

"Only dictators can afford to be unambiguous," said the French Second Secretary, speaking in that literary way that certain middle-class Frenchmen have. "But ambiguity is a necessity for survival with democratically elected leaders such as President Johnson and Mr. Wilson."

"What about General de Gaulle?" I asked.

The Second Secretary looked around, then lowered his voice. "Is ambiguity in God's nature?"

I grinned, and Lucille and I moved on, dog-paddling our way through the slow whirlpool of guests. The French Embassy had planned this reception weeks before and had not felt that the crisis tension of the past weeks demanded that it should be cancelled. Their sublime poise in the current situation seemed just another extension of the supreme arrogance that stared out at us from the big portrait hung at the end of the room; I had the feeling that if ever the Arab mobs broke in here even they would be daunted by the General's haughty stare. But the mobs had shown no sign yet of wanting to attack the French, and this evening the room was full of Arab dignitaries. Somehow the French had succeeded in persuading the Arabs to forget 1956 and Suez; more remarkably they had succeeded in getting them to ignore the fact that practically all the Israeli armament was French-supplied. The General might not feel the need of ambiguity but his diplomats were practised masters of it.

Lucille said, "I feel it's all unreal. All this cocktail-drinking and social chatter—don't they *care* if a war might break out at any moment? What would the soldiers down on the Gaza Strip think if they could see all this?"

"As I remember it, when we were in Korea we didn't give a thought to the diplomats. When soldiers think about the home front, it's usually only about girls, draft dodgers and profiteers."

"I hope one or two of the soldiers, then, are thinking about your friend."

"Why do you dislike him so much?"

"I don't like people who try to play both sides."

"You don't like neutrals, you mean?"

"That's a different thing. Your friend Briggs isn't neutral."

The Maronite bishop gave me a smile as we passed him, then he turned back to the group he was with, saying, "Of course, our problem is that Jesus Christ was a Jew ——"

I said to Lucille, "You see? Everyone could be suspected of the wrong sort of neutrality."

She gave me the sort of look that a woman gives when she has no answer to an argument, but which somehow gives you the feeling you have lost the argument anyway. I shrugged and smiled, and we moved on across the packed room. It was quite a crowd, the sort my mother would have been thrilled with; to have had a gathering like this in her drawing-room (we were the sort of family that still had a drawing-room), she would have even invited Stokeley Carmichael, if he had been the price she had to pay. There were oil sheiks from the Arabian Gulf and one from the Gulf fields of Texas: he stood in one corner all by himself, tall, thin and abashed: he was just a poor millionaire in the company of the billionaires standing near him. Husain al-Qataba nodded to me, remotely, as if I were a Fourth Secretary from Patagonia; yesterday he had been all smiles and cajolery, but to-day he was standing with two Egyptians; they glared at me as if I were wearing the Star of David on my forehead. The Greek diplomat, Lucasta, wandered around like someone who had lost the way to Mount Olympus: the coup in Athens had left him out on a limb trying to explain what had happened to democracy in the birthplace of democracy: he was going through the real test of a diplomat, trying to excuse a government that had betrayed him. Grimsby-Orr bounced among a group of Iraqis and Jordanians: there seemed to be a desperate gaiety about him, like that of a man making what he knew to be his last farewell to friends who no longer looked upon him as a friend. He saw me, waved like a drowning man, but I kept moving: I didn't feel capable of saving anyone.

The crowd continued to mill around through its slow tribal dance: the rich business men keeping up their contacts, the highest-priced whore in the Lebanon keeping up *hers*, the African diplomats trying too hard to state their support of the Arabs' cause, hoping that the Arabs would not remember how much support the African governments were getting from the Israelis.

"The Americans think their foreign aid entitles them to make us over in their image," said the Harvard-educated African, one eye on me as I sidled past. "They believe manna maketh the man."

"Very good, that," I said, stopping for a moment, smiling broadly, even though it hurt, to show that I wasn't offended. "You should try it on *Reader's Digest*."

He gave me a big smile in return, a hundred gleaming

white teeth spread right across his face: it made my smile look like a tiny curl of the lip. "They pay very well, don't they?"

"Better than *Pravda*," I said snidely, and moved on: you get a little tired of being diplomatic all the time. Cocktail chatter is often as flippant as that of disc jockeys, but you put up with it, always looking for a hint beneath the froth that something deeper might be discussed in a side room. But there was nothing to be gained by staying listening to this particular African; what he didn't yet know was that both we and the Russians had written off his government. His Prime Minister was known in both Moscow and Washington as the cannibal ingrate: he took delight in eating the hand that fed him.

Aldanov, one of the Russian Secretaries, was talking to Hacobian, Naami Zaid and Elias Hasbani when Lucille and I bumped against them.

"Mademoiselle!" Aldanov bent from the waist and put his lips to Lucille's hand; St. Petersburg would have been proud of him, if Leningrad wouldn't have been. "I have just been telling your father he doesn't have a diamond in his collection to compare with you."

Lucille had too much poise to blush at such extravagant compliments. "M'sieu Aldanov, they must be training you to be your country's ambassador in Paris."

"The compliment was sincere, but to tell you the truth, Paris would be a nice assignment." He winked at me, smoothing back his dark hair with his well-manicured peasant's hand. He was a small man, with the trim build of a lightweight boxer, and his silk-and-mohair suits were made by the best Armenian tailor in town. It was said that he had a sackcloth wardrobe for wearing when he went home to Moscow, but here in Beirut he was more dandified than even the Italians. "Though I'd prefer Washington."

"I'll see what I can do," I said.

He hadn't shaken hands with me nor had he smiled when he had winked at me. Each of us knew that every Arab in the room was watching us, and each of us knew who was supposed to be the Arabs' friend. He couldn't betray them by shaking hands with an infidel like me; and in turn I couldn't betray him by making him shake hands with me. I might need him some time: in international relations you never know who your next friend is going to be. We were on opposite sides of the fence over Vietnam and the war that might occur at any moment here in the Middle East. But each of us had to take the long view: there was still China.

"You are indeed looking beautiful this evening," said Hasbani to Lucille.

She gravely inclined her head. "May God forgive me, you are too kind, M'sieu Hasbani."

Hasbani was a short squat man with enormously broad shoulders and a completely bald head that sat on them like a brown, almost mapless globe. His face did have the normal features, but somehow it gave the impression of being blank; not the blankness of stupidity but that of a man who would give nothing of himself away to the world. And he was rumoured never to have given anything away; it was one of the reasons he was reputed to be the richest man in the Lebanon. No one knew where he came from; he had appeared in Beirut ten years ago, already rich, and in Beirut no one asks for further references than the money you hold in your hand. Now he was said to be ten times richer, able to match dollar for dollar with any of the oil sheiks who came to town, and still no one knew anything about his past history. No one believed that his real name was Hasbani. The Hasbani is a river that flows down out of the Lebanon into Jordan, and it was taken for granted that he had crossed the river, given himself its name, and come on into Beirut. He lived in a palatial mansion on the road up to Aley and twice a year threw parties that made even the oil sheiks' wing-dings look like cucumber-sandwich picnics.

Naami Zaid smiled with pride at his daughter. She was drawn into the conversation of him, Hasbani and Aldanov; and Hacobian and I were left on the outskirts. "Did the ship sail?" I asked.

"Went out at five o'clock. Mr. Barrington-Briggs wasn't on it."

"What about planes out of the airport?"

He shook his head. "I'm afraid he's still here somewhere."

"Has he contacted Miss Holden?"

"He may have telephoned her, but we wouldn't know that. You see, we don't have the facilities of your FBI——"

He smiled without malice. "For wire-tapping, I mean."

"If he does turn up, what are you going to do?"

"Arrest him at once. Isn't that what you would want me to do?"

"I'll help you drive him out to the airport."

"That won't be necessary, Mr. Tancred. After all, what we are trying to do is keep you from being involved at all, isn't that right?"

Then Aldanov turned to me and said, "There is a rumour that your Sixth Fleet is steaming east. Is it going to show the Stars and Stripes in Tel Aviv?"

"The last I heard the Fleet was still off Crete. Your intelligence seems to be better than ours."

"You gentlemen shouldn't quarrel." Hasbani's deep breathy voice was like a magnified whisper from the echo chamber of his big chest. "If it had not been for the broken promises of big Powers like your countries, we here in the Middle East might have worked out our own problems. After all, we Arabs have treated the Jews better throughout history than the Christian countries ever have. And you Russians don't have an enviable record towards them, Mr. Aldanov."

Hasbani was one of the few men here to-night who could afford to be as frank as he was: he was rich and powerful enough to play his own game of neutrality. But now that he had spoken, Zaid and Hacobian behind him were nodding their heads in agreement.

"There was a case for the establishment of a Jewish National Home and we Arabs might have agreed to it, if all the promises in the Balfour Declaration had been kept."

"We had nothing to do with the Balfour Declaration," said Aldanov smugly. "We broke no promises."

"Your sins started after Suez," said Hasbani, his face still showing no sign of expression. "That is, if Communists admit to sin. It was you who started the armaments race in this region after Suez. If all the money that has gone into planes and tanks and missiles had gone into other things, dams, irrigation projects, things like that, we might be more prepared to talk rather than to fight."

"We give your governments only what they ask for," said Aldanov, not looking at me. "What you are saying now might be considered as treason in Cairo, Hasbani."

"I am not in Cairo," said Hasbani. "I am one of those

Arabs who does not think President Nasser is the new Mohammed. He is the Saviour of Egypt, but I do not think he is the saviour of the Arabs."

"Who is?" Aldanov said.

"I do not know. We are still waiting, as we have been for almost a thousand years, or even longer. Back to the time of the Prophet himself. I think perhaps King Hussein of Jordan could be. But he has, as Mr. Tancred would say, two strikes against him. He comes from the poorest Arab country of them all and he is a king. Poor kings have never captured the imagination."

"Are you not in favour of the Arabs fighting for their rights?" Aldanov said.

"Oh, we shall fight for our rights and, God willing, we shall win. But I'm a peaceful man, Mr. Aldanov. I wish there were other ways to achieve our aims." He bowed gravely to us all, his face still expressionless. "Now if you will excuse me, I have a house guest. I see he has just arrived."

He walked across the room, the crowd opening up about him like the Red Sea before Moses (the wrong analogy for an Arab), nodding expressionlessly to Ambassadors, Third Secretaries, businessmen and the high-priced whore alike. He reached the door of the room and put out a hand to his house guest, Caradoc Briggs.

I looked at Hacobian. "Are you going to arrest him now?"

Hacobian smiled his beautiful sad smile. "You must be joking, Mr. Tancred. What could the police possibly want with a house guest of Mr. Hasbani's?"

CHAPTER 6

I drove Lucille and her father home in the Mustang. Zaid's chauffeur-driven Cadillac had been waiting outside the French Embassy for him, but he had dismissed it and asked if he could ride home with Lucille and me. He lolled in the back seat, spread sideways across it, and now and again I caught a glimpse of him in the rear-vision mirror looking at Lucille and me with a troubled look on his face. I began to feel I was in for one of those father-to-suitor talks.

Out at sea the lights of the fishing boats were strung out like the promenade lights on a distant shore, an invisible foreign land where there was peace and no one had any problems. Some families strolled on *our* promenade, silently and stiffly, like people aware that this might be their last night for strolling before the air raids began. Against the lights I could see Lucille's profile, severe with some concentration of thought.

"Your friend Mr. Briggs has some influential friends," Zaid said.

His remark surprised me; I had been expecting some question about myself and Lucille. "What influence has Hasbani got in a situation like this one?"

Zaid smiled, a slightly cynical smile. "The influence of any man who has unlimited credit. Mr. Briggs is like any private businessman, if he sells something he is not prepared to wait years for payment. Not like governments. The Russians, for instance, may never be paid for what they have supplied to Egypt." Then he added without any irony, 'Nor you Americans, either."

"Who would Hasbani be backing? The Lebanon doesn't want to spend any money on armaments."

I saw him smile in the rear-view mirror. "No one is more in favour of peace than us. War will ruin our trade and our tourist business."

"It won't ruin *your* business," Lucille said with no expression in her voice; it was impossible to tell whether she was disapproving of her father or just stating a fact. "Especially if you stay."

"No," he conceded good-humouredly. "Wartime is always a good time for diamond dealers. As soon as money is threatened, people like to invest in non-perishable investments. I've sold three hundred thousand dollars' worth of diamonds just in the past week."

"How do you protect your money?" I asked.

"Buy more diamonds," he said, and smiled again. He blew his nose on a large silk handkerchief and said worriedly, "I am getting a cold. One has to watch a cold in this humid weather."

"Do you think there will be war? Were any of your customers influential people?"

"You shouldn't ask my father that," Lucille said sharply.

Zaid answered for me. "Why not, my dear? Paul has to do his job, he has to get information where and when he can. He can ask, but that doesn't say I'm going to answer him." He looked at me in the mirror. "A diamond merchant is something like a priest, Paul. The whole business of selling diamonds is built on trust. I get packages of diamonds in the mail, worth anything from ten thousand to a hundred thousand dollars. The packages come from dealers all over the world, most of whom have never even met me. They send their packages to me, asking no guarantee from me, just that I try and sell them to my clients, adding a bit to the price for myself. Dealer trusts dealer, and in turn the customer trusts the dealer. If a man comes into my office and wants to change his money for diamonds, I don't ask him why nor where he got his money from. My office is like a priest's confessional. So I'm not going to tell you, Paul, who has been buying diamonds in the past week." He was silent a moment, then he said, "But you asked me if I thought there was going to be war. Yes, I think there will be."

Briggs had thought the same thing. I had managed to get him away from Hasbani when the latter had been intercepted by a German businessman. We had retreated to a small balcony that looked out on to a garden; but not before Briggs had picked up two glasses of champagne on the way. 'Its not vintage stuff. The Frogs are canny hosts. All the people here that they're trying to butter-up are Muslims so they don't drink alcohol. The rest of us don't matter, so why waste good bubbly on us?"

"I thought *you* mattered, judging by the reception Hasbani gave you."

He grinned and sipped his drink. "I might matter to Hasbani, but not to the Frogs. No Englishman matters to them these days."

"I wouldn't blame them, if all Englishmen were like you. You're developing into a prize sonofabitch, you know that? I've got an authority in my pocket, worth a quarter of a million bucks to you, and when I came to give it to you this afternoon, you'd run out on the deal."

He shook his head. "You got it wrong, chum. I made no deal nor any promises. You think back to what was said this afternoon. You did all the promising."

"You asked me to see if my boss would okay the deal."

"I was covering myself. Now don't get excited——" He waved a restraining hand as he saw me stiffen. "You're playing with government money. U.S. government money at that, the biggest pile of loot the world has ever known. It wouldn't miss a quarter of a million dollars, the quick and easy way you got that much this afternoon proves that. But a quarter of a million dollars to me and my partners ——" He shook his head again. "No, Paul. I've got to cover every angle."

Ethically he may have been dead wrong, but in strictly business terms I knew he was talking sense. America's wealth leaves us without argument in so many corners of the world: a poor man always has the most defensible position. Not that Briggs was a poor man; only relatively so. "What's changed things since I saw you last?"

"War's got that much closer. Nasser's put the Arabs right out on the end of a limb and I don't think he can keep them from falling off. And the Israelis are the same. There are blokes in their Cabinet just itching to have a go."

"How do you know what's going on in the Israeli Cabinet?"

He had drained his glass. I had put mine down on the balustrade of the balcony untouched and he picked it up. "You don't want this? It's piss, but I'm thirsty. I'd give a quid for a nice cold milk-and-bitter. How do I know what's going on in the Israeli Cabinet? I don't know for sure, but let's say I've got an antenna that picks up messages occasionally."

"That must go over well with your Arab buddies," I said sourly. "Dealing with a guy who's on a wavelength to Tel Aviv."

He grinned. "I don't tell 'em. Anyhow, here in Beirut they're different men from what they are back home in Cairo and Damascus and Baghdad. They're more practical, less emotional. They're not selling propaganda here, they're buying military hardware. Look inside there." I looked back into the room. "Who's this reception for? That bunch of Krauts over there in the corner." For a man who depended on international trade he had a load of prejudices: Krauts, Frogs, Yids and Wogs. "The West German trade delegation. The Wogs broke off diplomatic relations with them back in 1965 because they took up with the Israelis. That's why the Frogs are handling all their diplomatic business for them. It doesn't worry the Wogs that the Frogs recognise Israel—Arab logic can turn a blind eye to that. And it doesn't stop them from buying as much German stuff as the Krauts want to sell them. Trade is what counts in the long run, chum, not politics. When war breaks out, you can bet the Wogs will boycott selling oil to Britain and the U.S. But if the war goes on too long, you can take another bet that the oil-producing countries will want to lift the boycott. It's human nature, Paul, and human nature is what buggers all principle in the end."

I struggled against such cynicism, but I was like a man trying to walk cat-footed over a quicksand: it would get me in the end. I looked at the German trade mission, six sleek, well-fed men in their middle age, all old enough to have fought in the war they had lost but now with not a scar nor a sign of defeat on them. I didn't hate them, only envied them. Victory is as much a burden as defeat. You have to go on justifying what you have fought for; the defeated have to admit nothing; I am still not sure what was gained by the Nuremberg trials. I wondered how burdened the victors would be in the coming war by their justifications.

I looked beyond the Germans at the two Japanese businessmen, two tiny figures standing, it seemed, under the overhang of Husain al-Qataba's belly. What were they selling him? I wondered. They, too, had lost a war, but there were no scars on them either. They were our friends now and back home in the States it was always played down how much they were making out of the war we were fighting in Vietnam; you shouldn't be too critical of a friend if he wants to make a buck or two on the side, especially if it's your side. In a classified memorandum that had come in just this past week it was estimated that the Japanese would sell one and a half billion dollars' worth of goods to Vietnam this year, most of it paid for by us. They were selling everything that was asked for, from rolled steel to the pastic bags in which the dead GIs were shipped home to their tax-paying American Moms and Pops. After all, in a war *someone* had to make a profit, so why not our friends? We could forget Hiroshima if they could.

I looked back at Briggs almost with respect; at least I no longer resented him so much. "Well, I take it you're no longer interested in my measly quarter of a million bucks?"

"Keep it, Paul. Spend it on propaganda. You may need it when all this is over."

"Then you and I had better say good-bye."

He held the empty second champagne glass in front of him like a chalice: I waited for him to bless me, he looked so sympathetic and benign. "Go home, Paul. Get them to transfer you back home as quick as you can. You Yanks can't win here. And I don't like to see you one of the losers."

"Good-bye, Doc," I said, and half-turned ready to walk out on him. "Don't take any wooden nickels. When war breaks out, I wouldn't want you to be lying awake nights thinking you'd been gypped."

"I lie awake a lot," he said quietly, still with the glass held in front of him. But now the empty chalice gave me another image of him: a man who had lost all faith. "My life has had more wooden nickels in it than you could count. Not all of them made out of second-hand planes and tanks."

I had turned back then and put out my hand. "I'm sorry, Doc. I wish it *had* been Paris or Rome."

Then I had left him and five minutes later Lucille, her father and I had left the reception. And now Naami Zaid was saying, "Lucille's mother always wanted us to go back to Paris to live. Perhaps we should have. But I love Beirut. Lucille doesn't, do you, my dear?" In the mirror I saw the expression on his face as he looked at her, an almost shattered expression as if he had already seen a tragedy that had not yet occurred. It shocked me and my hand jerked on the wheel.

"Be careful, darling," Lucille said, then looked back at her father. "It isn't that I don't love Beirut, you know that. It's just that I don't trust it any more. I'm a very simple girl, Papa. I can only love those I can trust."

She turned back to look straight ahead again, not even glancing at me. Without looking in the mirror I was aware of Zaid staring at both of us from the back seat. *You're wrong, Zaid*, I thought, *she loves me and trusts me*. There and then I made up my mind to ask for a transfer; or if it

94

came to a showdown, I'd resign. The Department frowns on its officials marrying other nationals, especially women of the country where a man is posted. It doesn't categorically bar such marriages, but it does its best to suggest, with all the subtlety of those *What Makes A Good Marriage* books that cluttered up the bestseller list a few years ago, that a nice clean American girl, preferably white, churchgoing and unopinionated, is the best mate for an American diplomat. Except, of course, in African countries where she can be black, church-going and unopinionated. They might frown on Lucille, but not if I volunteered to take her to Finland, Australia or the Argentine.

I turned the car up the ramp over the sidewalk and tooted the horn for Ahmed to open the garage doors. I had the headlights switched on and I could see the overhead door of the garage was open about six inches from the ground. I tooted again, but Ahmed didn't emerge from the garage. Then I remembered this was the day he went out to the colony of shacks to see his parents. He was usually back by this time but perhaps he had been delayed. He never travelled by bus but always walked or thumbed a lift.

I got out of the car, swung the door up with a clatter. I was about to go back to the car when I saw the bundle of rags in the back corner of the garage. I stood there a moment, the car lights blazing on me, my shadow flung like that of a menacing giant over the bundle in the corner. Even before I had taken two paces towards him I knew that it was Ahmed and I felt the sickness come up in my throat before I even knelt down to touch him.

There was a knife in his chest. He had been stabbed twice, the first time to kill him, the second time to pin a note to him. The note, though bloodstained, was easily legible. The Arabic script, roughly translated, said: *Tell your friend to go home.*

2

I saw the huge shadow appear on the wall, merging into mine, then Zaid was standing beside me. Behind us Lucille said, "What is it?"; then I heard her open her door of the car. I looked over my shoulder and said, too sharply, "Stay there!"

Zaid noticed the tremor in my voice. "Steady, Paul."

"But good Christ, why kill Ahmed? Why did they have

to do that? What harm could he do anyone?" I could feel myself trembling; I wanted to vomit, but I knew that all that would come out would be a hysteria of words.

Zaid stared down at the dead boy. He seemed to be as affected as I was by Ahmed's murder, but in a much quieter way. "Does he have a family? Who are they?"

"They live out in the Kurd colony. But I don't know who they are. I never knew his family name."

Then Lucille, still in the car, said, "There's some sort of procession coming along the road."

Zaid and I went out and looked along the sea front. In the lights of the occasional passing car we could see the procession, maybe a hundred of them, coming towards us from the direction of Pigeons' Grotto. Those at the head of the procession had flares that lit up the big banner that rode like a dragon's head above the chanting, weaving body of demonstrators. They were less than a hundred yards away and when they saw us they began to hurry, their chanting quickening and rising to a shout.

"Out, Lucille! Quick!"

She didn't argue, but tumbled out of the car as I jumped in behind the wheel. I had left the engine running; I slipped it into gear and almost drove the car into the back wall of the garage in my panic. I slammed on the brakes, switched off the lights and the engine, fell out of the car and two seconds later had crashed down the door of the garage. I fumbled for the lock, shoved it through the staple on the concrete floor, and snapped it shut. I stood up, breathing heavily as the demonstrators arrived in front of the house.

They didn't come close enough to push us around. They stood in the roadway, strung out along the kerb, still chanting but now looking a little uncertain, as if they didn't know what to do next. The men were waving the banner: *Go Home* rippled in the light of the flares like a silent, hysterical threat. I was sickeningly aware of the other threat that lay behind the door of the garage.

Zaid, drawn up to his full height, impressive and almost majestic in his quiet dignity, looked at the demonstrators from one end of the procession to the other. Then he stared straight at the leaders congregated under the banner.

"Who sent you here?" he said, cold and unafraid.

Most of the demonstrators were young enough to be

students; some looked no more than schoolboys. But the leaders beneath the banner were older men, old enough to have marched in demonstrations in Beirut against the French and in other cities in Arab countries against the British. Their spokesman was a thin, hungry-looking man who knew every move and speech required. Professional demonstrators are like professional boxers: they have always to be in training, always ready to fight from the gut.

"The people sent us! The people who are tired of American imperialism——" He went on, shouting the old clichés with the fervour of a man coining new phrases: this is another trick of the professional. He would stop a moment and look around, and the crowd would join in with their chant: "Go home! Go home!" It was all most impressive, as organised as the Yale Glee Club. It was *too* organised, that was the trouble. Who had sent them here right at this moment? Why *now*? I could feel the presence of the dead Ahmed behind the closed garage door almost as if he were sitting there in a floodlit store window. If they moved in, they could knock down the door without any trouble; if they found Ahmed, my life, and perhaps those of Lucille and Zaid, would not be worth a wooden nickel. How much had the demonstrators been told? I looked along the rows of chanting angry faces, felt the violence surging there, and tried to control the shiver that ran through me.

The leader was still shouting, working himself slowly into a frenzy. He did it beautifully, climbing to a climax like an actor; despite my fear of what was about to explode, I had to admire him. I stood behind Zaid, Lucille by my side, and watched the crowd respond. It seemed to congeal, became a giant fist that would in a moment smash all three of us against the garage door. The flares were swung about, sending a yellow spume of light over the billowing sea of faces. The faces merged, became a blur of screaming mouths, bulging eyes, shining contorted cheeks. The din seemed to push us back: I felt the garage door against my shoulder blades. Lucille's hand grabbed mine, her fingers digging into me. I thought, *Christ, are they going to kill her, too*? Ahmed, Lucille, Zaid: did they really hate us Americans so much that they would also kill all our friends? Even as I thought it, staring at the kids working themselves up to be murderers, I remembered the friend, the one who deserved to be killed, who would get away. I would bet the authorisation I still had in my pocket, the quarter of a million dollars, that there would be no demonstrators crying for Briggs' blood outside Hasbani's house.

Then suddenly Zaid shouted, a roar that drowned even the frenzied noise of the crowd. It was a roar of command, as violent in its threat as theirs, and it worked: one man silenced a hundred. He grabbed the leader by his shirt front, pulled him forward, shouted at him till the man looked deafened and stunned by the tirade hitting him in the face. It is impossible to tell you exactly what Zaid said; it was Arab rhetoric at its best and angriest. But the gist of it was that I was a man just like them, that if they wanted to demonstrate against America the place to do it was outside the embassy, that he, Zaid, was as patriotic an Arab as any of them, and that I, the American, was his friend and that he personally, by Allah and in the name of the Prophet, would die for me. And if *he* died, how would they explain that to the riot police of Squad 16? Go and demonstrate by all means, but demonstrate where President Johnson and the American government would get the message! Then he let the leader go, flung him back against those behind him. He staggered into one of the men holding a pole of the banner; the pole-holder sat down, pulling his opposite number with him. The banner collapsed, sinking into the crowd like a sail suddenly left limp by a gale that had died. The demonstration was over.

Zaid turned sharply, taking advantage of the moment, and went up the steps towards the house. Lucille and I followed, aware of the sullen stares of the crowd, but not turning to look back. We reached the front door and only then did we turn around. Already most of the crowd was beginning to drift away, going back to the interrupted coffee and talk in the cafés above Pigeons' Grotto. But some remained, the banner holders and the spokesman among them, though they had retreated now to the other side of the road and stood with their backs to the sea wall, staring across at us in the fixed pose of sentries on guard.

"Do you think they know Ahmed's body is down there in the garage?"

Zaid was putting his key in the door. He was no longer cold and majestic; his quick nervous gestures had come back. He stabbed at the lock, flung the door back. "I think not, Paul. If they had known that, then we couldn't have stopped them."

We went into the house and I went upstairs with them to their apartment. Lucille's mother had left her legacy here, too: Arabia was spread all over the living-room. She smiled out at us from a large photo on a table decorated with pearl inlay: a plump beautiful woman who might have been Arab or Jewish. She had the long Semetic nose and heavy-lidded eyes, and her hair was the black, tightly-waved hair you find on many of the Lebanese Arab women. There was nothing in the photo to suggest that she was not Arab, except that she did not have that placid, acquiescent look that was so familiar on the faces of Arab women of her class. Despite the heavy lids, her eyes were shrewd and bright, were those of a sophisticated European woman. I could not imagine that Zaid had had one word to say about how this home of theirs had been furnished.

I sank down on to a couch straight out of a harem. Lucille brought me a drink, then sat down beside me. Zaid poured himself an *arak* and sat down opposite us. He looked across at the photo of his dead wife, as if asking her opinion of what happened. Then blew his nose noisily on his handkerchief and said to Lucille, "My cold is getting worse. Get me some aspirin, my dear. And some of that medicine Dr. Jafet gave me last time."

Lucille got up and went out of the room and I looked at Zaid shaking his head worriedly at the thought of the cold that was about to strike him down. As he had told the demonstrators, he was as much of an Arab as any of them. Only an Arab could have faced possible death as coldly and fatalistically as he had down in the street, yet now behave like an abject hypochondriac in the face of a common cold. Lucille came back with the aspirin and a bottle of medicine. Zaid took three aspirin, swallowed a mouthful of the medicine, then washed it all down with a drink of *arak*. Then he relaxed, safe for the time being.

"Whoever sent those people here," he said, "I don't think he told them about the murder of Ahmed. That might have meant giving too much away. Perhaps he had hoped that you would be found bending over Ahmed. Though that would have meant perfect timing."

"Their timing was nearly good enough as it was. If Lucille hadn't stayed in the car and seen them coming———"

I felt the shiver run through me again. If the crowd had arrived with me and Zaid still in the garage, still bending over Ahmed, the cheer-leader wouldn't have needed to go into his routine. The mob would have acted on instinct, stomped me, and possibly Zaid, to death within seconds. The Negro rioters were doing it back home to white men found too close to dead or injured coloured kids. It could happen here just as easily. Mob hate has the same low boiling point anywhere in the world. "They probably hadn't counted on you and Lucille being with me."

"But why should they do such a thing? Why such a roundabout way of trying to——" Lucille's voice trembled just slightly "——to dispose of you?"

"They could make more propaganda of it this way," said Zaid, blowing his nose again, warding off death by cold germ.

Lucille sank back on the couch, put her hand in mine. "And you still don't want to leave here?"

She was pale and her eyes looked large, as if they were still distended from the shock she had had down in the street. But she was in control of herself; the hand in mine, though cold, was firm in its grip.

"No. I do want to leave here. I'd made up my mind before we even found Ahmed——"

"When? When do you want to go?"

I smiled at her impatience; but it was also a smile to relieve the tension in me, like a man stretching his limbs to ease muscles that have stiffened. "It will take a little time. I can't just pack a bag and go. Washington will have to okay it——"

"Why can't you just resign? How long does it take you to resign?"

I looked at Zaid for support. "Explain to her, please. A man can't run out without a moment's notice. And I don't want to leave the Department—not unless I have to——"

"I think Lucille is right, Paul." He gave his nose a wipe, but did not put the handkerchief away: the germ might strike at any moment. "You should get away from here as soon as you can."

"It's not that easy." I could feel myself getting angry

with both of them; reaction was setting in to what I had just been through. "There's Ahmed, for instance. You think I can just walk out, leave him down there in the garage——?" I stopped, almost spilled my drink as I thumped it down on the table beside me. "What *do* we do about him, anyway? Leave him down there till—when? Till that mob goes away? They might be there for weeks, taking shifts. The bastards who killed Ahmed will know his body is still down there, they'll keep those guys there in front of the house——" I stood up abruptly. "Can I use your phone?"

Zaid nodded. "Whom are you calling?"

"Hacobian. He'll get rid of them pretty damn' quick. Then I'll tell him what happened. He'll see the body is taken away without any fuss."

But I couldn't get Hacobian. The Sûreté told me he was out of town, could someone else help me? "No, thanks," I said. "But please ask Captain Hacobian to call me as soon as he returns."

"Yes, Mr. Tancred." They were all friendly politeness; war hadn't yet broken out between us and the Beirut police. "But are you sure no one else can help you?"

"No. It was a personal matter." Then I remembered I had to protect Hacobian's neutrality as an Armenian; if war did break out, they must not remember what police captain had been called at the Sûreté by a staff member of the American embassy. "We were to have played tennis to-morrow."

"And now you want to cancel the game, Mr. Tancred?"

"Yes. No——" They were being too friendly, especially for police. "No, just ask him to call me."

I hung up. Zaid sipped his *arak* and looked across at me. "You let yourself get too involved for a diplomat, Paul. President Johnson does not expect you to take everything personally."

"Maybe that's why I'll never make it to the top as a diplomat. But it's the way I am." I looked at Lucille. "Would you want me any other way?"

She hesitated, then she said, "No. But be careful, darling."

I said good night to Zaid, kissed Lucille at the door, and went downstairs to my apartment. I didn't switch on the lights at once. I walked across the living-room, opened the french doors and stepped out on to the small veranda. Down on the promenade, on the other side of the road, there were now only three of them: the two banner carriers and the professional spokesman. They stood leaning against the sea wall, the banner furled like a struck sail: they could have been fishermen who had come in early, disappointed because there had been no catch. Then the two banner carriers went off along the promenade towards Pigeons' Grotto, one man carrying the furled banner on his shoulder, a workman going home from the job. The professional sank down on to the sidewalk, sat with his back against the wall, staring across at the garage and the house.

Out at sea the lights of the fishing fleet hadn't moved, were still spaced out like the fixed lights along a distant shore. They had been there for ever: it was a shore peopled by ghosts stretching back six thousand years: Phoenicians, Greeks, Romans and Saracens and a score of others. They all sat there, invisible but tangible, staring through the night and history at the Levant, waiting for the next convulsion in man's attempt to live with his neighbours. I wanted to cry out to them, but what is there to say to ghosts who have seen it all before?

CHAPTER 7

When I got up in the morning the professional was still there, still sitting with his back against the wall but with his head sunk on his chest. It was somehow comforting to know that he had to sleep; that at least suggested he was human. I made coffee, breakfasted on fruit and the white goat's cheese that I like so much, showered and dressed, then called the Sûreté again. Captain Hacobian was still out of town. Could someone else help me? I thanked them, hung up and went upstairs to the Zaids' apartment.

Lucille answered the door. She was in a red silk housecoat buttoned high to the throat; she wore no make-up, but the housecoat gave her all the colour she needed. She kissed me, her lips cool and soft, but I could feel her fingers digging into my arm. "It's Sunday. Why are you up so early?"

"I want to borrow your car."

"Mine or Father's?"

"Yours." She had a Volkswagen; an air-conditioned chauffeur-driven Cadillac wouldn't be appropriate for where I was headed. "I shouldn't be more than an hour."

"Where are you going?"

"You're sounding like a wife again." I grinned, but I really wasn't in the mood for joking.

But neither was she. "Darling, where are you going?"

"I'm looking for Ahmed's family. I've got to tell them what happened, *how* it happened—I wish to Christ I could tell them *why* it happened——" I felt myself beginning to tremble again.

"Paul, please——" She clutched my arm again.

"Don't ask me not to go."

"I'm not going to. I know you have to go——" She raised a hand to my face, stroked my jaw. "In a way I'm glad you're like this. It's part of why I love you. But don't tear yourself apart over Ahmed. He may be better off. Life wasn't much for him."

"Nobody's better off dead."

"That's American optimism, isn't it?"

"None of your Arab fatalism. All I asked for was your car."

She went away, came back with the key of the car. She kissed me. "Will you always be young and charming and kind, darling?"

"Thirty-six isn't so young."

"You're young, darling, no matter how many birthdays you've had. So many Americans are. Young all their lives."

They're so damned superior towards us, I thought, *these people from the Old World*. They can't see the other side of the coin; that so many of *them* are born old, so that they know only pessimism and have never experienced the exhilaration of optimism. Pessimism may forestall disappointment; but shouldn't a man reach for the sun once in his lifetime? I kissed her, not angry with her, indeed a little sorry for her. "I'll take you to lunch."

"Pick me up at the university."

I looked at her in surprise. "Sunday?"

"I have a lot of work to clear up."

"What sort of advice are counsellors supposed to give at a time like this?"

She shrugged. "Just the non-Arab come for advice now, the Africans and the Asians. All they want to know is should they go home."

"What do you tell them?"

But she avoided the question. I was outside the door when she said, "How are you going to find Ahmed's family?"

"Briggs will help me. He knows the leaders out in the Kurd colony."

I heard her say something, but I went down the stairs quickly, not wanting any further argument. I had had enough argument with myself. I had said good-bye to Briggs last night, glad to see the last of him. But I needed him now. And in a way he owed me and Ahmed something. The note pinned to Ahmed's chest had said: *Tell your friend to go home.* Briggs was the friend.

I went out the front door, crossed the patio and opened the side gate. I looked back down towards the promenade, saw the professional still sitting with his back against the wall. He was awake now, having a cigarette for breakfast, still intent on his vigil. Ahmed was safe for a while yet.

I ran up the narrow flight of stone steps that led to the street at the back of the house. There was a double garage fronting on to this street; it sheltered the Cadillac and the Volkswagen. I took out the Volkswagen, turned down the street and drove down through the city and out along the road that led up to Aley. Cars were already moving out of town, heading for the mountains and some respite from the heat. But the traffic was not as heavy as it usually was. Most people were staying home, prepared to put up with the heat. They didn't want to be picnicking in the mountains when the bombers blew up their homes. They probably hadn't reasoned it that way, but it seemed that they would rather die among their possessions than come back and find they had none.

Lucille was like most women with a car: she put it in for maintenance only when she was reminded. It laboured up the long climb of the Aley road, wheezing as if at any moment it would stop and run backwards down into the sea. The road twisted and turned, past olive groves;

ultra-modern houses, all glass and concrete; an old Roman tower decorated with a historical plaque: Freshen Up With 7-Up; it ran past the Jesuit College, and I saw the priests on their way to mass, walking in tight dark little groups like mourners on their way to a burial. This road to Aley was also the road to Damascus, but who since Paul had seen any visions on it? I expected none. Optimism was dead this morning.

A high stone wall surrounded Hasbani's house. I pulled up outside the big wooden gates and blew a blast on the horn. A young boy in a white uniform and a red tarboosh came down to the gates, and asked who I was, then took a phone from a box on the inside of the wall and called the house. Then he nodded at me, opened the gates and I drove up the curving gravel drive to the house. House is too much of an under-statement; even mansion doesn't fit it. It was a modern castle, built of the pale local stone; Saladin would have felt at home in it, if a little out of period. Two white-uniformed, tarbooshed servants met me at the steps that led up to the wide terrace in front of the place. They escorted me through huge rooms, hung with abstract paintings (I recognised a Pollock: at least one American was welcome here), and out on to another wide terrace in the middle of which was a swimming pool large enough to have accommodated the entire Kennedy clan. In the middle of it Briggs floated on his back, serene as a great hairy water lily.

Hasbani, in a white terry-cloth robe, sat beneath an umbrella at the side of the pool. "Welcome to my humble house, Mr. Tancred," he said, and had the grace to smile. The smile was so unexpected on that featureless face that I missed my step and almost walked into the pool. The smile widened still further, but it was an ugly sight; friendly humour did not sit well on Hasbani. "You are up early. I hope you don't have bad news for Mr. Briggs? War hasn't broken out, has it, and we humble ones have not heard of it?"

"The war, when it breaks out, Mr. Hasbani, won't be a secret one. No, I need Mr. Briggs' help."

Briggs had swum to the side of the pool, moving with a slow side-arm stroke, somehow managing to keep his wounded arm out of the water. He clambered up the ladder and then I saw the collodion skin that had been sprayed over his wound. He picked up a towel and came towards us. "Hel-*lo*, chum, I thought we'd said good-bye."

I hesitated a moment, looking at Hasbani, then I took the plunge, explained why I was here. All I left out was mention of the note that had been pinned to Ahmed's chest and my suspicion that it had been as much a warning to Briggs as to myself. "You have contacts down there with the Kurds, Doc. I want you to come down with me, help me find Ahmed's parents."

Hasbani said, "I don't think it would be wise for you to go down there, either of you. The Kurds don't like strangers, especially Europeans."

"I'm sorry, Paul. I'm afraid Mr. Hasbani is right. I'd forget it if I were you."

"That's not so easy, at least not for me. It might not be for you, Doc, if you had seen him. He's dead, a poor innocent little bugger——" I succeeded in imitating Briggs' accent. "You're as much to blame for his death as I am."

Hasbani's face was expressionless once more. Briggs' face closed up again like a fist and he paused, the towel held to his head as he had been drying his hair. "How's that, Paul?"

I told him about the note. "They meant you, Doc. I think the other night when they attacked us, they were going for you, not me."

He finished drying his hair, his face still tight, then he looked at Hasbani. "Do you know anyone who would want to knock me off?"

Hasbani's deep whispering voice was faintly sarcastic. "What sort of friends do you think I have? If someone is trying to, er, knock you off, I suggest your safest place is here. Not down in the Kurd village."

"You're a good bloke, Elias." Somehow I had never expected anyone to call Hasbani by his first name; but Briggs did it as easily as if he had never called Hasbani anything else. "But I think Paul is right. I do owe that kid, or anyway his parents, something."

"Sympathy won't help them," Hasbani said. "And if you offer them money, they'll be insulted."

"I still have to go, Elias," Briggs said, and looked at me. "If only to prove to Paul here that I'm not all sonofabitch. Which is what he thinks I am."

Hasbani shrugged and stood up. His robe fell open and

only then did I see the gold cross on the chain round his neck. I should have known from his name: he was a Christian Arab. Yet last night, arguing with Aldanov, he had sounded as Muslim as any other Arab in the room. These people were too complicated, and I began to doubt that I would ever understand them. A hundred years ago the Christian Arabs in the Lebanon had been massacred in tens of thousands; but that had been forgotten, at least by this one Christian. He was an Arab, linked with every other Arab in the fight against Israel and the West. Then I wondered at my own surprise. White Americans and black Americans were dying side by side in Vietnam. And from what was happening in America itself, you might wonder what they had in common.

"Good luck," Hasbani said. "You must come again sometime, Mr. Tancred. I lived in America once, a long time ago."

"Where?"

"All over." He smiled again, just a fissure in the great globe of his face. "I was seeking my fortune."

"Did you find it?" I asked, facing the small sea of his swimming pool, my back to the castle, full of treasure but empty of people.

"Not there, Mr. Tancred," he said. "America doesn't reward everyone who comes to it."

I wondered what America had done to him a long time ago and why he hated it so much.

2

"How did you meet up with him?" I took the Volkswagen down the long hill, plunging towards the glittering sea. High up two bombers flew west, their contrails drawn like a skier's trail across the blue field of the sky. Westward, out over the sea, is the safest flight pattern for the Lebanese air force. The country is so small that within minutes of take-off they can find themselves flying in foreign air space, not all of it friendly. From Beirut airport it is less than five minutes' flying time to the Israeli border.

"I ferried in an aircraft for him some years ago. That was the first time I met him. A couple of years ago I sold him two dozen Shermans."

"Where's he got them stored? In that castle?"

"The last time I heard of them they were in the Congo."

"Whose side?"

"I never ask those sort of questions." He looked out of the car, then back at me. "What are we going to say to Ahmed's mum and dad? Christ, I'm sorry it had to happen to the kid. I really am, Paul."

"I know that, Doc. Otherwise you wouldn't have come with me. I'm glad you did."

"So am I," he said, and suddenly we were friends again.

The Kurds' shack village comes right to the edge of the road that leads north out of Beirut. When you pass it in a car it seems that all the shacks are jammed together in one vast many-roomed building, a one-storied castle of poverty; only when you pull up do you see the narrow alleys running crookedly away among the shacks, like gullies of erosion in a mesa of tin, timber and cardboard. When I pulled the Volkswagen into the side of the road I could look back up towards the mountains and see Hasbani's home, its pale stone bright as gold in the brilliant sunlight.

The narrow space between the road and the outer row of shacks, not really a sidewalk but just a long stretch of dirt, was crowded with men sitting on rickety chairs. They played backgammon on tables made of packing cases, huddled together in conspiratorial talk, were grouped around static-splintered transistor radios, or sat and gazed up at the mountains, their eyes blank with hopeless dreams. When Briggs and I got out of the car they suddenly all had a common focal point: five hundred pairs of eyes glared their hostility. Foreigners, especially an Englishman and an American, were not welcomed on this boulevard of the dispossessed.

"You better find your contact quick," I said. "Otherwise we're not going to make it past these guys on the barricades."

Briggs walked straight across to the nearest group of men. He was not wearing the Italian silk suit this morning, just slacks and an open-necked shirt; but beside the patched clothes of the Kurd men he looked richly dressed. They didn't stand up as he approached them, just stared at him waiting for him to state his business. I began to despair of seeing Ahmed's parents, began to wonder at the wisdom of our coming. What would be gained anyway? Then I shook that thought out of my head. I hadn't come here to gain anything, but to give something of myself away.

Briggs' Arabic seemed to surprise the men with its fluency; you wear down a little of a xenophobe's resistance to you when you speak to him in his own tongue. Though all the other men were still staring at us with hostility, the group Briggs was talking to slowly relaxed. Then one of them stood up, jerked his head at Briggs and me, and opened a way for us through the barricade of chairs. We went down a long alley no more than three feet wide, a winding roofless corridor off which a hundred or more rooms opened. Disembodied eyes stared out at us from the dark hovels, gazing at us with a mixture of hatred and fear: one emotion was not strong enough to drive out the other. Flies hung like thin ground fog above the garbage outside each door; the almost tangible stench forced its way up your nostrils like invisible fingers. Radios blared, every song seemingly a sad one, and occasionally in the darkness of a shack we would see the flickering screen of a television set, the grey, ghostly image of a world that was as unreal to these people as the other side of the moon.

"Christ!" Briggs said, and his voice wept.

"These are the people you were selling those rifles to, at twenty-five bucks a piece."

"Don't rub it in. What do you want me to do—give them the rifles, so they can all blow their heads off and get out of this hell?"

The guide, a tall bony man with a bald skull that was dotted with lumps, looked back at us, but it was evident that he did not speak English. Briggs smiled at him, the man nodded and went on leading the way.

"No," I said. "Just don't make a profit out of them. Don't take money from them for something that's hopeless."

Briggs said nothing, and then we came to a slightly larger shack. Our guide called out, and a moment later a man emerged from the hut. He was middle-aged and would have been a middleweight if there had been any flesh on his frame; but this one was a revolutionary and fanaticism had him burned down to the bones. His right hand was missing (was he a thief who had experienced old-style Muslim justice? Or had he lost it in the cause of revolution?), and there was a cast in his right eye. There was a look of evil about him, yet in his way he was probably just as honest as Briggs and myself. Perhaps even more so: at least he was not bothered by compromise.

His name was Kaseb and he greeted us both coldly. Briggs explained whom we were looking for, and Kaseb knew the family at once. I had the idea that he knew everyone in this whole crawling hive of people, every one card-indexed in his mind as to their support for the cause. "Why do you want to see them?"

"We have some bad news for them," Briggs said. "Mr. Tancred thought it right that he should bring the news himself, instead of sending someone else."

Kaseb looked at me, his good eye as blank as the one with the squint. Then he dismissed the guide. "I shall take you to the family myself."

There was no arguing with him. He turned away at once and there was nothing to do but follow him. We went deeper and deeper into the great rubbish dump of hovels. If he suddenly abandoned us I knew we would never find our way out of here. Briggs must have read my thoughts, because he looked over my shoulder and winked encouragingly at me. He had more faith in his ex-client, Kaseb, than I had.

At last we came to a shack no different from scores of those we had passed. As if they had been expecting us, as if some sort of bush telegraph worked here in these twisting alleys as it does in slum alleys all over the world, Ahmed's family were waiting for us outside their door. There was the father, the mother and three small children. The family resemblance was only that of the same malnutrition: hunger had marked them all with the same dulled expression. I had thought Ahmed had looked skinny and undernourished, but beside his parents and his brothers and sister he must have looked sleek and well-fed. The scraps from my table had raised him to another identity.

Briggs looked at me. I was the one who had suggested coming here; now it was my turn to do the talking. It would have been difficult enough in English; in Arabic the words were like rough pebbles in my mouth. I told them how Ahmed had died, but not the whole truth: "We do not know who killed him. It could have been a thief whom he found trying to break into my house. All I can say is——" the formal rhetoric almost crippled my tongue, but it was what was expected of me "——my heart bleeds for his death and for your misery. He was my son as much as yours. May God reward him."

The mother sat down on her haunches as if someone had hit her suddenly behind the knees. She threw her black veil over her head and began to rock back and forth, moaning like an animal in pain. The children clung to her, the little girl weeping silently, the boys staring stonefaced at me and Briggs. The father, a skeleton of a man in black trousers, black vest and a patched collarless shirt, took off the black peaked cap he wore; he snatched it off, as if he had suddenly found himself at his son's graveside. He looked at me and when his voice came out it was just a whisper that whistled softly through his broken teeth.

"Have you brought my son with you?"

"No. I thought——" I hadn't really thought of anything up till now. "You cannot bury him here. I should like to pay for the funeral and the grave in the cemetery." Otherwise they would have to take him up into the hills, bury him among the rocks and hope that the jackals did not find him.

"You are too kind, sir."

But now the alley was full of people; all of them had got the message and none of them looked as if he thought I was kind at all. I could hear them murmuring among themselves, a volatile building-up of anger.

"I think we'd better get out of here," Briggs said.

I wanted to take out my wallet, give Ahmed's family everything I had in it; but charity, dollar charity, would have been the match needed to set off the explosion. There was nothing I could do to help them escape from here; my only concern now was to see that Briggs and I escaped. The crowd pressed in, filling up the alley; the walls of the shacks threatened to buckle at any moment. The family had only grief, but the crowd wanted revenge.

Someone pushed me in the back and I fell forward against the wall of the rough shack. The wall shuddered and for one awful moment I thought I was going to knock the whole hut down with my fall. I clutched at a gap in the wall, dug in my heels as if trying to hold up the flimsy house. It was built of sheets of tin, kerosene drums hammered out flat, of thick corrugated cardboard and even newspapers and magazines wadded together: Svetlana Alliluyeva smiled comfortingly out at me from the cover of *Newsweek*: Stalin's daughter, I was assured, had chosen the U.S. I straightened up, looked urgently at Kaseb.

"Get us out of here—please!" *LBJ should see me now*, I thought: an American diplomat pleading for his life. It was no use shouting at these people to tell them I was on their side, that I wanted to help them. They weren't even concerned with the Arabs' fight against the Israelis; they just hated me because I was an American, because everything America touched ended in disaster for those who had already had enough of disaster. What had gone wrong with the shining example we had once tried to set?

Kaseb said nothing. He just stared coldly at both of us, enjoying our torture. *You sonofabitch*, I thought; and straightened still further, leaning back defiantly now against those shoving against me from behind. Anger gave me some sort of courage. I wouldn't let them kill me on my knees. Briggs had the same idea. He, too, was leaning back against the press of people, his face closed in that tight fist-like expression, his eyes black with murder.

Then without a word Kaseb jerked his head at us. He turned and the crowd opened up as if he had slashed at it with a sword. He led the way through and we followed him. I glanced back hurriedly at Ahmed's family. The mother was still rocking back and forth on her haunches, her head still covered, the children still clinging to her, moving back and forth with her to the rhythm of her grief. The father stood with his back to the walls of home: the tin, the cardboard, the magazines that were somehow a sneer from another world. He looked after me, not hating me, stupefied by fatalism: he had nothing to expect but the worst.

Five minutes later we were out on the road, standing beside the Volkswagen. "Bring the boy's body here tomorrow at ten o'clock," Kaseb said. "We shall see he is buried in the proper way."

"Is there anything I can do to help the family?" I said.

"Nothing." He nodded at the hundreds of shacks behind him. The inference was plain: what could one man do to relieve all that misery? Ahmed's family were part of the whole. He looked at Briggs. "Have you sold the guns yet?"

"Yes," Briggs said. "I'm sorry you couldn't have had them, Kaseb."

"We can wait," said Kaseb, and I remembered that the Kurds had been fighting for centuries. They would probably still be fighting when the war between the Arabs and the Israelis was long over.

I drove Briggs back up the mountain road to Hasbani's. I dropped him at the gate. "I won't come in. Hasbani will only say he told me so. That we'd get nowhere, I mean."

"You have too much conscience, Paul. You'd sleep better if you could forget it." He stood leaning on the side of the car looking in at me; then he said, "I'd sleep better myself if you got out of Beirut. Next time those blokes might put the knife in you."

"Who are you dealing with, Doc? Who's going to buy those planes and tanks from you?"

"You'll know soon enough. I've had half a dozen offers. Every one of them a friend of yours." He grinned, but without humour.

"I didn't think we had any friends in these parts."

"Are you going to get out of Beirut?"

Everyone wanted me out of Beirut. "I'll think about it."

"Well, while you're thinking about it, keep your head down. If one of those bastards knocked you off, I'd never forgive myself."

"The note on Ahmed said for you to go home. If you did, maybe they wouldn't be interested in me any more."

"It's too late now, Paul. If I was going to go, I should have gone two days ago. Before I met you."

He abruptly swung round and went in through the tall gates before I had time to ask him the question that would worry me the rest of the day. What had happened after he had met me that had kept him in Beirut?

CHAPTER 8

I drove home. I had long ago stopped thinking of Charleston as home; it was only the city where my parents lived. Home now was where my bed and my books happened to be; I was a Foreign Service bedouin, pitching my air-conditioned tent wherever the Fate that was State happened to send me. But no matter how temporary it was, I always found it a comfort to have a place of my own to go back to. I am the sort of man who needs some reassurance of permanence.

As I drove down the Place des Martyrs people were hurrying to mass at St. George's Cathedral; the sidewalk merchants were already out trying to sell them penknives, toothbrushes, fountain pens, trying to grab the churchgoers' loose change before it was dropped into the collection box. My foot lifted momentarily from the accelerator; it was as if I had caught a whiff of incense, heard an echo of a chant from the past. That was another of the things the Beaudines had found hard to take, that my mother had married a Catholic, even though a lapsed one; Dad had made it up to them by allowing me to be brought up as a French Protestant. Mother still went every Sunday to the Beaudine pew in the Huguenot Church on Church Street in downtown Charleston; but I had realised at an early age that with her church-going was a social and not a religious custom. A French Protestant had been looked upon as something strange and exotic at Groton, on a par with a Spanish Holy Roller; I had been encouraged enough to hint that our services were sometimes a bit spicy, a sort of Folies Bergère with the lid on. By the time I reached Yale I had no religion at all, but I didn't take any position on it. In the Air Force and now in the State Department I was listed as Episcopalian; it was easier than trying to explain that a French Protestant was not a foreign subversive. But in the past year my father had gone back to Catholicism, and I had found myself beginning to wonder about it. It was something I had promised myself I would look into when I had more time; not because I thought it might be *the* religion, but because it was *a* religion. When I momentarily slowed the Volkswagen as I saw the people hurrying to St. George's Cathedral, it was because I subconsciously envied them. Some of them, if not all of them, had something in which they believed. All I had was doubt.

When I drove past the embassy there was another file of demonstrators lined up on the opposite side of the road. I caught a glimpse of the professional; he was a seven-day-a-week man. I was glad to see him there picketing the embassy; that meant I could get Ahmed's body out of the garage without causing a riot. I speeded up along the Corniche.

There was a car parked outside the steps leading up to the Zaid house. I had drawn up behind it before I recognised it as Hacobian's unmarked police car. The garage door was up and he and Zaid came out as I got out of the Volkswagen. I looked into the empty garage, then into the police car. Ahmed's body was on the back seat covered by a rug.

"I tried to return your phone call," Hacobian explained. "I knew there must be something wrong when you left a message about our tennis game. I have never played tennis in my life. Football is, or was, my game, Mr. Tancred."

"I'll remember that next time."

"I hope there isn't a next time." He glanced at the heap on the back seat of his car, then looked back at me. "I drove out here and met Mr. Zaid. He explained to me what had happened. They shouldn't murder children," he said sadly; he looked too weary for anger. "One does not make any point at all by killing the innocent."

"You saw the note?"

He patted his pocket. He looked as if he was wearing his Sunday best; I wondered if he too, had been on his way to mass when he had got my message. "I have it and the knife. They will be disposed of."

Zaid had been standing watching us, almost warily, I thought; as if he half-expected Hacobian to arrest me. I would have to explain to him about diplomatic immunity, hollow as the principle might be in some parts of the world to-day. Lebanon was a civilised country and Hacobian was a civilised policeman. Zaid seemed to appreciate the latter fact because he said, "Captain Hacobian is going to take Ahmed's body up to the morgue. He doesn't feel it necessary to put all the facts into the record. The less complications, the better."

Hacobian said, "I think it would be best if we did not even look for the murderers. You understand, Mr. Tancred?"

"Perfectly," I said.

"I have suggested to Captain Hacobian that perhaps he does not even need to report that Ahmed worked for you."

Zaid will make a good father-in-law, I thought; he's got my welfare at heart. It was a pity I had to complicate things for him: "That may be difficult. I mean, up at the morgue. I'll have to go there to-morrow morning to claim the body. I've promised to deliver it to his parents for burial."

"I can do that." Hacobian, too, seemed to have my welfare at heart.

"I'm sorry," I said, and explained how I had promised to pay for the funeral and burial. "I can't back out now."

Zaid and Hacobian looked at each other. I could read the message to each other on their faces: what makes Americans so innocent? Zaid said impatiently, a father-in-law who had begun to wonder if his daughter had made the wrong choice, "Paul, if Ahmed had died naturally, from pneumonia, some disease, been run over by a car, anything at all, he would not have had a funeral. He would have been buried somewhere up in the hills and his parents would not have hoped for anything more. They would have accepted it."

"Maybe so. But it's not what *they* will accept," I said stubbornly, "it's what *I'll* accept. If he hadn't been working for me, Ahmed would not have died the way he did."

You do not ask much of me, he had said. *My parents are good people who have had a very bad time. But we pray things will get better.* And now his mother was keening to herself in the darkness of the hovel they called home, grief like a sharp-edged rock in her breast, and the father was asking himself how much more God was going to ask them to bear. I suddenly felt a grief of my own, as if Ahmed had been a son of mine. "I have to take him out there to-morrow. I have to see him buried decently."

A bus went by on the way to the airport, maybe the

last of the American tourists on their way home. They stared out at us, sullen disappointment on their faces: they had been robbed of their vacation, of all that the travel advertisements had promised them.

"I owe him that," I said.

"I'm sorry, Mr. Tancred." Hacobian looked as if he were making an effort not to sigh; I could have been an old crook whom he was trying to persuade to plead Not Guilty. "But if you want to do that, you will have to take him up to the morgue yourself. We can't give them two stories of what happened."

"Leave it with Captain Hacobian, Paul. *Please*." Zaid's gestures were even more nervous than usual; his large plump hands snapped at each other like quarrelling birds. "You mustn't think only of yourself." He saw the look on my face and he went on hastily: "I don't mean it that way, Paul. May God strike me down if I should offend you. But think of Lucille—I ask you humbly to think of me—there could be trouble right here where we stand, demonstrations—the atmosphere in the city is all wrong, Paul, for personal gestures like yours—at any other time Captain Hacobian and I should admire you—we *do* admire you——" I had never seen him like this before, almost incoherent; not even the night before last when Briggs and I had been attacked. *He's ready to leave Beirut now*, I thought; and looked up and saw Lucille standing at the top of the steps watching us. "Please, Paul. Leave it with Captain Hacobian."

"I think your embassy would prefer it that way," said Hacobian, and Zaid nodded eagerly, glad of the further argument.

We can't win, I thought. *We try so goddam hard to do good, but every time it fouls up on us, even the personal effort*. "Okay," I said resignedly. "I'll leave it to you, Captain. But what happens to him?"

"I'll see that someone from the morgue tells his parents. What is their name?"

I shook my head: nothing was going right. "I don't know. I didn't get their name. I was to deliver the body to a guy named Kaseb. He was the one who found Ahmed's parents for us."

"Us?" Hacobian's thick eyebrows went up.

I'm tired, I thought; *I'm giving too much away*. "Briggs.

I had to go to him. I knew he had contacts with the Kurds."

"So do I," said Hacobian. "Including Kaseb. You haven't been very diplomatic, have you, Mr. Tancred? Were you trying to invite trouble for yourself?"

"Believe it or not," I said, "I was trying to do some good. But it seems that's almost impossible in this part of the world."

"At a time like this, it is," Hacobian agreed. "Especially for Americans."

"So you will handle the matter?" Zaid rubbed the dark stubble on his cheeks. "I must shave and be off." He looked at the large gold watch on his wrist; it was one of those watches that told you everything but the time of your death. "I have an appointment in half an hour. I haven't sold so many diamonds since the trouble in 1958. Business was brisk then, but now I just can't keep up with the demand."

"What have you to sell a policeman if war breaks out?" said Hacobian, but he didn't sound bitter. Maybe he compared himself with Ahmed or Ahmed's parents: at least he knew he was better off than they were. He smiled at the look on Zaid's face. "Don't be embarrassed. No one blames you for other people's greed and cowardice."

"For a moment you made me feel a profiteer," said Zaid.

"I didn't mean to," Hacobian said gently. "If war does break out, you won't grab your possessions and run like these others."

"No," said Zaid, but he half-turned and looked up towards Lucille still standing at the top of the steps. Then he smiled the dislocated smile of a man making a weak joke: "But I must run now." Then he looked at me, his face at once sober. "I understand how you feel about Ahmed, Paul. But what Captain Hacobian is doing is for the best. Believe me, it is for the best."

Then he went up the steps, moving quickly and with grace for such a big man. Lucille waved to me, then she took her father's hand and they went into the house.

"He is a good man," said Hacobian. "But I should not blame him if he did leave Beirut. It is not easy for his daughter, being only half-Arab. They spat on her the other day at the university."

"Who told you that?" I looked at him in surprise.

"We have our sources. Just like Mr. Criska." He smiled, but without malice.

"Mlle Zaid is not happy," I said, preparing him, hoping he would understand if Lucille and her father did leave when war broke out. "A mouthful of spittle isn't much reward for what she's been trying to do up at the university."

"I know, Mr. Tancred. But the young to-day don't think gratitude is a virtue. I believe it is that way in your country also, is that right?"

It was time to change the subject. "Have you heard anything more of the *Dobbs Ferry*?"

"Mr. Barrington-Briggs didn't tell you anything this morning?"

"We had something else on our mind besides rifles."

"I thought when you saw Kaseb——" He shrugged, then went on: "One of our air force planes shadowed the *Dobbs Ferry* up till dark last night. Then it lost it during the night——" He smiled apologetically. "Our air force is not very experienced. When they went looking for the ship this morning it had disappeared."

I laid out a map of the eastern Mediterranean in my mind. "Eight or nine hours of darkness. There wouldn't be many ports they could make in that time. Limassol, Famagusta, Latakia. Unless they headed up the coast to Tripoli. But you'd hear about that from your own Customs people."

"Yes, we'd hear about that," he said. "We should not hear about it if the ship made for Haifa. Mr. Barrington-Briggs is like Zaid, a business man. If the price is right ——" He gestured expressively.

"Are you putting Zaid in the same class as Briggs? I thought you said Zaid was a good man?"

"He is. Selling diamonds is not a criminal business. I was just making the comparison that each man goes to the highest bidder. Zaid would not sell diamonds to the Jews, but I think your Mr. Barrington-Briggs would sell guns to anyone."

"You're wrong," I said, remembering Briggs' refusal to sell arms to the Aden terrorists. "He has morals, of a sort. Anyhow, if he sold those rifles to the Israelis, he wouldn't still be here. He'd have his throat cut before morning if the word got through that the rifles were down there in Haifa."

"There's still time."

I shook my head. "No, I won't buy that one, Captain. The Israeli agent is dead—someone told me yesterday that you fished him out of the sea with his throat cut a couple of weeks ago. The Israelis wouldn't have risked smuggling in another buying agent so soon. They'd wait a while."

"At a time like this, perhaps they can't afford to wait. If you don't think the *Dobbs Ferry* went to Haifa, Mr. Tancred, where *do* you think it went?"

"I'm only guessing, but I'd say Latakia."

He raised an eyebrow. "Syria? Then do you think the Syrians might also be bidding for the planes and tanks he is trying to sell?" He mused a moment, then smiled. "That would be something to see, would it not? Russian MiGs and American Starfighters side by side in the air. Is there such a thing as warlike co-existence?"

Then he got into his car, glanced back at the rug-covered heap on the back seat, then looked at me. "Let's hope we can bury the boy without too much trouble, Mr. Tancred. You have enough to worry about as it is."

2

"Those cruds in Boston," said Joe Oxford, and I waited for a fusillade of buttons to crack the window in front of us. "They're no better than that mob down there. What do they think they're gonna gain, burning and rioting like that? How are we gonna reason with this mob down there when those cruds back home are tearing up the place?"

"Maybe the Negroes back home don't care about our relations with the mob down there." Bill Lebow's voice was mild. "Where do you come from, Joe? Somewhere in Minnesota, isn't it?"

"Pipestone."

"Nice place? Any Negroes there?"

Oxford pursed his big lips. "None that I recall. But I've been gone from there ten, eleven years now. Maybe the town is full of them. They're coming north all the time. There are Indians there."

"Then I'd tell your folks to watch out." Bill Lebow's

smile was tentative; he never trusted his humour. "Those Indians get it into their heads to riot, they might go back to scalping."

Oxford struggled to keep his belligerence under control. I wondered what sort of an officer he had been in action; the aggressive ones are not necessarily the best. "I take it you don't blame the Negroes for what they're doing to America?"

"I don't think it's my place to hand out blame." Lebow's voice was still cool. "I just *understand*, that's all. I come from New York, uptown, not far from Harlem. If I lived there and my skin was black, I might start rioting, too." It was hard to believe that he would ever raise his voice in protest at anything; but his very mildness somehow seemed to add weight to his words. "Blessing people doesn't solve the problem they've raised."

Oxford wasn't convinced; he turned away and looked down through the window at the crowd below. "Something's gone wrong with the world," he said in bafflement; they had missed out too many subjects at West Point, "Why can't you reason with people any more?"

None of us had an answer, least of all Paul Tancred, the man who believed in reason and negotiation. I sat down at the long conference table, closed my eyes and tried to relax. Though it was Sunday the whole staff was on duty and the Ambassador had called the usual morning conference. He had been delayed in his office and now we were all here waiting for him.

I had arrived at my office twenty minutes before. I had given her car back to Lucille and had driven in in the Mustang. It was perhaps not the sensible thing to do, in view of the demonstrators I had seen in front of the embassy when driving home in the Volkswagen, but the frustrations of the morning had begun to build up a perversity in me. I had done my best to play down my Americanism and had got nowhere. From now on I was going to be no more and no less than what I was, an American, take it or leave it.

The demonstrators had acted predictably, if with more violence than I had expected. As soon as they had seen my car approaching they had run across the road in front of me. I slowed down, trying to push my way through the human wall that blocked my way, but I had gone no more than half a dozen yards when I had to stop. They were crowded around the car, banging on it with sticks, rocks, even their fists. A boy, he couldn't have been more than fourteen or fifteen, scrambled up on the hood and began to jump up and down on it. I had put up the convertible top and that had been a mistake; I heard a ripping sound and looked up to see a knife tearing through the canvas. The car was being rocked like a small boat in a wild sea; a gale of screaming and shouting drowned out any noise beyond the crowd. That was why I didn't hear the police sirens. I had suddenly become frightened; in a panic I tried to open the door and fight my way out of the hate-filled mob. Then all at once the demonstrators in front of me fell back and I saw the red berets of the riot police. I flopped back into the driver's seat and had to restrain myself from gunning the car through the lane that had opened up. I kept the car in low gear, myself under restraint, slowly followed the police through the still-jeering crowd and up to the embassy car compound.

When I got upstairs I learned I was not the only one whose car had been attacked. Joe Oxford's Barracuda had had all its windows and the windshield smashed and the mob had managed to puncture all four of his tyres. He had only managed to escape because the Marines on guard duty in the embassy had come out into the road and escorted his battered car around into the compound; the Marines had still been with him when I had come along and I had been fortunate that the police, who had been phoned five minutes earlier, had arrived just at that moment. Then Oxford had come upstairs, read Saturday's edition of the *New York Times* which had just arrived in the diplomatic bag, seen that the rioting Negroes in the Roxbury district of Boston had smashed and burned cars, and then had erupted, lumping the Negroes and Arabs together as his common enemy.

"I think I'd like to be the Icelandic Ambassador." I opened my eyes. Bredgar had come into the room and sat down at the head of the table. "They have no trouble at home and I believe they're friends with everyone abroad. Sorry I'm late, gentlemen, but some news has just come in about things down south." He looked at Ben Criska; one of Ben's agents must have sent in the news. "Things seem to be a little easier down there. Israeli troops have been sent on leave. Not all of them, of course. But there are reports that several hundred soldiers were picnicking on the beaches near Tel Aviv yesterday with their families."

"It's true," Bill Lebow said. "I was tuned in to Tel Aviv this morning. They put it out as a news item."

"I don't believe it," said Oxford; he was having a bad morning. "Not now they've got Moshe Dayan as Defence Minister. He's not the sort of guy who's likely to start backing down."

"There are some Israelis who think they've missed the boat by not going in a week ago," Bredgar said. "Maybe Dayan is one of them. He's too good a soldier to risk a war if he doesn't think he can win it. And win it quickly, because that's what they'll have to do. They'll never win a long war."

"Someone should send those guys down in the street out to the beaches," Oxford said, backing down himself now; he never argued with his senior officer. "They're already at war with us."

"You can charge the damages to your car to the embassy, Joe. You too, Paul. Anything else been happening?"

Everyone had something to report. I held back, not because I wanted to be dramatic and top everyone's story but because I was so depressed I didn't want to have to talk about what had happened to Ahmed. But I knew I couldn't keep it to myself. I was treating everything that had happened over the past two days as much too personal an involvement.

Ted Sinden, the Consul, was the last to report: "I've got people arriving from everywhere, most of them from Syria and Iraq. Families of oil men, people like that. We're trying to charter planes to fly them out, get them to Rome or Athens or Istanbul. If we have to accommodate any of them overnight, we'll keep them up at the university. They'll be better off there all together than trying to spread them around in hotels."

I wondered if Lucille would be called upon to help. It wouldn't improve her reputation with the militant Arab students, helping refugee Americans to escape. I'd advise her at lunch that it might be better for her to stay away from the university.

"Well, is that the lot?" Bredgar said.

"No," I said, and saw everyone look at me with irritation.

"Well, what is it, Paul?" Even Bredgar sounded impatient with me.

I drew a breath, tried to calm myself. Then I told them everything that had happened, flatly and undramatically as I could.

"Why didn't you get in touch with me last night?" Bredgar demanded. "As soon as you found the boy, what's-his-name's, body? You haven't acted very smart, Paul. Are you trying to conduct a one-man war or something?"

I knew I hadn't been very smart, but everyone seemed ready to misjudge my motives. "I was trying to keep the whole thing as quiet as possible, sir. What could we have done? I mean, we couldn't have made an American operation out of it. The Marines couldn't have handled this one."

"Take it easy, Mr. Tancred." Bredgar's voice was cool and quiet, but he let me know that I was talking to the Ambassador.

"I'm sorry, sir." I wasn't being very smart now, either. I took another deep breath, tried to damp down the trembling inside me. Though the U.S. Marines had been invited into the Lebanon in 1958 by President Chamoun, there were still many Lebanese, both Christian and Muslim, who remembered the fact with bitterness. Bredgar had not been the Ambassador then, and I knew that he was privately glad that it had not been he who had had to agree to Chamoun's request. He was one of our Ambassadors who did not believe in the Big Stick. This, I knew, was one reason why he might try to understand why I had done what I had.

I went on, talking to him as if the others were not in the room: I could sense the disapproval of them all, even Criska and Lebow: "If I'd been able to get in touch with Captain Hacobian, sir, everything would have been all right. Well, not all right——" I couldn't abandon Ahmed altogether. "The boy was still dead. But we couldn't have moved him till the police had got rid of those pickets outside my house. I don't even know who got them along there just at that time."

"What about this morning? Why did you go out to the Kurd village?"

I was having to defend myself to everyone. It struck me that only Briggs understood what I had done, and even he had been against me at the start. "That was wrong, sir, I admit that. I was just trying to, well, do the decent thing, that was all. I felt responsible for the boy's death."

There was silence for a while, then Bredgar said, "In future, Paul, forget about the decent thing. Do the sensible thing, instead. You don't have to carry the ball all the way yourself."

I nodded, knowing now that he understood, "Thank you, sir."

Then Criska said, "What about Barrington-Briggs?"

"Call him Briggs, that's his real name." It was time now for no more deception, not even for a bogus name. I told them about the missing *Dobbs Ferry* with its load of rifles. "If you have a man in Latakia, Ben, you might check with him." Then I added as an afterthought: "Or Haifa."

There was a murmur from one or two of the men at the table when I mentioned Haifa, but neither Criska nor the Ambassador showed any expression. Criska just nodded. "I'll do that. In the meantime we've got to do what we can to stop Briggs."

"Can you get the British to withdraw his passport?" Lebow said.

"They might do it. But they've got to haul him in first, make sure he's got his passport with him to hand it over. If he doesn't have it on him, the only way they can grab it is when he presents it at the airport on his way out. And it will probably be too late then."

"What about having him arrested by the Lebanese?"

"I've suggested that to Hacobian," I said. "No go."

Bredgar took off his glasses, polished them. "Well, if we can't stop this man, then we have to find out who his possible buyers are, get to them and see if we can't make some sort of deal with them. Get them to forget the planes and tanks for some other sort of aid."

"Do you think any of the Ay-rabs want to talk to us at all, sir?" Oxford asked.

"Possibly not," said Bredgar. "But we have to try everything we can. We're not only trying to convince everyone here in the Middle East that we're neutral. We're trying to prove the same thing to the Russians."

Oxford's face showed what he thought of having to prove anything to the Russians; but he controlled himself remarkably well: the buttons on his shirt caught the light, but didn't look dangerous. "I was on the phone with their Military Attaché yesterday afternoon, sir. He told me they're still sticking to their bargain with us. No more arms for anyone. I'm not inclined to believe them, but there's nothing for us to do but go along with them."

"I do believe them," Criska said. "We're not sure, but we think it was they who started all this. We've got evidence that they warned Nasser early last month that the Israelis were building up to attack Syria. It was a lie, of course, but Nasser fell for it."

Bredgar showed no surprise at the information. But I could see that the others were like me: this was the first we had heard of it. We all got on well with Ben Criska, but it was obvious that in his own mind he did not see himself as working with us or for State. He worked for the CIA, another government altogether.

"Where we think things went wrong for the Russians was in the way Nasser reacted. Closing the Straits of Tiran, kicking out the UN force, moving eighty thousand troops up into Sinai. I don't know what they *had* expected, but I don't think they expected him to pull all the stops out like that. That's why I think Kosygin was prepared to listen to the President when he got in touch with him."

"Well, whether they precipitated the crisis or not," said Bredgar, "we have to go along with them. If Briggs does sell those planes and tanks, there's nothing to prevent the Russians doing the same thing. They might not sell them direct, they'd probably want to keep up the pretence of not being warmongers. But they have plenty of puppets who'd act for them." He looked at Criska, ignoring me. "I think you'd better get moving, Ben."

I sat back, not offended; in fact, I felt relieved. From now on Criska, secure against involvement, taught to see the whole international game in terms of pawns, could deal with Briggs.

Ben Criska and I were the last to leave the conference room. He had picked up the copy of the *New York Times*

Joe Oxford had left lying on the table, glanced at it, then dropped it back on the table.

"Sometimes I wonder if isolation isn't the best policy." I looked at him in surprise; perhaps he was not so secure after all. "Maybe we should all be home trying to learn to live with each other."

"Did it work in the Nineteen Thirties?"

He smiled humourlessly and shook his head. I looked at him more closely, for the first time caught a glimpse of the real man behind his cloak of anonymity. When his tour of duty abroad was finished and he had to return to CIA headquarters, to that concrete-and-glass spread in Langley, Virginia, that looks like a sanatorium for the dying, he would dry up with frustration and soured memories and the inevitable down-grading of status. It happened to all field men when they went back to a desk job; I knew it would happen to me when the time came. Foreign Service men have their own selfish reasons for fighting isolationism.

"No. That was when my old man was fighting U.S. Steel. And *they* sure enough weren't trying to live with *him*," he said wryly. "The past always seems so much simpler, when you remember it. But maybe that's only because you've managed to survive it. Who knows, ten years from now we may be thinking to-day was pretty simple."

"I wouldn't bet on it," I said. And tried to remember what problems had faced me ten years ago, back in 1957, and couldn't. But it still didn't give me much optimism about the present.

3

Janet Ponder was putting her face on when I got down to my office. "Karl, that's the new one, likes the sexy Continental type. Do you think a girl from Lincoln, Nebraska, can look sexy and Continental?"

"I knew a girl from Butte, Montana, who looked sexy and Oriental. Her old man ran a Chinese laundry."

She made a face in the mirror of her compact. "I suppose she gave herself one of those exotic Chinese names. Lotus Flower or something."

"No, she called herself Carmen Foo. She used to go down to Mexico every year looking for a Chinese bullfighter."

Ruth Hacker sat at her desk by the window, her pursed-up expression showing only too clearly what she thought of my conversation with Janet. These inanities were a regular routine with Janet and me; it was the one wavelength on which we were at home with each other. When you are working with people day after day you have to find some contact with them other than your work alone; I am not self-contained enough to be able to treat people as machines. But I had never been able to make contact with Ruth Hacker. It was almost as if she insisted on being a machine and nothing more.

Janet finished putting on her face, not making a very good job of being sexy and Continental: Lincoln, Nebraska was still there plain as the sun behind the mascara and the pale lipstick. "Karl has been advising me to leave, Mr. Tancred. He says if we don't get out soon, there won't be any planes for us to get on."

"Well, it's up to you, Janet. I'd be sorry to see you go, but if you feel——" I looked across at Ruth Hacker. "What about you, Ruth?"

"Where would I go?" she said, and for the first time since I had known her she sounded uncertain. "I haven't been home to the States in twelve years. There's no one there." She looked out the window; when she looked back at us the old mask was there on her face. She slipped an envelope into her typewriter, set the margin carefully for typing the address. "I'll be all right, Mr. Tancred. There's some personal mail for you. I put it on your desk."

I looked at Janet, who twitched an eyebrow as if to say: *What can you do with a woman like that?* Janet had evidently asked Ruth for advice on whether she should leave Beirut and had got no satisfactory answer. My own answer had been just as unsatisfactory. She snapped shut her compact, stood up and went out to lunch with Karl, the Swiss expert on evacuations.

I went into my office, picked up the letters on my desk. One was from my father, the other from my mother. Dad had his problem, too: "I am about to preside at the trial of a young man—Shepley Cooker, you may remember him—who is accused of raping a Negro girl. It is a most unfortunate case. Young Mr. Cooker, albeit the scion of a very good family, has been in trouble all his life. Before the war, in the 1930's, he would have been hustled out of town and the case allowed to lapse. Not justice, of course, but expediency that worked then. Of course it would not work to-day, and so young Mr. Cooker looks like being sentenced. It is all most unfortunate—not least for the Negro girl, of course . . ."

I felt a wave of sympathy for Dad, trying so hard to tear himself out of the past and bring himself into to-day. Despite himself, he still belonged to a time long gone; his thinking was as out of date as his prose style (*albeit a scion . . .*), but he struggled hard to be just and liberal (*not least for the Negro girl, of course . . .*). He would sentence young Mr. Cooker, whom I did not remember at all, to the maximum, but I knew that he would lie awake at night wondering why he had to prove his sense of justice and liberalism at the expense of the sentiment he felt for a simpler, if more unjust time. In the 1930's the South had had its own isolationism, and it had worked. At least for some people.

Mother had no problems: "The garden is looking beautiful. The azaleas were particularly good this year, though of course they are now almost gone. Old Mose asks after you. He is a dear old man, so contented, except I think he worries a great deal about his son, the youngest one, who is now up North and working for General Motors and getting involved in union politics or something. I feel so sorry for Mose, who is so gentle and easy going himself . . . In the meantime, I know you'll be delighted to know that Charlene hopes to attend the next St. Cecilia Ball. There is talk that they may relax the rule against divorcees attending the Ball—somehow I never think of Charlene as a divorcee, strange, isn't it?—it has always been a rule I have believed in in the past, but I suppose one must move with the times. It does seem unfair that a girl like Charlene should be excluded just because you and she could not live together . . ."

Ah, she's impregnable, I thought. Mother, not Charlene. Charlene, I hoped despite all the portents, was not burying herself in all the dust and trappings of the past; I could not imagine that she was breaking her neck to get to the St. Cecilia Ball, with the waltz and the slow fox-trot as its only dances and no alcohol for the ladies. But Mother would be there, as she had been for forty years, waltzing with Dad and dreaming of her grandmother's day, her mind drugged with magnolia-scented memories that were not her own, when coloured folk were all contented and when divorce was not for ladies. She was impregnable, all right, shielded by nostalgia and a lack of proper imagination.

I would write to them, but what would I say? "Dear Mother and Dad: Young Ahmed, so gentle and easy going, was stabbed in the chest last night . . ."

There was a knock on the door and Ruth ushered in Grimsby-Orr. "Sorry, old man. Always seem to be dropping in on you. Quite a crowd you have out there in the street. They waiting for Frank Sinatra or someone?"

"Knock it off. You British and your *Punch* sense of humour."

He flung himself into a chair, bounced a little, punched one hand into the other. "I've just come in from Shemlan. We're moving them all into town, you know. Just in case."

Shemlan was a village in the mountains just outside Beirut. The British had a school there, the Middle East Centre for Arabic Studies, and though it was supposed to be no more than an Arabic language school for Foreign Office staff, oil men and bank staff, there wasn't an Arab who knew of it who didn't believe that it was not a training school for spies. Blake, the double agent, had been attending it just before he was recalled to London and arrested; Philby, another double agent, was another who was said to have been at the school. Grimsby-Orr spent a lot of time out there, but I had never asked him what he did.

"One of our teachers out there, nice chap, an Iraqi, told me there is a meeting this afternoon. All the Arab commercial attachés are getting together. Not only them. Some of the unofficial agents, too. I gather they're all going to bury the hatchet, for this afternoon, anyway."

"What's the idea?"

"Your friend Briggs. Seems he's been doing some auctioneering. Now they all want to find out who's bidding against whom." He relaxed a moment, stared down at his open hand. Then he said fiercely, "Briggs is a clot. Why the bloody hell doesn't he wake up to what a bloody mess he's causing?"

He got up, went to the window, stared down into the

street. "I don't have much time for the town Arab. It's the *bedu* I'm fond of, the desert man. They're an absolutely marvellous people. But Christ, we've mucked them about, haven't we? We English always do mess things up when we're dealing with an emotional people." He looked back at me. "But you Yanks aren't much better, are you?"

I could see my office copy of the *New York Times* folded over in my *In* basket: a helmeted cop peered at me over a cocked pistol and behind him a Negro boy glared wild-eyed at me. "We're learning," I said. "The hard way."

He leaned back on the window ledge, only half-relaxing, like a man resting between squash games who didn't want his muscles to go cold. "I hope by to-night I'll know who Briggs' customers are. I'll be on the blower to you right off, Paul, soon's I know. I hope you'll do the same for me, if you get the gun first."

"Ben Criska is handling it now," I said, and only then did I realise how relieved I was.

"Oh." He looked disappointed. I knew he didn't get on well with Criska; he found him too secretive. Espionage agents, and I was pretty certain that Grimsby-Orr was one, don't appreciate having to gouge information out of other agents who are supposed to be their allies. Ben Criska was the sort who probably hated even to confide anything in a report to CIA headquarters. "Well, I'll keep in touch anyway. You never know."

As he moved towards the door I said, "Do you know where Briggs has got these aircraft and tanks stashed away? Mightn't it take him weeks to deliver them?"

"That's one of the flies in the ointment, old chap. He could deliver in about forty-eight hours. He has the planes and tanks on half a dozen ships spread round this end of the Mediterranean. Our only way to stop them getting wherever he wants them to go would be to pull them up on the high seas. You know what that would mean. The buyers, whoever they are, would be knocking on the UN's door next morning, accusing us of piracy."

"How come his company, Vulcan, could speculate so much money? They must be up for over three million dollars."

"A certain African country was going to buy the stuff. Reneged at the last minute. No cash in the exchequer, I shouldn't be surprised. Vulcan must have sized up the situation here, took a risk. They persuaded the NATO country who sold them the goods to extend their option. Briggs flew in here, coming here anyway because of those rifles and the Kurds. He was pretty certain he could close a deal within a day or two. But now he seems to be getting greedy."

"Where did you learn all this? Out at the school at Shemlan?"

His freckled face had enough innocence for an entire choir. "All we learn out there, Paul, is a few Arab phrases."

"Such as?"

"*Ana mitkaddir. Bass malzum.*" ("I am sorry. I have to go.")

I bunched my fist, but he had already skipped out the door.

CHAPTER 9

At lunchtime I walked up to the university. The demonstrators were still outside the embassy, still chanting their insults; but it had all become a ritual now, one that bored them as much as the watchers inside the embassy. But given any small provocation they could soon throw away their boredom; they looked for vexation as a beggar might look for charity. Uncharitably, I went out the back way from the embassy.

Across from the university groups of students lounged in the Rue Kennedy outside the hospital; I wondered if the street would still keep its name if war broke out. One or two of them shouted at me as I went in the gates, but these weren't demonstrators; they were only kids with nothing to do, filling in an idle Sunday. The gateman saluted me and I went on down between the Pharmacy and the Public Health buildings to Lucille's office. A couple of Pakistani girls passed me, soft and delicate as reeds, their long robes blowing like a green mist about them; two African boys went by, conversing in rich BBC English. Down through the trees I could see the soccer field and beyond it the baseball diamond:

some boys there were shagging fly-balls, shouting "I got it!" as the ball floated down into their gloves. The whole place suggested an oasis of peace and I could feel myself beginning to relax in its atmosphere. It was only when I reached the space between the Administration building and the Library that I saw the Americans, a couple of hundred of them, sitting on their belongings in the shade of the tree beyond.

Lucille was waiting for me outside the Administration building. She saw me looking at the group of women and children. "They came in this morning. They're mostly Aramco people from the oilfields. Two chartered planes are coming in this afternoon to pick them up."

"Have you had anything to do with them?"

"Not yet. But if any more arrive, and they're expected, I guess I'll have to." She smiled and put her hand in mine. "Don't worry, *chéri*. I know what you're thinking. But if the students are going to resent my being kind to women and children, then I think I might do some spitting myself."

I pressed her hand and we began to walk back up towards the gates. A young boy came running after us. "Sir!" He was about Ahmed's age, but twice as big; all his life he had had enough to eat, had got the right vitamins. *You're so lucky, kid,* I thought; *I hope you appreciate it.* Maybe he did, because there was a humility about him that I had not found among most American kids last time I was home. "Sir, my mother would like a word with you, please."

Lucille and I followed him over to the trees. A woman, two small children clinging to her hands, had been sitting on a suitcase. She rose as we approached, wearily, as if she might have spent the last week sitting on a suitcase waiting for planes that never seemed to arrive. She was in her late thirties, blonde, her skin dried out by years of exposure to the sun; she was one of the new-type pioneers, the women who follow their oilmen husbands into the deserts and jungles of the world. She introduced herself, Mrs. Watson, and her face seemed vaguely familiar.

"You met us on a trip you made down to Dhahran about a year ago. My husband had to take you around."

I remembered her now, but still only vaguely. I could not remember many of the people I had met there; it was the town itself that had made the impression. I am used to how we manage to stamp *America* on every part of the world where we gather in any sort of numbers: the air force bases in Britain, the army bases in Germany. All countries with any sort of wealth and power manage to do it: the British have their cricket grounds, their stuffy clubs, their conservative banks, still spread around the remains of their Empire; there are still relics of French influence here in the Lebanon, even though the French have been gone for more than twenty years. But we Americans had taken a stretch of desert and built on it an air-conditioned, deodorised, pre-shrunk town that looked as if it had escaped from the advertisement pages of the *Ladies Home Journal* and, somewhat to its own mystification, had finished up here at, as one man had described it to me, the ass-end of *Arabia Felix*. I had drunk a Coke (no liquor was allowed because of the local Wahhabi laws) at the Rolling Hills Country Club, had supper of a charcoal-broiled T-bone steak with French fries, followed by blueberry pie, at the restaurant, gone to the movies and eaten popcorn as Omar Sharif got frost-bitten in Siberia. I had been at home among Americans in a Little America and had found it all a fantasy and incredible. But it was now part of the American interest in the Middle East, a symbol of the two-and-a-half billion dollars we took out of Arabia each year. I was committed as much as Mrs. Watson's husband to its protection.

"We didn't want to leave," Mrs. Watson said, hushing the two tired and irritable younger children. "But they thought that those with children——" She shrugged, as if to say that oil companies could not be expected to understand that families do not like to be broken up. "Do you know where they are sending us, Mr. Tancred?"

"I heard London," said the boy. "Boy, that'll be great! I can let my hair grow."

His mother smiled with tired indulgence. "He wanted to grow it down in Dhahran, but his father wouldn't let him. Said it might create a bad impression with the Arab workers. We've had some trouble down there lately with——" She looked around, then lowered her voice. "You're not from Texas, are you, Mr. Tancred?"

"No. South Carolina, a long time ago. But I know what you mean, Mrs. Watson."

I remembered Watson now, a big, tough, soft-spoken

man who had been most careful always to treat the Arab workers with respect. He had told me how it was the company's policy never to act with superiority towards the Arabs, but how invariably they always had trouble with the Texans on the staff, how they brought their racialism with them as if it were some sort of disease for which there was no cure. I sometimes think Texas should be allowed to secede from the Union, given its own State Department. Texans give us Foreign Service men more trouble abroad than travellers from any other three States you care to name. But I smiled and wished the boy good luck with his long hair in London. At his age he shouldn't have had to carry the burden of America's image.

"How long do you think before we can go back? The children are already missing their father." She smiled again, the sun-wrinkles around her eyes making her look older. "So do I."

"I wouldn't even guess," I admitted. "But let's hope it isn't too long. The news is a little better this morning. The Israelis are supposed to have sent some of their troops on leave. So maybe it's all going to blow over."

"Darn!" said the boy, and ran his hand over his crew-cut. "I mightn't even get to London."

"Never mind," I said. "At the rate we're influencing them, the Arabs may soon have their own Beatles. Then your father won't have to worry how long your hair is."

Lucille and I said good-bye to them, walked up to the gates and caught a cab down to the St. Georges. Sitting beside me in the back of the cab, a late-model Chevrolet that the driver hurled through the narrow streets like a tank, Lucille said, "If they make the university a reception centre of refugees, I'm wondering if some of the demonstrators won't try to wreck the place. They'd be stupid enough to. They arrested two of the students trying to smuggle in Molotov cocktails this morning."

I cursed, sadly not angrily. "What's the matter with them? The university is run for *them*, not for us."

"Do you think the Israelis might bomb it, I mean if war does start?"

"I don't think so. One thing the Jews respect, maybe more than anyone else in the world, is education and learning. I don't think they'd bomb a university any more than they would one of their own temples."

"The British didn't in 1941. Papa told me that all the British pilots were given a map of Beirut with the university marked in red on it. They would have been court-martialled if they'd dropped any bombs on it."

The British and our own American bombers hadn't been so selective and considerate of German universities; and I wondered what had been the thoughts of any Jewish pilots in the RAF and USAF as they had heard the cry of "Bombs away!" as they had flown over the university districts of Berlin and Leipzig. But maybe by then they had despaired of German education and learning.

The cab driver, fat, bald, and radical only in his defence of what he would charge us, had been listening to our conversation. But he said nothing, and I wondered if he had marked Lucille for reference to someone if and when the real trouble began. I turned my head to give her a warning look, but she just smiled at me and snuggled closer. She seemed happier and more relaxed than for the past week, and after a moment I relaxed with her, squeezing her arm against my body. The news from Tel Aviv seemed to have reached everyone.

Even on the terrace of the St. Georges you could feel the lessening of tension. Usually by this time of the year the exodus to the mountain resorts of those who could afford it had begun. But the wealthy escapees from the summer heat were just like the one-day picnickers: it seemed that they, too, wanted to be at home when their homes were bombed. But they were not expecting bombs to-day. The terrace was crowded and the chatter almost drowned out the roar of the passing speedboat trolling its bikini-clad bait.

We managed to get a table overlooking the water; being an American has its advantages at least with waiters. The waiter adjusted the umbrella so that we sat in a pool of shade, took our order and scurried away. He had to make as many tips as he could while he could; no one knew when the season might end. The waiters were not relaxing because of the good news from Tel Aviv.

"I'm putting on weight. I have to watch it, otherwise I'll finish up like my father's mother. She had the Arab figure, big bosoms, wide across the hips. Great in bed, I suppose, for the man, I mean. But it wasn't meant for anything by Givenchy or Quant."

"Who are they?"

"*Chéri*. Don't you know *anything* about women?" She smiled, putting her hand on mine and digging her nails gently into me.

"I never read the fashion pages, if that's what you mean. They never tell a man anything about a woman. They only tell other women."

"Now you're just trying to sound like a cynic. You shouldn't, *chéri*. Americans don't make very good cynics. That's what I like about you." Her nails dug into me again; we were practically in bed there on the terrace. "It's not all I like about you."

"Easy. There are about fifty-seven *voyeurs* watching you trying to seduce me. Here, have an olive."

She laughed, scratched the back of my hand and sat back. It was weeks since I had seen her as gay as this. I suddenly loved her very much, and wondered how soon I could get away from the embassy this afternoon.

The pool of shadow in which we sat all at once darkened; I looked up at the bulk of Husain al-Qataba. He gave Lucille a cursory nod, his concession to her as an emancipated woman, then he looked at me. He was in Arab garb again to-day, an outfit that looked brand new, as if he had just had it run up for the occasion. I guessed that people could dress for crises as much as they might for weddings or funerals. It only occurred to me then that the most militant Arab of them all, Nasser, never wore anything but Western dress.

Husain gave me a flowery greeting, then said, "May I intrude for a moment, Mr. Tancred?" A waiter had appeared behind him with a chair and Husain lowered himself on to it without looking around; it was a simple thing, but it reminded me of how much this stout Yemeni still belonged to a medieval age; he was a *sayyid* who still believed in a need for slaves. I looked at the waiter, wondering if he was an ex-slave from Yemen, but I recognised him. He was just a Greek waiter who knew where the good tips came from.

Husain made a steeple of his long fingers; or perhaps it was a minaret. "Mr. Tancred, I am told you have had a visit from Fahad Aziz, one of the Imam's dogs. Am I right?"

"About the visit, yes. I am not going to make any comment one way or the other on your opinion of Fahad Aziz."

"I hope you are not going to sell him the planes and guns you refused to sell me?"

"We are selling nothing."

"Six weeks ago all we had to do was say we were in the market for arms, and salesmen came flocking like vultures."

"Not me. And please don't let's talk of vultures. M'amselle Zaid is about to have her lunch."

"I humbly apologise," Husain said, but his apology to Lucille was as cursory as his recognition of her had been. His eye was caught for a moment as the speedboat roared by again; the two skiers in their bikinis flashed by right below us, subliminal promises of sex. He pursed his lips as if tasting something, then looked back at me. "Is it that you are now looking for the highest bidder, Mr. Tancred?"

"I told you, we're selling to no one."

Out of the corner of my eye I saw Briggs come out on to the terrace with Hasbani, Sandra Holden and a stranger who was dressed in a dark suit, cut English style, but who wore Arab head-dress. The terrace was crowded, but somehow an empty table was conjured up by three waiters who appeared like genies. Americans were not the only ones who had the magic touch; Hasbani had it too. I must have turned my head slightly to look at the newcomers, because when I looked back at Husain he was watching me curiously.

"Of course, Mr. Tancred! I had forgotten. Mr. Barrington-Briggs is a friend of yours, isn't he?" He stood up, looming over us, shutting out my view of Briggs. He had taken out his worry-beads and they were crawling in and out of his fingers like a small yellow snake. "You are playing the wrong sort of game, Mr. Tancred. And so is your friend. You should tell him so."

He went across the terrace, waddling between the tables, and disappeared into the hotel. Lucille looked at me. "What was that all about?"

I looked across at Briggs and said slowly, "Husain

thinks Briggs is an agent for us. I wonder how many others think the same?"

2

I didn't enjoy my lunch, light though it was. I kept looking across at Briggs and after a while he sensed it; he turned round, saw me and waved. He said something to Hasbani and the others, got up and came across to Lucille and me.

"Lucille." He kissed her hand, with none of the self-consciousness that English and American men usually show when they go in for Continental gallantries. He saw my raised eyebrow and winked. "It's the Celt in me."

"I didn't think the Celts had much time for women. Wasn't it a woman who gave away the original Caradoc to the Romans? That's what you told me in Korea."

"I've mellowed since then, chum, take another view of history altogether." He winked at Lucille. I looked at her, waiting for her reaction. But instead of the chilliness I had expected, she was smiling at him. Was it her own rediscovered gaiety or was his goddam charm at last beginning to work on her, too? "There was this bird Cartismandua, a bit of a wanton as they called them in those days——" Then he glanced back at his own table, straightened up. "I'll tell you another time, Lucille. Paul, I'm without the ready again. Left my wallet up at Hasbani's. I'm supposed to be the host at this little luncheon. Could you——?"

"Why the hell don't you join the Diners' Club?"

"I belong to it, and half a dozen others. All their cards are in my wallet."

I had taken out my wallet. "I haven't got enough. Look, put it on my Diners' card——"

"I'll lend it to you, Mr. Briggs." Lucille had taken her wallet out of her handbag.

Briggs was not embarrassed. "I'll only take it if you call me by my first name. I never borrow from women who call me Mr. Briggs."

They smiled at each other like old friends. "Caradoc—I like that much better than Doc—take what you want."

Briggs extracted some notes from her wallet. "We're being watched by everyone here on the terrace. They probably think I'm being paid off for something."

"They must be thinking I'm the only guy in the Lebanon who sits quietly by while his girl pays off their blackmailer. How are you going to explain it to Sandra and your friends?"

"I'll be just as frank as I ever am." He smiled impudently; he seemed as gay as Lucille. "Tell them it was blackmail——" He kissed Lucille's hand again. "Thank you, Lucille. You'll have it back this afternoon, I promise. I owe you a couple of quid, too, Paul."

"Forget it. But there's just one thing——" But he had gone, before I could warn him what Husain al-Qataba had told me. If he was playing a dangerous game, he was either unaware of it or he did not care. He was back with Hasbani, Sandra and the stranger, laughing and joking with them as if the four of them were all tourists without a care in the world, as if this terrace were somewhere on the Riviera, far from the threat of war. The news from Tel Aviv this morning seemed to be infectious.

I looked back at Lucille. "All of a sudden you like him?"

She was still looking across at him. It was a moment before she turned back to me. She stared at me, then suddenly she smiled and impulsively put her hand on mine. "Darling, you're not jealous!"

It hadn't occurred to me that I might be. I considered it for a moment, then I smiled and shook my head. "I'm too smug and conceited to feel jealous. I *know* I'm the only man you could love."

"I know it, too. Even if that is a stupid thing for a girl to say to a man as sure of me as you are." Her nails dug into me. "I'll be finished at the university by four. What time can you get away from your office?"

"Blackmailed, seduced—all in public. Life was never like this back in Charleston. But you still haven't told me why you've changed your mind about Doc."

She looked across at him before she replied. She never at once gave an opinion when asked for it; she was a girl of considered judgements, unlike most women (or is that a man's unconsidered judgement?). "I don't really know. Perhaps it's because I've just come to realise that he likes you. *Really* likes you, I mean. Were you very close friends when you were in that prison camp together?"

Sitting here on this sun-drenched terrace, amid the chatter, the abundant food and drink, the expensively dressed men and women, it was not easy to conjure up that cold, grey encampment of fifteen years ago. It was also not easy to conjure up just how strong the bond had been between Briggs and myself. Friendship was a word that had been devalued in the circle in which I moved, the society of surface contacts: the meaningless kiss on the cheek on meeting and parting; the endless talk, no matter how serious, that rarely exposed the real person beneath; the dinner parties and salon gatherings, the manifestations of group friendships that were no real substitutes for true understanding between two people. I had come to the conclusion that deep, understanding friendship was not possible between more than two people; the complexity of human nature made it impossible for even three people to understand and love each other with the same depth and patience as two could bring to their relationship. Briggs and I had not separated ourselves from the other men in that camp; there had always been a group, sometimes four or five of us, sometimes more; but Briggs and I had always been the constant nucleus of whoever made up the group. I looked across at the promenade and saw two men strolling along together, hands linked together by their little fingers. There is a fair amount of homosexuality among town Arabs, but this did not mean that those two men were lovers. They were probably just two poor, lonely men who felt a need of each other, who were friends. It struck me then that it is possible that only the poor now have the time and the social isolation to indulge in true friendship: it is the one luxury they can afford that escapes the rich and well-to-do, who are afraid of lost time and the terrors of isolation. Briggs and I had both been poor in that prison camp, yet both of us rich in time and solitude. The conditions had been ideal for friendship.

"Yes," I said. "We were very close."

"I think he would like to be that close again. He's a very lonely man, Paul."

I looked across at Briggs, the life of the party at the other table: he even had Hasbani smiling. "Maybe," I said, and remembered that he had been the life of the party at

Pyongyang, where he had once confessed to me that, among five hundred men, he had never felt so lonely in all his life.

Later, driving back to the university in a cab, Lucille said, "If you and Caradoc could become friends again, I should like that. When you and I are married, I'd like you to have a close friend." She must have thought she sounded too serious, because she smiled. "I mean a close man friend. I'm not going to let you have a mistress."

"There goes another illusion. I thought all Frenchwomen took their husband's mistresses for granted."

"I'm only half-French."

"Well, what about the half of you that's Arab? Aren't Arab women supposed to be tolerant, too?"

"Not the emancipated ones, like me." She smiled; this was how it had been between us up till a few weeks ago. Then she said, "But I would like it if you and Caradoc were friends again like you used to be."

"We'll never be that close again. Our worlds are too far apart. I don't mean what he does as opposed to what I do—though that doesn't help." Careers are something else these days that, as Briggs would have put it, have buggered friendships. "We'd never be in the same place long enough to pick up the threads again."

"You're picking them up now. Or at least he is trying to."

"No, I don't think he is trying to, at all. He *would* like to." I was silent for a moment, watching Beirut slide quickly by outside the car: the curio shops empty of tourists, the peddlers reduced to talking to each other, a town waiting for a war that it really didn't think was any of its business. "So would I. But this isn't the time or place. We won't become friends again here," I said with a regret that surprised me. "Not real friends like we used to be."

She studied me as the cab slowed down, horned its way through a group of demonstrators that was marching up the street, gay and light-hearted as carnival-goers: they didn't have to put up their aggressive face till they reached the scene of the intended demonstration. "You'd be upset if something happened to him, wouldn't you?"

We were through the demonstrators. I looked back at them, then turned back to her. "I'll be more upset if something happens to you. Those fellers are on their way up to the university—they must have heard about those American families up there. I don't think they'll get nasty with women and kids, but they could get nasty towards anyone who looks as if they're helping them. Do me a favour. Go home, don't go near the university till we've got all the refugees out of there." Refugees: the word sounded strange on my tongue when applied to Americans. For too long it had been a word we applied only to other people; we were gradually being educated in the lexicon of the unfortunate. I leaned forward, told the driver to take us down to the Corniche de Chouran. Then I sat back beside Lucille, took her arm in mine, squeezed it. "I'll try and get away from the office within the next hour."

She got my message. She squeezed my arm in reply, smiling at me. We both knew the cab driver had his ears pinned back, but we were going to give him no more for him to gossip about to other cab drivers back on the rank where we had picked him up. He had enough already: that I and some other man wished we could become friends again, that I was afraid that Lucille might be accused of being pro-American. I didn't want him to have proof of that last fact by letting him know that she was so pro-American she was prepared to go to bed with one.

Lucille turned her body slightly so that her breast pressed against my elbow. It's a hell of a place for sexual contact, but the feeling still got through to me. Her lips moved soundlessly, but I read them clearly as if she had said the words aloud: "I love you, *chéri*."

I wouldn't bother to hang about at the office for an hour. I'd tell Janet and Ruth that I had some work to do at home, then beat it at once. Even at the height of international crisis, a diplomat should be entitled to some personal involvement of his own.

3

That, of course, was the trouble: personal involvement of my own, but in a different way from which I had expected.

When I got back to my office Grimsby-Orr was waiting for me, moving restlessly up and down the room like a man whose squash opponent had suddenly had to go to the washroom in the middle of a game. "God, I've been wondering when you'd get back! You chaps take long lunch hours, don't you? I thought we English were supposed to be the offenders in that respect."

"It's Sunday and I've been to lunch with my girl," I said smugly; even the surprise of seeing him here again so soon didn't upset me. "Where have you been—out learning some more of your smart Arabic phrases?"

"I've been learning something a bloody sight more important than that. And disturbing too." He was at the window, glancing for a moment down at the few demonstrators still there in the street; most of them must have gone home for lunch, a long Sunday lunch with their girl. Then he raised his eyes, stared out at the sea as if searching for a ship or perhaps even an invasion fleet, then he turned quickly back to me. "Paul, two of those bloody ships of Briggs' look as if they're headed this way. I've just got word. One of them left Izmir yesterday afternoon and another left Rhodes this morning. The others are also supposed to be ready to leave."

"There's no guarantee they're coming this way."

"There's no guarantee they're not. Don't be negative about this, Paul. We have to think positively. You'd better get Criska on the blower."

He got Criska's name out with reluctance, but the mere fact that he mentioned Ben Criska at all showed me how serious he thought the situation had become. I could see my Sunday afternoon personal involvement with Lucille going out the window. I picked up the phone, asked for Criska's extension. But he wasn't in.

"I'm afraid I don't know where he is, Mr. Tancred." That was his secretary, a girl as anonymous as her boss; I could never remember her name, she was always just a pleasant, non-committal voice on the phone. "He went out right after the meeting this morning, said he wouldn't be back till late this afternoon. I think he went out of town."

"Have you any idea where he might be?"

"None at all, Mr. Tancred." Christ, did the CIA teach even its secretaries to be secretive towards other embassy personnel? I was about to blow her head off, then thought better of it. If she was being secretive, then it was only because she was doing her job, because Ben Criska had told her to give nothing away. Then again, she might be telling the truth. Maybe she didn't know where

Criska was, maybe he was secretive with her, too. "I'll have him get in touch with you as soon as he get back, Mr. Tancred."

I hung up. "Looks like he's out of town. What do we do now?"

He was staring out the window again, still scanning the empty horizon. "You know, I had the chance of being political adviser to one of the sheiks down on the Trucial Oman coast. I'd have loved the life. Plenty of desert to roam around in, tribesmen there still unspoiled, genuine *bedu*, a spot of hunting occasionally with falcons. I trained falcons, you know," he added irrelevantly. He continued to stare out the window, not seeing the sea any longer but a desert landscape that would be hell to most people but was obviously heaven for him. At last he turned round. "I turned down the job. Thought I couldn't stomach the old sheik, that he would be a bit too unprincipled for my taste. I'm a bit of a prig, you know, when it comes to principles," he added, not irrelevantly this time: he was bringing this dilemma that faced us down to a personal level, because each of us knew that in the end that would be the only way we could approach it. "I didn't appreciate at the time that governments, *our* governments, don't always stick to principle. I was very naïve in those days. Should have taken the job, really. The old sheik was a villain, but he was a simple villain. Life's too bloody complicated here."

"So what do we do?" I repeated.

"I think you had better find out who's bought the planes and tanks from friend Briggs. Talk them out of it, threaten them or buy them off, anything at all. But bugger up the deal." I was surprised when he used Briggs' favourite word; he gave it a slightly different sound, but as with Briggs it had exactly the right emphasis. "That's the important thing. Those planes and tanks must never get to their destination." He sighed, took one last look out at the sea. "If war is on the cards, Paul, there is nothing you or I or God Almighty can do to stop it. But there is a chance we can stop these planes and tanks going to the wrong side."

"Which is the wrong side?"

He shrugged. "We'll only know that when we find out who's bought them."

CHAPTER 10

When Grimsby-Orr left I called Lucille. "So soon?" she said, and she laughed. "I'll go downstairs now, get the bed ready."

"Easy. This line may be open at the switchboard." In the outer office the typewriters of Janet and Ruth were suddenly, coincidentally, silent. I knew they couldn't hear me, but I instinctively lowered my voice.

"Ah, you're always so careful, darling. Are all diplomats like this in their love affairs?" She laughed again, a soft sound loaded with all the sex that I knew was in her; she was like a girl with no care in the world but making herself and me happy in bed. "How soon will you be home?"

"That's the point——" And I explained to her what I had to do. "I'm sorry, darling. I'll make it as soon as I can."

There was silence on the other end of the phone, then at last she said, "Paul, why don't you let someone else handle it? This isn't going to help things between you and Caradoc."

I gave a coughing laugh, one of disbelief. "Lucille, this isn't just something between me and Briggs. Can't you understand, it's much bigger than whether he and I——"

"I understand, Paul," she interrupted, her voice quiet and cool now. "Call me later." And she hung up.

I stared at the phone for a moment, angry at her for what seemed her lack of proportion: everything to her was a matter of personal relationships. Then I calmed down. Why shouldn't she see everything that way? Why should I expect her to take the broad impersonal view that I had to take? But even as I found excuses for her, I wondered how it would be when we were married and she was a diplomat's wife. If ever I got to be an ambassador, would she expect me to approach heads of government on a personal level? Once she might have been right: it had worked with Talleyrand and Metternich; there would have been no Israel if Weizmann had not been able to work on the personal level. But each of them had been aiming for something more than personal return; friendship had been the means, not the end. And times then had been different: foreign policy was often something that the country, even sometimes the government, was only told about after it had been implemented. Governments to-day included too many politicians who were suspicious of their ambassadors who were too friendly with the heads of state to which they were posted. Diplomats, like football referees and brothel madames, are always suspected by both sides.

I went first to Fahad Aziz. His suite in the St. Georges looked straight across the harbour to the mountains: a view that he would probably remember with nostalgia when he got back to the sun-bleached bony mountains of the Yemen. He was not wearing his Brooks Brothers suit to-day; he was dressed Arab style, even to the sandals on his feet. Four air-weight suitcases stood just inside the door.

"My caravan is waiting for me, Mr. Tancred, but all my time is yours." He gave me the blank smile.

"The Pan Am caravan?"

"Pan Am do not fly into Riyadh, Mr. Tancred. I am going home."

"Riyadh is a long way from home. How do you get from there down to the Yemen?"

"We have ways and means, Mr. Tancred. Of course, if you had sold me those planes we asked for, I could have gone home in one of those. Is that why you are here? Have you come to tell me you have changed your mind?"

The suite was furnished in what I took to be a French period style; I sat down on a chaise-longue that seemed more appropriate for a reclining duchess than a stiff-backed, impatient junior diplomat. "Fahad Aziz, have you bought any planes and tanks from someone else? From Mr. Briggs, for instance?"

"If I had, Mr. Tancred, would it be any business of yours? You do not recognise us, remember?" He sat down in a chair opposite me, a deep comfortable chair that looked to have silk covers; it struck me then that we were in the best suite in the hotel: the Royal Suite, it would be called, if it had a name. Fahad would be reluctant to leave all this: the Yemeni royalists might try to live royally in their mountains, but they would have no luxury like this.

"I appreciate your attitude, Fahad Aziz, and perhaps we were not as wise as we might have been." *Christ I thought, here we go again through all the rigmarole of flattery, rhetoric, what-have-you. Why couldn't I have a posting to some straightforward country such as, say Australia where, as one of their representatives here had told me, bullshit got you nowhere?* "But at the time, it was logical that we should recognise the other side——".

"Logic is of no use in diplomacy, Mr. Tancred. Lord Salisbury said that. You Americans should take a lesson from the English in diplomacy, Mr. Tancred."

"We're attending regular classes in Whitehall all the time," I said tartly. "I understand they keep places open for the Arabs, too."

"We don't need them, Mr. Tancred." His smile was still blank, but I thought I could detect a tiny glint in his dark eyes; he was enjoying my discomfiture. His fingernails scratched on the silk of the chair, a sound that made me shiver. "We learned everything we had to learn from the English—in the field, as I think you would call it. Perfidy is their main accomplishment and that is easily learned."

I was glad Grimsby-Orr was not here. He might have been angry, but more probably he would have been sad: he had devoted his life honestly to these people and this opinion was his reward. I stood up, convinced now that Fahad Aziz was going back to the Yemen empty-handed.

"You sound bitter, Fahad Aziz. Was Briggs' price too high for you to meet?"

He stood up, drawing himself up to his full height; with his tall conical hat he topped me by almost a foot. There was no smile now on his thin, hook-nosed face; he looked like a bird of prey that had been robbed just at the moment it was about to feast; I had seen the same look in the eyes of falcons in the Jordan desert when their owners had snatched them from the quarry they had just struck down. "We shall win our war without your help, Mr. Tancred, or that of anyone else." He put his hand on something at his belt; for the first time I noticed the gold dagger there. "Mr. Barrington-Briggs has made a mistake.

Outsiders who meddle in wars can expect to be among the casualties. You should tell him so if you should meet him."

Husain al-Qataba and now Fahad Aziz: Briggs wasn't playing favourites, he was building up enmity from all sides. "I'll tell him that," I said. "May you have a safe and pleasant return to your home, Fahad Aziz, and may your war go well."

"Thank you, Mr. Tancred. And yours, too." I looked at him blankly and he gave me the blank smile in return. "In Vietnam."

"Thank you," I said, and wondered if he knew how far I felt myself removed from that war: Vietnam was as if it were the problem of another country altogether.

One of Fahad Aziz's bodyguards ushered me out of the suite. He, too, was in Arab dress, but with a purple turban wound around his head instead of the conical hat; bearded, scar-faced, he looked like something out of an old print, a fighting tribesman from another age. Which, of course, he was: the war in the Yemen was a war from another time. But it was fast being brought up to date. There had been many medieval refinements of cruelty towards your enemy, but none to equal poison gas or napalm bombing. The bodyguard, evil as he might look, probably still fought an honourable, if not chivalric, war and wondered at the savageries introduced from a world that called him uncivilised.

The door of the suite closed behind me and I waited for the elevator to come up. Its doors slid open and Naami Zaid stepped out.

"A client here?" I asked.

He hesitated, then nodded at the door to Fahad's suite. "A good one, I hope."

"He should have a lot to spend. He wasn't able to spend it on arms."

Zaid smiled. "What would you rather they all bought, Paul? Diamonds or arms?"

"Diamonds every time. But you can't have much stock left."

"Not much. I may be cleaned out by to-night." He looked hot and tired, as if he had been on the run ever since he had left Hacobian and me this morning outside the garage. He took out a handkerchief, blew his nose, then produced an inhaler and sniffed it. He said apologetically, "My cold is worse."

"Can't you get some more diamonds?"

"I doubt it. Not yet awhile, anyway. From now on diamonds won't be coming through the mail, just in case war should break out. They'll be brought in by couriers. Even then it will only be when we put in specific orders."

"What will you do when you run out of stock?"

"Relax and wait." He sniffed, wiped the end of his nose again.

"For what?"

He shrugged. "Peace or war. Or orders for more diamonds. I'm philosophical, Paul. I don't try to fight events as you do."

I left him, went in the elevator, stood outside the hotel and wondered where next to go. Fahad Aziz and Husain al-Qataba were off the list; who else might be a buyer?

I went back into the hotel and out on to the terrace; but it was almost deserted. There was no sign of Briggs and the others. In my mind I ran down the list of whom else he might be dealing with: Kaseb, Hasbani, the stranger with whom they had lunched to-day, the Syrian ex-Minister. Kaseb was out: the Kurds would have no one to fly the planes or to man the tanks: their ambition was for no more than a small, old-fashioned war. Hasbani and the stranger would be a stronger bet, but I wouldn't get into Hasbani's castle as easily again as I had this morning. While I thought of a way to get to see them, the best thing was to check on another suspect, the Syrian.

The next stop was Sandra Holden's apartment. I didn't really expect to find her there, but I had to be systematic; and I still wanted time to reason out some way of getting to Hasbani and the stranger. But when I pressed the bell of her apartment it was Sandra herself who opened the door.

"Paul, how nice!" But she didn't open the door any wider.

"Aren't you going to ask me in?" She hesitated, then stood aside while I entered the apartment. The first thing I saw was her luggage, half a dozen suitcases and a trunk all in the process of being packed. "When are you leaving?"

She sat down, lit a cigarette. She was dressed in a brief pair of shorts and the brassière of her bikini outfit; perhaps she had to be as briefly dressed as possible when she was working; the years of her profession had bred the habit. Her blonde hair had fallen down from the pins that held it up off her neck and there was a sheen of perspiration on her face and chest.

"I've been flat out." She drew heavily on the cigarette, blew out smoke. "I'm on the plane for London to-night."

"When did you make up your mind to leave? At lunch?" She nodded. "Doc going with you?"

"You'd better ask him, Paul."

"Was he the one who advised you to go?"

She drew on the cigarette, blew out smoke again before she replied. "He gave me my ticket. As a going-away present, I suppose."

"Where is he now?"

"With Hasbani."

"And the other guy, too? Who's he?"

"Paul, why do you want to know so much? Why can't you leave Doc alone? I'm frightened enough for him as it is——" She uncrossed, then re-crossed her legs; somehow I had not expected her to be a nervous woman. She looked older this afternoon: not in the body, that was still good and firm, but in the face. Particularly around the neck where, Lucille had told me, some women always age first: the highly strung women who have struggled to present a calm face to the world. For seventeen years Sandra had been presenting a calm, bright face to the world, at beauty contests from Hammersmith to Aberystwyth, as a showgirl from Blackpool to Beirut. And now the years were asking payment. She stubbed out the cigarette, got up, began to move restlessly about the apartment. She picked up a green silk blouse, looked at it as if she wondered whose it was, then stuffed it negligently into one of the suitcases. "He brought me home from the Casino early this morning—he'd borrowed one of Hasbani's cars. Someone tried to run us off the road just the other side of Juniye as you come down from the

151

Casino. It wasn't an accident, it was deliberate. I've been a bundle of nerves ever since."

"I saw Doc this morning. We were alone for quite a time. He didn't mention anything about it."

"You know what he's like. He tried to tell me it was nothing, it was some drunk, but I knew better. Especially when he called for me to take me to lunch and gave me a ticket for London, told me to get out of Beirut to-night." She stopped, turned and looked back at me; even as wrought up as she was, she still managed to look graceful. "Paul, if you have to see him at all, try and persuade him to be on that plane with me to-night."

I nodded. "Do me a favour first. Tell me where that Syrian is, the ex-Minister you had up here the other day."

"That's easy. Rashid went back to Damascus this morning."

"Damascus? But they'll cut his throat."

"He didn't seem to think so. That man at lunch with us arrived from Damascus late last night—he had an invitation for Rashid to go back to join the government. I didn't know it, but Rashid is some sort of defence expert."

"Who's the other guy?"

"He's a colonel in the Syrian army. Colonel Marik."

"So Hasbani is financing the Syrians?"

She shook her head impatiently; more hair fell down out of the pins. "Paul, I don't know! All I want is to get out of Beirut—and I want Doc to go with me! Please try and persuade him—please!"

She was on the verge of tears; her love for Briggs was all at once as visible as a scar on her lovely body. *Here's the girl who'll give you the marriage you want, Doc, I* thought; and determined to have him on that plane for London with her to-night. But that was reducing everything again to the personal level: first, I had to get to Hasbani and the Syrian colonel.

"He'll be on the plane. I'll deliver him personally to you at the airport." I looked at the six suitcases and the trunk. "You might have to leave some of this behind to get him on the plane. They're all overloaded as it is."

"I'll go out just in what I stand up in, if it means Doc will go with me." Then she looked down at herself.

She blinked, cleared her beautiful eyes of tears, and smiled. "Well, not exactly like this. And thank you, Paul."

"Thank me at the airport. I haven't got him there yet."

I went back to the embassy. There was really no need to, because I had already made up my mind what was to be done next. But the embassy was a base, the one constant factor in all the perplexities that had confronted me over the past three days; it was as if I went back there each time for re-orientation. As if to find a practical excuse for going back, I turned into the parking lot before I reached the embassy. My car was scratched and dented, but Danny Nahmad had told me there was nothing seriously wrong with it.

"Not like Major Oxford's. Boy, they did a job on his car." Danny was a wizened Lebanese in his early sixties; he always reminded me of a gnarled olive tree, with black olives for eyes. He had lived in San Francisco for thirty years, running a gas station there, then come back home to Beirut to retire. But retirement had bored him and he had missed contact with Americans—"I talk to my brothers, and what we got to talk about? You know? Nothing. So I come here to the embassy, get a job. I talk baseball to you, Mr. Tancred, or politics or cars or anything. American talk, you know?" So now he looked after the embassy transport and was content, a man back in his own country but still in touch with his adopted country. I never held long conversations with him, but sometimes I wondered if you ever really could go home again after a long absence. Looking and listening to him, Charleston seemed more and more a town I'd never know again.

Danny scratched his head and pulled his long nose. "Things are gonna get worse, Mr. Tancred. Those young punks out front——" He spat disgustedly. "How you gonna get the message across to them?"

I didn't ask him what message he meant; I wasn't quite sure that I had got it myself. Washington sent us lots of words, but never any real message. "Could you take the top off and get that rip repaired, Danny?"

"What about a new top? I can get you one first thing to-morrow."

"Let's wait a while, Danny. I don't want to go buying new tops every few days."

Danny spat again. "I hate to admit this, you know? But I got a nephew out there in that crowd out front. Eighteen years old and he's a judge of America, tells me everything that's wrong with it. He's right half the time. I gotta admit that. But he's not right *all* the time. What country ain't made mistakes?"

"There are a few, Danny. Unfortunately for our image, they aren't countries that *these* countries, the Arab ones, ever approach for any sort of aid. The way your nephew and his buddies see it, the only sonsofbitches among countries are the wealthy ones."

"Sounds just like real Commie propaganda."

I stifled the sigh that welled up in me. Danny still talked American, still thought American. The sort of American thought and talk that blinkered our outlook towards the rest of the world, that made it so difficult for us who had to talk to the rest of the world on America's behalf. "Yes, Danny," I said, and tried not to sound weary.

"We oughta all just go home and leave the bums to starve." Home: America was still home to him, then.

"Yes, Danny."

I went up to my office. Janet and Ruth sat at their desks, each of them reading a copy of *Time*. Israel's Premier Eshkol was on the cover, looking very worried. "I used to date a Jewish boy once," Janet said. "He was anti-Zionist. I could never understand him. I mean, if I was a Jew—though thank God I'm not——" Then she blushed. "I didn't mean to say that. Not that way, anyway."

"Don't apologise," said Ruth. "At a time like this, anyone should be glad they're not a Jew. It saves having to make a decision."

That's it, Ruth, I thought, *always the cool, practical one*. Except, of course, that some of us, Jewish or not, *had* to make decisions. I looked out the window. The crowd had grown again; the deserters had come back from their long lunch. It was the biggest crowd of the week and the best dressed: this was a Sunday-best demonstration. But it was much better tempered than this morning's mob had been; it reminded me of the crowds I had seen at London's Speakers' Corner on Sunday afternoons. People had evidently heard the news from Tel Aviv on their radios and, like the soldiers and citizens down there, had decided to relax. Shouting a little mild abuse at Americans on a Sunday afternoon was cheaper than going to the movies.

Janet said, "Captain Hacobian called. He said the matter had been taken care of. He said you'd understand."

I felt a sense of shame. I hadn't thought at all of Ahmed for the last two hours; I had a moment of doubt that perhaps my concern for his death was not so deep after all. I had never had to mourn anyone before: perhaps grief was like a cold in the head, you woke up one morning and suddenly it was gone. But not the sense of guilt: I knew *that* would remain. It came back now, strong enough to make me feel physically weak. I went into my office, sat down and closed my eyes. Whatever else happened in the next twenty-four hours I must not let myself forget my promise to Ahmed's parents. Sensible or not, I'd be at his funeral to-morrow. There are some gestures as necessary to yourself as deeds.

I rang Criska's office again, but the anonymous secretary told me he was still out. I hung up, went down to the parking lot, took out my car and drove up through the town and out on to the Aley Road. Danny had taken off the top. Funny thing was, I felt so exposed. I drove most of the time with the top down, but now that the top had been completely removed the car seemed almost stripped. I felt I was driving on a bare chassis, open to everyone who wanted to hurl abuse or a stone at me.

Nobody did. I pulled up outside Hasbani's place, tooted the horn and the gatekeeper in the red tarboosh came down to greet me again. He got on the phone to the house, then the gates were opened and I drove up the gravelled drive between rose bushes that held flowers that looked like red plastic Brussels sprouts. I had half-expected Hasbani either to refuse to see me or at least to inquire my business. It had all been too easy so far.

The two servants who had met me this morning met me again. They took me across the wide front marbled terrace, as brightly glaring as a skating rink, and into the house. But instead of going straight through this time we turned left into a side room. It could not have been called a living-room; nobody really lived on a scale like this any more; it was not a drawing-room, either, because no one any longer withdrew into such surroundings as this. Maybe it was a departure room, a luxurious one such as no airport ever saw. It was furnished in perfect taste, a combination of several periods and nationalities that merged smoothly, but it had the transient, unlived-in look of airport departure lounges: Hasbani and Colonel Marik, standing at the far end of the room, were waiting to be told that their own luxury aircraft was waiting for them at the end of the gravelled drive. I come from a family that is a long way from being poor, but I still can't get over a feeling of being slightly uncomfortable in the midst of extravagance. Perhaps, for all Danny Nahmad knew, the Commie propaganda had got to me, too.

Hasbani introduced Marik, who didn't put out his hand but coldly inclined his head. I recognised that the battle-lines had been drawn at once: it had been easy to get in here, but that was where it stopped.

One of the servants brought me a lemonade and some dates. I don't have a sweet tooth, but Hasbani evidently did. He began to munch some of the dates and, following the rules of Arab hospitality, I bit into one. It could have been worse: I once had to eat a sheep's eyeball.

I looked around. "Mr. Briggs is not here?"

"Mr. Briggs left us after lunch to take Miss Holden back to her apartment. We are still waiting on him." Hasbani's deep whisper of a voice had an impatient edge to it. "Was it Mr. Briggs you wanted to see?"

Briggs hadn't been in Sandra's apartment when I was there; I was sure of that. Wherever he was, I was glad he wasn't here. That had been part of the problem I had expected to face: "It's better that he isn't here. You see ——" I had rehearsed several ways of broaching this subject on the way up here, but now I came out with it bluntly: "Mr. Hasbani, are you arranging a deal between Briggs and Colonel Marik?"

Marik turned his head slightly to look at Hasbani, then he looked back at me; but his black eyes showed no expression, were as opaque as the black marble table that stood between us. He was a short narrow man with a long narrow face; you had the feeling you were looking at him through a distorting mirror. His clothes fitted him as if the tailor had built them on him; you almost expected the dark worsted to turn out to be dark metal. There was something unyielding about him, a man who found it far easier to hate than to love.

Hasbani ran his tongue round inside his lips, cleaning his teeth of dates. "Is it any business of yours, Mr. Tancred?"

I was getting used to that question. "I think so, especially if Briggs is trying to sell you American arms."

Marik spoke for the first time, in a voice that suited the image of him, thin and squeezed out. "Are you against supplying arms to Syria?"

"We are against supplying arms to anyone. At this moment, anyway."

"This is when they are needed most."

"The Russians and we don't think so." I had to get the Russians into the act; Marik had to be reminded that the moratorium on armaments supplying was not just an American deal. "It's possibly the first time we've ever been in complete agreement."

"The Russians are getting soft in the head."

It wasn't my place to defend Moscow: after all, we were not yet one hundred per cent allies. I sipped my lemonade, wishing it were something more fortifying. "Could be. Washington hasn't had as much to do with them as Damascus has."

Something like a smile started on Hasbani's face; the corner of his mouth twitched, but he got it under control almost at once. "Why are you so concerned that Colonel Marik should not buy American arms?"

"It's a question of neutrality. And morality, too, maybe."

He let the smile have its way this time, but it was no pleasure to look at: gold glinted in each corner of his mouth as if the light had caught on hinges. "Neutrality?"

"We're trying not to take sides." Through an open window I could see a wide expanse of lawn; in the bright vertical sunlight the grass looked unnaturally green, as if it had just been sprayed with chlorophyll. Suddenly hidden sprinklers began to play; the lawn looked as if it were giving off a silver steam. A gardener moved across the lawn, as oblivious of the spray as of the sunshine. Once he stopped, opened his mouth against the spray, then moved on. "We have no fight with the Arabs."

"America is the Arabs' friend? And you are the Israelis' friend, too? Is that what you call neutrality?" Hasbani's smile neither widened nor lessened; it remained fixed, as if the hinges of his mouth had stuck.

"It's what is recognised internationally as being neutral. It's not just the American conception of it."

"And what about morality? Is that American morality you are talking about?"

I shrugged. "There must be an international morality."

"I doubt it, Mr. Tancred." The smile vanished; you could almost hear the golden hinges click shut. I wondered why he wore the gold teeth; everything else about him was in such good taste. But maybe he had a sentimental attachment to them; perhaps they were the first extravagance he had been able to afford. "Getting back to Mr. Briggs. Yesterday he was talking a deal with me. He seemed in sympathy with the Arab cause for justice—at least he did not talk of neutrality." His tone put the word in quotes. "That was why I got in touch with Colonel Marik, why he came down from Damascus at once. But to-day at lunch Mr. Briggs began to hedge. What did you have to say to him this morning, Mr. Tancred?"

So here was another one who thought Briggs was an agent for us. I put down the dates I still held in my hand; even their sweetness could not take away the sour taste that was now in my mouth. I began to wonder how much use Briggs had made of my name. "You are mistaken, Mr. Hasbani. What I had to say to Briggs this morning was purely personal. It had only to do with the dead boy."

"A Kurdish ragamuffin? A street arab?" He looked at Marik, the grimace of a smile again splitting his face. "That's what they call them in America. Street arabs."

"We didn't invent the term, if it offends you. I believe it was a British invention." Grimsby-Orr, Harold Wilson *et al* would thank me for that little bit of treachery. "And Ahmed was more than a street arab, as you called him. He worked for me."

"No sensible man would do what you suggested doing this morning, risking his neck among a miserable pack of revolutionaries to see that some urchin got a proper burial."

I looked at Marik to see how he reacted to the remark about revolutionaries; I wondered how many of Syria's fourteen coups he had figured in. But he showed no reaction at all. Revolutionaries are only to be sneered at when they are still out of power. The Kurds, poor bastards, would always be good for a sneer and a laugh. But then so had the Jews for almost two thousand years, and no one was laughing at them to-day. Maybe Marik had more respect for the Kurds than Hasbani had.

Hasbani's deep whisper had turned into a rising growl. "Where did you and Briggs go? I do not like being made a fool of, Mr. Tancred. Tell Briggs that when you see him——"

I put down my half-finished lemonade. "I made a mistake in coming here, Mr. Hasbani, and I ask you to forgive the intrusion." It suddenly seemed easier to retreat behind a barrier of formality. I began to back toward the door, keeping a careful eye on Hasbani as rage began to shake him. "Strict neutrality should keep me within my own house. I regret having intruded into yours. Good-bye, Colonel Marik——"

I had reached the door; the length of the room separated us. "Where is Briggs?" Hasbani shouted, and the room had an echo. *Christ,* I thought, *all that money and he has only echoes for company.* "Where is Briggs? Tell him he'll regret what he's done—tell him Arabs have long memories——"

The two tarbooshed servants caught up with me as I was half-way across the marble skating rink. I faltered, waiting for them to attack me, but they only smiled and escorted me down to my car. I drove down between the roses, bright as blood on their bushes; but I had the feeling that if I stopped to smell them, they would have no perfume at all. Over to my right the sprinklers still spun their shimmering carousels and the gardener still moved unconcernedly among them, his face shining and his clothes dark with water. When I stopped for the gateman to open the gates I looked back. The huge house looked unreal and uninhabited, a dream world for a man who had no dreams left. Not even the dream of Arab unity. For Hasbani was no more interested in the Arab cause than Briggs was. He was a financier, interested only in putting his money on what he thought would be the winning side. And living here in an Arab country, entertaining a top man from the most fanatic Arab country of them all, that meant he had already placed his bet on what he thought would be the winning side.

If Briggs had walked out on him, that meant Briggs was going to sell his planes and tanks to someone else. And there was only one other buyer left.

2

I climbed the steps to the house, put my key in my apartment door, and had the door opened by Briggs. "Saw you coming up the steps. I've been waiting and watching for you for the last hour."

"How did you get in here?"

"Picked the lock on your kitchen door. It was something I learned to do when we were in that prison camp. It was in a Red Cross book on hobbies and crafts."

"That Red Cross, they really look after you, don't they? What else did they teach you? How to double-cross everyone in business deals?"

"You sound as if you've had a hard day at the office." He clucked like a solicitous wife. "What do you want to drink? Scotch?"

I flopped down on the couch, too weak even to bawl him out. Frustration and now exasperation had rendered me impotent. He brought me a Scotch, then sat down on a chair opposite me. He leaned forward with his elbows on his knees, holding his glass in both hands, and looked at me as if he were seeing me for the first time.

"I brought you back the money I owe you, yours and Lucille's. I've put it all on the one cheque—you can pay her for me. It's there on the table." He nodded at the table at the end of the couch. "I'm sorry it's got to be a cheque. But I didn't go back to Hasbani's for my wallet."

"I know. I've been to see him. And Sandra, too. Cheers." I held up my glass, and he raised his in acknowledgment. I glanced at the cheque without picking it up, saw the amount. "You don't owe us that much! Why the bonus?"

"It's for Ahmed's funeral. My share. I shan't be able to come along to-morrow. I have to leave to-night, unfortunately."

"It would be better if you left right now. Go out to the airport and get on the first plane that's headed for London, Rome, Paris, anywhere. Anywhere at all but some Arab country." I took another drink, looked at him with weary impatience. "They'll kill you before long, you know that?"

At first he seemed to show no reaction at all. Then I noticed the tiny splashing in his glass; his hands were trembling like those of an old man. He ran his tongue around his lips and said, "They might, at that. The Wogs aren't the most patient buggers on earth."

"How the hell could you expect them to be patient?" The Scotch splashed in my own glass. "You lead them up the garden path, then all at once turn around and sell to the Jews——"

He raised an eyebrow. "Where did you get that?"

"Well, where's the *Dobbs Ferry* if it isn't in Haifa?"

"Don't start spreading yarns like that, chum. Whose side are you on, anyway?"

"I'm getting pretty sick and tired of that question. Don't *you* start." I looked at my drink, wondering what good it was doing me; the Scotch crutch is one of the myths I've found hard to swallow. Then I said, "Why didn't you ask yourself what side *you* were on before you got here?"

"To tell you the truth, I never thought the question would arise. It might not have, if I hadn't met you. You're a disturbing bugger."

He made an effort to relax, and did a good job of it. He sat back in the chair, hooked one leg over the other, exposing about six inches of bare hairy leg above his sock. He was wearing the Italian silk suit, but had taken off the jacket and thrown it over the back of the couch on which I sat. For the first time I saw his briefcase, a black leather one bulging with papers and lying on a chair just across from him. He would be travelling light, but he looked ready to leave the country at a moment's notice. But I had given him that notice and he hadn't budged.

"When I get back to London this time, Paul, I'm going to chuck the whole business." His tone was casually conversational; we could have been filling in time before going out to dinner. "Yes, I thought you'd be pleased to hear that. It's not one of my fibs this time, either. I mean it. I've had enough. I'm going to sell out and I'm going out to the Caribbean, Jamaica, Trinidad, somewhere like that, and I'm going to be a retired gent. Pity I didn't make better than flying-officer in the RAF. Wing-Commander Barrington-Briggs would sound well out there among the old colonial relics."

"You taking Sandra with you?"

"I could do worse, as I've told you. But don't start any match-making. I like to make up my own mind——" For just an instant there was an edge to his voice, then he smiled, raised his glass to me again and took another drink. "I shan't be rich, not stinking rich like that old bugger Hasbani. But I'll have enough. Enough for my needs and maybe a bit left over to help other people."

"Forgive me, Doc, but I don't quite see you as a philanthropist."

He laughed, and the whisky in his glass splashed again. "You're right, chum. But out there this morning at that Kurd village——" He blinked and shook his head, like a man remembering a punch. "There was a poet I used to recite once, a Welshman. Not Dylan Thomas. *Everyone* recites him. A bloke named Davies, W. H. Davies. In that dingy bloody café in Earl's Court Road, on these days when I was at the arse-end of despair, I used to say two lines of his to myself. *I stare at dewdrops till they close their eyes/I stare at grass till all the world is green*." He was silent for a moment, staring into a past that belonged to him alone. Then he blinked again and looked at me. "When will the world ever be green for those poor buggers out in that shanty town?"

Under the armour of the silk suit and the bulging business-like briefcase there was still some pity left. "Why the hell did you ever go into the arms game?"

But it was a rhetorical question and he knew it. He put down his glass, stood up and looked at his watch. He went across, put on his jacket, then came back and held out his hand. "It's really good-bye this time, Paul."

"I could come out to the airport to-night. What time does your plane go?"

"Better not. You have to stay here in this town. You've been trying so bloody hard to be neutral." He picked up his briefcase, hefted it as a gunfighter might test the weight of his weapon. "Don't spoil it at the last minute just for the sake of sentiment."

"You were always the sentimental one. I'm no Celt."

"Maybe. Matter of fact, I think I've remembered more than you have of what happened in that P.O.W. camp."

I doubted that, but I wasn't going to contradict him. Perhaps Lucille had been right: he had been more moved by our reunion than I had. I might have felt the same if only... If only he had been a theatrical agent?

"Remember that week-end we had in Tokyo after they repatriated us? When we were waiting to come home? You had to pay, too, remember? I'd mislaid my paybook, same old bloody carelessness. I never paid you back for that, either, did I? We didn't really have the strength for a binge, but we tried anyway." He chuckled, winked appreciatively. "We went looking for a brothel, remember, but you wouldn't go in because it didn't have the *Good Housekeeping Seal* over the door. We were so drunk then, on half a dozen beers, that was all, I don't think I could have got the old feller to stand up anyway. Then the M.P.'s picked us up and threw us in the cooler. Out of one cooler into another. They didn't like it, remember, when we told them we'd known a better gaol in Pyongyang."

I nodded, smiling as the long dead years came back; but even as I smiled I knew it was too late for memories now. "So long, Doc. Take care, for Christ's sake." I gripped his hand hard. "Don't be a stupid sonofabitch. Get out of Beirut as soon as you can. And maybe some day I'll see you in Jamaica or Trinidad."

He nodded and returned the pressure of my grip. He stared at me hard, then he shook his head. "Don't let them make you carry the can all the time, chum. Good luck."

"Don't let who?" I said, but he was already moving out of the room, heading for the back of the apartment.

"You'd better get that lock fixed on your kitchen door. I didn't do a very good job on it. Cheerio, Paul."

I stood in the middle of the room, aware of a feeling that was vaguely familiar. Then I remembered: I had felt exactly like this fifteen years ago when I had stood in the airport lounge at Tokyo and watched him walk out to the plane that was taking him home to London. A sense of loss.

I picked up the cheque from the table. The amount, above what he owed me and Lucille, would more than pay for his share of the funeral: it would keep Ahmed's family for a year. It was made out on the British Bank and there wasn't a doubt in my mind that Briggs had enough money there to honour it. He might be a liar and unethical in business, but he had never been one who tried to profit by making empty gestures towards the unfortunate. Whenever he had promised anything in the prison camp, he had delivered.

Then I looked at the cheque again. His old carelessness had let him down again: he had forgotten to sign it.

CHAPTER 11

"Of course it's Israel," Ben Criska said. "We've got no proof so far, but who else could it be?"

"What about the *Dobbs Ferry*? Have you traced that yet?"

"It's in Haifa. The Israelis don't want those old Lee-Enfields—they have enough World War Two stuff of their own with their Kar 98K's. But they'd pay out a quarter of a million bucks just to make sure no one else got them. The same as we'd have done."

"Why didn't he sell them back to us then?"

"Maybe he'd already made the deal before you got to him. For all we know, he may be an ethical businessman. Isn't there something about an Englishman's word is his bond?" Criska did not like the British, but I had never discovered why; national prejudices are harder to define and less defensible than personal ones. "The thing now is, it's a safe bet he's selling them the planes and tanks. They'll be buying them for the same reason as they bought the rifles—so no one else can have them."

I had come back to the embassy, driving down the back streets to avoid the demonstrators, to find a message that Ben Criska wanted to see me in his office. For a moment I had been riled; I was senior to Criska and I was not used to being summoned to the office of a junior. It sounds petty, I know, but no matter how much you rebel against the system, it gets into *your* system: protocol becomes part of your way of life. I got as far as picking up the phone to tell Criska I'd see him in *my* office, then thought better of it. What the hell did it matter who called on whom at a time like this? I was as bad as my mother, at whom I laughed for her insistence upon proper social etiquette.

Criska's office was smaller than mine and two floors

below: a demonstrator, even without a Willie Mays arm, could throw a stone through his window without any trouble. It was furnished with the stock government desk and steel filing cabinets; I wondered if he separated his Agriculture and CIA reports, if *Espionage* and *Erosion* were in the same file. Two of the walls were hung with government issue prints; the wall behind his desk was papered with maps. There was nothing in the room that represented the personal side of Ben Criska: it seemed that he never relaxed his anonymity.

I sat facing the window, so that if the stone came I'd have at least an instant's warning. The crowd outside had grown bigger and, bored with no reaction from within the embassy, was becoming restless. This was the time when kids chose to throw stones.

"Where did you go this afternoon?" I asked.

"Out."

I nodded. "What did you do? Nothing. Okay, Ben. Sorry I asked. But you didn't call me down here to tell me nothing."

He got the minor point. "I'm sorry about that. Asking you to come down here, I mean. But it was the only way I could guarantee we wouldn't be interrupted."

The anonymous secretary hadn't been in the outside office when I had come through, and after I had entered his office Criska had locked the door behind me. Mollified and yet ashamed at the same time, I nodded. "All right. What is it?"

"Your friend Briggs." Criska looked away from me, stared at the Andrew Wyeth print hanging on the wall opposite him. He was holding a brass dagger that he used as a letter opener and he tapped on his desk with it while he continued to stare at Wyeth's picture of rural serenity in an America that seemed more of a memory than anything else. I was suddenly aware of his nervousness, something I had never seen in him before. At last he looked back at me, held the dagger still with its point pushed hard into the desk edge in front of him. "He is going to be attended to to-night."

"Attended to?" The phrase sounded ridiculous and I didn't at once catch his meaning.

He irritably threw the dagger on the desk. "Don't be dense, Paul! Do I have to spell it out for you?"

I could feel my own nerves beginning to quiver, but I held tight to myself. "You're going to kill him, is that what you're trying to say? No wonder you didn't want any interruption." I gestured at the locked door.

"Not *us*! We aren't the ones——" He got up, leaned against the wall behind the desk; I noticed he stayed away from the window. "Look, Paul. The Arabs suspect he's selling to the Jews—and I've got a suspicion they think he's our agent——" He stopped, watching me closely. "What's the matter?"

"They do," I said reluctantly, and told him of Husain's and Hasbani's reactions.

"Well, you see? We can't win. But maybe we can cut our losses. If he gets away with this deal, Christ knows where he'll stop. If the price is right, there's enough second-hand arms around the world to equip half a dozen armies." He paused, heaved himself away from the wall and leaned forward across the desk. Behind him a map of the Middle East looked like a primitive abstract: the yellow of Saudi Arabia, the orange of Iraq, the brown of Syria, the green of Israel. I wondered who the cartographer had been who had chosen the colours. Why had he chosen green, the colour of promise, for Israel? Was he another man who had stared at the grass till all the world, or anyway Israel, was green? "The Arabs are going to get rid of Briggs to-night. Don't ask me how I know—I just do, that's all. I gather they've made a couple of attempts already. This time they're going to make sure."

"Where?"

"I don't know for sure, but even if I did I wouldn't tell you." He looked out the window wistfully, as if he wished he were a long way from here. *I wonder what your old man thinks of you*, I thought, *the old guy who picketed U.S. Steel for its disregard of human dignity*.

"Why are you telling me anything, then?"

He scratched his thinning hair, not in perplexity but because he was still nervous. For the first time I began to look at him closely, going over his face as I might over a large-scale map, seeing the blood vessels, like contour markings, too close to the skin, the sharply sculptured shape of the nostrils, the redness that showed in the corners of the eyes when he looked sideways. This plain anonymous face was that of a man who condoned murder. Or might even have contrived it . . .

"You didn't plan this, did you? Put the Arabs on to Briggs?"

"I'm telling you all this, Paul, because I don't want you to be anywhere near him to-night. Because they might kill you as well. If you had planned any meeting with him to-night, stay away——"

"You didn't answer my question! Have you CIA jokers arranged this?" Suddenly I lost control of myself. I stood up, banged the desk; down in the street shouting had begun, but I heard it only with the edge of my mind. I shouted at Criska: "For Christ's sake, answer me! Are you having him killed?"

"Take it easy, Paul——"

"Take it easy!" I vomited an obscenity. The yelling down in the street had increased, swelled to an angry roar. Criska glanced nervously at the window, but I had eyes only for him. I reached across the desk for him, made a futile grab at him, but he had leaned away out of my reach. "You're going to kill a man—a man I *know*—and you tell me to take it easy! Jesus, what do they do to you in CIA? Do they cut your guts and heart out?"

"Paul, stay out of it——"

Stay out of it. Be neutral. Outside the shouting was now a storm. Something thudded against the wall of the building. I spun round, fumbled with the key of the door, then wrenched the door open. As I almost ran out of the office there was a crash of glass behind me, but I didn't look back. I found myself hoping that the stone had hit Criska right between the eyes.

I was still trembling with rage when I got into my car and drove it out of the parking lot. I slammed it down the ramp, bounced over the kerb and swung right, driving away from the embassy. In the rear-view mirror I caught a glimpse of the crowd surging like a dark sea about the front gates of the embassy. Stones flew up like birds against the yellow cliff of the building; squares of sunlight were abruptly blacked out as windows were shattered. Then the view was gone from the mirror, and I didn't care at all what happened to the embassy or anyone in it.

I drove home through the back streets, driving slowly,

as if by restraining myself from speeding I was also putting the brake on my rage. I was suffering from more than just rage; shock had also set me trembling. I was not unaccustomed to callousness; in international relations we call it expediency. Diem's assassination in Saigon had not been regretted in Washington; we had actively helped towards the overthrow of Mossadegh in Teheran. On a less violent scale I had once drawn up a scheme to alleviate the poverty and distress of the thousands of Palestine refugees; I had not demurred when it had been pointed out that such a proposal might be interpreted as an admission on our part that we were at least partly responsible for the refugee problem; the scheme had been torn up and, for all I knew, perhaps a thousand refugees had died because expediency had denied them succour. I knew callousness was a necessary part of the make-up of anyone who wanted to survive in foreign service; but I was not accustomed to straight-out, cold-blooded murder. They had never talked about that in the briefing sessions in Foggy Bottom.

I drove the car into the garage. I sat for a while staring at the corner where I had found Ahmed. Rage began to stir in me again, dully this time, the sort of fire that would burn for a long time. I got out of the car, slammed down the door and locked it. I stood and looked across at the Sunday afternoon strollers moving slowly up and down, as in a ritual dance, on the promenade on the other side of the road. One or two of them glanced across at me, but none of them stopped to shout at me. These were not demonstrators, people concerned with a cause, infected with hatred. These were ordinary people like Ahmed, the ones who would be expected to take their unearned, undeserved places among the casualties when the bombs fell. I could do nothing about them, as I had been unable to do anything about the Palestine refugees, but I could, *must*, do something about Briggs.

2

I went straight up past my own front door to the Zaid's apartment. I had no intention of telling Lucille what I had just learned, but right now I did not want to be alone. I am not self-contained enough to be able to bear rage or shock or despair, or the mixture of all three, alone.

I didn't know what Lucille's capacity to help would be, but somehow I never doubted that she would help. I had not fallen in love with her just for her talent for making love. Even if I could not yet define her truly, if there was still some mystery in her that I might never solve (and what man ever solves any woman, even the brainless, shallow ones who are unhappy without men? Women will always be more of a mystery than a man; even her genitals, the physical instruments of love, are more secretive than his); as incompletely as I knew her, I still trusted her to make me happy, to be able to sustain me when I needed her. It would be enough now just to be with her.

But when she opened the door I knew at once that something was wrong. All the gaiety that had been there at lunchtime had gone out of her face; she was like she had been yesterday, only worse. "What's the matter? Those students haven't been down *here*, have they?"

She turned and walked back into the apartment without a word. I followed her, took her by the shoulders and turned her around to face me. "Darling, what's the matter ——?" Then behind her I saw the suitcase at the foot of the stairs that led up to the bedrooms. "Whose is that? Your father's? Is he going somewhere?"

"Can't you see it's mine?" She sounded irritable, impatient with me. "Come upstairs, Paul."

She broke out of my hands and ran up the stairs. I went after her, baffled and angry: the rage in me was being stoked by another sort of fuel. Her bedroom was huge, opening out on to a balcony; its hugeness was magnified by the mirrors lining all one wall. It was a feminine room, all mirrors and frills and thick fluffy carpets, one where Madame Zaid had not been able to introduce Arabia. It was a wonderful room for love-making or, as now, a lovers' fight.

"What's all this? Where the hell do you think you're going?" I made a wild sweeping gesture at the clothes scattered about the room, on the bed, on the chairs, even on the floor. The mirrored doors of the wall cupboards were slid back; the drawers of the dressing-table were open; the room looked as if it were in the middle of being looted. "For Christ's sake, Lucille, what's going on?"

"Don't swear at me!" She looked on the verge of tears;

I had never seen her like this before, so young and uncertain. The anger began to die down in me.

"I'm sorry. I didn't think Christ meant anything to——" I stopped, but she had already heard the word I hadn't yet spoken.

"An Arab?" A small radio on her dressing-table had been playing: it was Um Kalthoum again, this time singing one of her sad love songs. Lucille crossed to the radio and switched it off, stood beside it as if finishing off the last words of the song in her mind. Then she turned back to me. "You can forget I am an Arab. From now on I'm going to forget it myself."

I wondered how people could do that, forget their race or their nationality. I knew I could never forget I was an American, even if I wanted to: the die of history had moulded me too strongly. Some men make good jobs of taking on another nationality: T. S. Eliot had become almost an archetype of an Englishman, Sam Gompers had become an archetypal American labour leader; but had the one ever forgotten he had been born an American, the other forgotten he had been an Englishman? Perhaps it would be easier for Lucille: by inheritance she had a choice.

"What are you going to be? French?"

She shrugged, which I suppose is a French gesture. "What else? Or would you like to marry me and make me an American?"

"I can do just that. But we can't get married if you're going to run off like this."

"It will have to wait, then."

"How is your father going to like it? I mean, forgetting you're an Arab?"

She was packing clothes in one of the suitcases, neatly and methodically; that would be the provincial French coming out in her; it was almost as if, now she had decided to forget she was half-Arab, she was going to be French all the way. I began to watch for other signs of her newly adopted nationality, but I am not educated in the subtleties of other peoples' characteristics; we are not a subtle people ourselves and we tend too much to take foreigners at face value. We might *suspect* them, but suspicion doesn't always educate. After a while I tired of looking for the French and Arab in her: she was just

Lucille, whom I was still trying to understand after six months of knowing her.

She said, "Papa will get used to it. There are other things he will have to learn to live with."

"What things?"

But she didn't answer, and I said, "What's got into you since lunch? Did you know then that you were leaving?"

She stopped packing, looked at me across the bed that separated us. She brushed her hair back from her brow and it was as if she had drawn a veil away from her face: it exposed more than just weariness and concern: she was afraid, too. "Yes, I knew then, Paul. I didn't know *when* we'd be leaving but Papa told me this morning he'd changed his mind about wanting to stay on in Beirut. We're going out on a plane to-night."

"Why didn't you tell me, then?"

"I don't really know. I think I was afraid we might argue. You don't want me to leave, do you?" I wasn't sure now what I wanted her to do; but she didn't wait for my answer: "It isn't as easy for me as it is for you, Paul. I mean the decision whether to stay here or not. Being here for you is not really a personal decision—and you don't have to commit yourself for the rest of your life. You can always fall back on Washington. Or even Charleston." She half-smiled, not quizzically but almost sympathetically. "Sometimes, I think, deep inside you you want to go back there."

"To Charleston? You're crazy."

"Perhaps. But you criticize it too much, darling, talk about it too much. You must be nostalgic for something there. Is it your ex-wife?"

"You know better than that."

"I'm sorry, I shouldn't have said that. Yes, I do know better than that. But whatever it is, I don't think you'd be entirely unhappy if you went back to Charleston. At least it is somewhere for you to go, somewhere you *know*. That's what I mean when I say is isn't really much of a decision for you as to whether you stay in Beirut or not."

"You don't give me any credit for having——" I tried to think of a less pompous phrase, but couldn't: "An official conscience?"

The phrase must have sounded pompous to her, too,

because she smiled. "No, I don't, darling. It's not that I don't give you credit—it's just that I can't believe it. It's like—like a Catholic trying to explain to me some of the things he believes. All that business about bread and wine turning into the body of Christ, the Virgin Birth, all that. I just couldn't believe it, but I don't sneer at them for believing it. I don't sneer at you for your—official conscience—" there was just a slight pause, as if she found the phrase difficult to say. "It's just that I think people are more important than governments. And, when it finally comes down to it, if what I do doesn't hurt other people, then I'm the most important one of the lot. You and me."

I had never been any good at arguing with her; or with Charlene. You need a streak of cruelty to be good at argument, and I don't have it: at least not with the women I have loved. Which may perhaps be a weakness. Psychologists are always telling us that women look for cruelty in their lovers; but those psychologists are usually men. Weak or not, I took another tack now: "Were you going to tell me at all?"

"Of course. At lunch I was just feeling so good—Papa saying he was going to leave Beirut with me, the news from Tel Aviv——" She sat down on the bed beside the suitcase, wearily, as if her legs had given out on her. "I was going to tell you this afternoon in bed. It's a very good place for persuasion. I was going to try and persuade you to come with me. Oh, not right away, I knew you wouldn't—couldn't do that, not at once. But soon, as soon as your conscience would let you. But we didn't go to bed, did we?"

"Is that why your mood has changed? Because I didn't make it to bed?" I did have a streak of cruelty in me, after all; but it was only petty cruelty and it made no mark on her at all. She just shook her head without looking at me, picked up some things from the bed and went on with her packing. I said, "Where's your father now?"

She still didn't look up at me. "He had to go out of town." She held a scarf in her hand, a St. Laurent one that I had bought on the spur of the moment one day when she had complained about her hair being blown about in my car when the top was down. She folded it carefully and put it in the suitcase. "He has one last client to see before he leaves."

"Maybe when I do leave here I should go into business with your father. The diamond game seems so uncomplicated."

She got up suddenly, came around the bed and put her arms around my neck. She stared at me, then abruptly, savagely, she kissed me. I held her to me and tasted the salt of her tears as they ran down her cheeks. Gently I pushed her away, but still kept my arms around her. "I didn't mean to sound sour about your father. There's nothing wrong with the diamond game. He told me it's all based on trust. Maybe we could do with some of that in our game."

"That isn't why I'm weeping."

"Why then?" We stood between the large mirror on her dressing-table and the mirrored wall: we were reflected *ad infinitum*, one mirror within another, lovers multiplied X times over in an endless room.

"You are always asking questions, *chéri*. Why don't you sometimes just accept things as they are? You help to make things complicated for yourself by always asking *why*."

"It's an old American habit. It's probably how we came to have so much know-how."

"Know-how doesn't always help with people, *chéri*. They aren't like engines and mechanical things." She kissed me again, lightly this time, wiped her eyes and went back around the bed. She snapped shut the lid of the suitcase, put it on the floor and picked up another one. "I think it is better if we sometimes don't know everything there is to be known about each other."

Maybe she was right. I wondered how much better I would feel now if I had known less than I did about Briggs. I wanted to tell her about him, but what good would it do? Some of the anger at what they were going to do to Briggs came back into me. I went out on to the balcony while I tried to control it. If it escaped from me in some way, I did not want Lucille to mistake it as meant for her. I was determined that from now till she got on the plane to-night I would do nothing to disturb the brittle harmony that we had established between us. The farewell to-night might be for longer than I cared to think about.

The late afternoon sun was turning the sea to gold. The fishing fleet was heading out towards the horizon, a broken string of shadow chasing the sunset. Some gulls went home, sleek and silent as the breeze through which they flew; far out, a dark reflection of them, five fighter planes also headed home. Down on the promenade the strollers moved in solemn silence; even the children now seemed quiet and restrained; perhaps the news from Tel Aviv had changed even since I had come home. A tourist bus went by, the people in it sitting back in their seats tired and bored; they had seen the wonders of Baalbek, digested the history of Byblos, but now their day of exploration had been reduced to the discovery of blistered feet, tired eyes and aching backs. I wondered who the tourists were, if they were Germans, French or even some adventurous Americans; and even as I wondered about the last, I saw the Pan Am plane coming in (bringing more refugees from other, less hospitable places than Beirut?). It went low overhead, its jets whistling, and down below the faces of the strollers turned up in a long line, like the white edge of a wave that had just broken over the promenade wall.

I went back into the bedroom. 'What time does your plane go? You might have a bit of trouble getting on, you know. You aren't the only ones wanting to get out of here in a hurry."

"Is Caradoc Briggs going out, too?"

"What made you ask about him?" I said cautiously.

She dropped a bikini carelessly into the suitcase; it is one article of clothing about which it is difficult to be neat. "I saw him leaving here. He came up the side lane. He didn't see me, I was just putting my car away. I went down to your apartment, but you must have just gone out again. Had he been to see you?"

"He brought me a cheque. Us. For what we'd lent him."

"Didn't you tell him there was no hurry?"

"He's leaving to-night, maybe on the same plane as you and your father." I wished it were true; and did my best to keep the despair out of my voice. "But there wasn't just what he owed us. There was some extra, quite a lot extra, to pay for Ahmed's funeral." I didn't mention that the cheque was unsigned: you don't scale down a man's charity because of his carelessness.

"I wish you two could get together. I mean, more permanently."

"It's too late now." Then abruptly the full horror of what lay in store for Briggs came back, and I blurted out: "They're going to kill him!"

She froze, her hands full of a froth of blue silk nightgown; without moving she suddenly seemed to become angular, a manikin with a dead-white plaster face. "When? Where?"

"I don't know for sure. To-night, I guess, but I don't know where."

"How do you know?"

"Don't ask me that. I just know." Some sense of loyalty stopped me from mentioning Criska: I owed him nothing, except that we were both Americans. If she had been American, I might have told her. But she wasn't, and some sort of national pride stopped me. Expediency is not a national characteristic poets sing about or diplomats boast about, and Sousa could never have set it to music.

"Is it down at Sidon?"

"Sidon? I don't know. Why, what's going on down there?"

Then downstairs the doorbell rang. She squeezed the nightgown, her hands tightening without her realising it, then she dropped it into the suitcase and went quickly out of the bedroom. I hesitated a moment, then I went downstairs after her.

She opened the front door of the apartment. Captain Hacobian stood on the landing outside, dressed still in his Sunday best suit. With him were two other men, also in civilian clothes, but not so well dressed. Their suits were of the same brown material: it could have been a uniform: even the wrinkles seemed to be in the same places, like badges of office. They were of the same age, in their early thirties, and they had the same blank, hard expression. Hacobian didn't have to name them: these were government men, policemen who were concerned with more than just ordinary crime.

Hacobian introduced the two strangers, but I didn't hear their names. I was looking at him: he looked worried and said, like a man who had just been betrayed by a friend. "We are looking for your father, M'amselle Zaid."

"He is not here." Lucille's voice was almost indistinct, caught in her throat. "Why do you want him?"

"These gentlemen want him for questioning," said Hacobian. Then he looked directly at me: "Zaid is the chief Israeli agent in this country."

CHAPTER 12

"Where have they taken Miss Zaid?" the Ambassador asked.

"Up to one of the Ministries. I'm not sure which one, they wouldn't let me go with her."

"A wise thing. You didn't try to insist on going with her, did you?"

I had, at first; but I wasn't going to admit it. "No, sir. Captain Hacobian was there. He politely pointed out to me that as a foreigner it was no business of mine."

"It certainly isn't. Oh, I know how you feel, Paul, she being your girl and all that——" He took off his glasses, began to polish them. "I'm not going to give you any lecture on getting involved with a local girl. I know what it's like. Pretty girls don't wear flags." That was one of his lesser aphorisms, but he seemed pleased with it. "But you stay out of it, Paul. I'll make some inquiries of one or two of the Ministers. But I don't think they'll do anything to her. This country isn't like some of the others. They don't have fanatics who go in for torturing to get information."

"There's nothing she could tell them."

"She could tell them where her father is right now," said Ben Criska.

"Maybe you could tell them."

Criska said nothing, but Bredgar had noticed the bitterness in my voice. "That's enough of that, Paul. I think you could do with a little more objectivity in regard to this matter."

"That's not easy, sir. Do you know what they're planning to do?"

"What *who* planning to do?"

The coldness of his voice warned me. I glanced at Criska, but there was no expression at all on his face; at least he wasn't waiting, with any sort of grisly anticipation, for me to plunge in over my head. His decency, no matter how negative, and the Ambassador's warning made me back off: I couldn't come right out and accuse Criska of engineering the intended murder of Briggs. "I'm not sure. Ben told me he knows of a plan to kill Briggs to-night. That means they'll kill Zaid, too."

"How do you know Briggs is meeting Zaid?"

"I just took it for granted——" I looked at Criska. "Is he meeting him?"

Criska spread a hand. "I don't know. All my information said was that Briggs had a meeting somewhere to-night and that he was going to be knocked off."

The rage was taking hold of me again. "How the hell can you be so cold-blooded about it? Can't we do something to stop it? What if he is meeting Zaid, if they kill both of them?"

Criska didn't answer, just glanced at Bredgar. The Ambassador had been about to put his glasses back on, but now he stopped, took out his handkerchief and began to polish them again. I wanted to snatch them from him and hurl them against the wall. Then I saw the pain in his eyes and I knew he was as frustrated and baffled as I was. "Paul, what good will it do if we interfere?"

This is a time for Arab rhetoric, I thought; but rhetoric never wins serious arguments, only mobs. "It might save the lives of two people."

Bredgar nodded, still polishing his glasses. "Agreed. And I understand your concern for these two particular people —we'll assume that Zaid *is* going to meet your friend Briggs. But if we do save them—and there's no guarantee we can, we don't even know where the meeting is to be —if we do save them, who thanks us?"

"Briggs and Zaid."

"Not enough. We're not looking for the thanks of individuals right now, Paul."

"What are we looking for, sir? The thanks of murderers for minding our own business?"

"I'll overlook that one, Paul. If I were in your position I'd be upset and flying off the handle, too." *He's trying to help me,* I thought, *and I'm making it hard as I can for him.* "But I don't happen to be in your position, and whatever you may think about objectivity in a case like this, I have to do my best to see we have it. We aren't here to save individuals, friends or otherwise. Especially non-American individuals." There was a photo on his desk of his family: a dark-haired pretty woman, two teenage boys, a small girl. I wondered at what time in his daily official life he stopped thinking of them as individuals. Misunderstanding the look on my face, he held up a hand, anticipating some sarcasm from me. "Hold it, Paul. Even if they were Americans, I don't know that we'd interfere. What they are doing is against American policy here in the Middle East. That, and only that, can be our yardstick."

I leaned forward, then abruptly I thought better of what I was about to say. I sat back in my chair, beaten.

"You were going to say something?"

I hesitated, then I thought: *What the hell? I just don't care any more.* I could see Bredgar's decision on me in his face: I would be on a plane out of here as soon as they could get a replacement for me. "I was going to say, sir, that I didn't think we had a policy here."

His mouth tightened, and so did his hand: there was a sudden sharp crack and the glasses snapped apart at the bridge. He looked down at them blankly, showing no annoyance at all at what had happened. Then he looked up at me: he had no annoyance, or rather anger, for anything or anyone but me. And I recognised, or thought I recognised, the reason for it: not for making a treasonable remark such as I had, but for stating the truth in a situation where he had to deny it. He didn't trust Ben Criska, but he had to go along with him.

"I think you'd better go, Paul. I'll see what I can do about Miss Zaid. In the meantime, leave the Briggs affair alone. Stay out of it."

Stay out of it. That was what Hacobian had told me after the two strangers had taken Lucille away. There had been no hysterics from Lucille after Hacobian had announced why they had come, and no emotion at all from the two government men; I had been the one surging with emotion and that had been as much from an accumulation of the day's events as from this latest shock. Somehow I had kept control of myself, and that seemed to impress the strangers; perhaps they had expected me, as an American, to put on some sort of act. I had looked at Lucille and said, "Did you know this about your father?"

"Not till this afternoon." We had gone back to the living-room, Hacobian and the two men standing awkwardly by, like undertakers who had arrived for a funeral for which the household was unprepared. "He came in about an hour ago, just after you'd called. He told me then we'd have to fly out to-night, and he told me why." She managed a tiny smile of sad wryness. "That was why my mood had changed since lunch."

I looked at Hacobin. "Are you *sure*? What proof have you got?"

One of the men spoke to Hacobian in Arabic, who answered him. Then the man looked at me. "Do you speak Arabic?"

"A little. But you must go slowly."

He did speak slowly, with maddening enunciation, but I didn't interrupt him. "We have the most positive proof, Mr. Tancred. You have also heard what M'amselle Zaid has just said—isn't that proof enough for you?" I learned later his name was Qassab. He had thick bushy eyebrows and an old-fashioned toothbrush moustache: they looked as if they had been pasted on to his dull blank face to give him some identity. He was not unsympathetic, just unimaginative, an ideal man for the job he had to do. "Zaid was married to a Jewish woman——"

I whirled on Lucille, said in English, "Is that true? Your mother?"

"She was a French Jew. Most people had forgotten, but Mama never did. But she was not a Jew who hated Arabs——" She said this last in Arabic to Qassab and his companion, who accepted the information without any reaction: they were not here to arrest a dead Jewish woman. Lucille seemed to understand that they were not interested in her mother, but she went on arguing for her. She waved a hand at the Arabiana in the living-room, the brass tables, the inlaid boxes and trays, the carpets, as if she were offering evidence for the defendant: "You can see what she was like——"

"It is your father we want," said Qassab. "He is an Arab. Why does he hate the Arabs?"

"He doesn't! He——" Lucille was about to argue; the passion in her came to the surface for just a moment. Then she shrugged, subsided and turned away. "It doesn't matter. I'll let him explain——" She looked at me, broke back into English. "This makes it bad for you, doesn't it? Living in the house of an Arab traitor, in love with his half-Jewish daughter——"

Suddenly she broke down, began to weep. I put my arms around her, looked over her head at Hacobian; somehow I couldn't bring myself to accept that the other two men were the real masters of this situation. "Can you leave us alone now? Zaid isn't here."

Hacobian shook his head, glanced at Qassab and translated. The second man seemed to show no interest in what was said, but, a block of wood in a brown suit, just stared fixedly at Lucille and me. Then Qassab said, "We shall take M'amselle Zaid with us. She is wanted for questioning. She will not be harmed."

Lucille disengaged herself from my arms, wiped her eyes.

"I'll come with you," I said.

Hacobian cleared his throat. "I think it would be better if you didn't, Mr. Tancred," he said in English, and Qassab and his companion looked sharply at him. But they said nothing, just waited for Lucille.

"Captain Hacobian is right, Paul," Lucille said, and pressed my hand. "Stay here."

I wanted to insist that I go with her, but the pressure of her hand had been as much a warning as anything else. I had no ammunition for argument; my thoughts were just an incoherent mess. At this moment I had not even connected Zaid with Briggs; that only came later when they had taken Lucille away. Qassab and his colleague were not gallant towards her, but at least they treated her as if they had not already judged her guilty. She came downstairs from her bedroom with a light coat thrown over her shoulders, gave me a wan smile and went out with the two government men.

I looked at Hacobian. "What will happen to her? Are they likely to try some force on her, get her to tell them where her father is?"

"Does she know where her father is?"

"I don't know." I suddenly remembered something she had said just before the doorbell had rung: *Is it down at Sidon?* I turned my back on Hacobian, hoping nothing had shown in my face. "She didn't say anything to me when we were talking about him. Why couldn't you have come on your own, Captain? You didn't have to bring those fellers with you. You could have questioned her here——"

"I didn't bring them, Mr. Tancred. They brought *me*. They thought you might be here and they knew I knew you. They wanted me here to talk to you, to——" he smiled "——to reason with you if you tried to interfere. You see, Mr. Tancred, our government doesn't really want a fight with the American government. The Lebanese are not anti-American."

"Have you seen the crowd outside the embassy?"

"A few demonstrators, Mr. Tancred. Does the John Birch Society speak for America? Or the hippies of San Francisco? You see? We know much more about America than you know about us." Part of my mind was settled enough to recognise the truth of that. "M'amselle Zaid will be all right. They don't suspect her of anything. Not even because she has been your friend."

"I still wish you'd come alone."

"I am no longer on cases like this, Mr. Tancred. Not even the one to do with your Mr. Briggs and the rifles." There was no rancour in his voice; he spoke with the mild resignation of a minority who had learned to shrug and accept everything. "They have put me on to the hashish growers. They think I'll be safe there, an Armenian. They won't have to suspect my political or racial loyalties. All I have to do is go up to the Beqaa Valley occasionally, pat the hashish growers on the head and tell them to grow sunflowers instead——" He laughed and wobbled his head in wonder. "They will laugh at me and say yes, but as soon as I have gone they will be out cultivating the Indian hemp again. They've been doing it for centuries now. Why change? Sunflowers." He laughed again. "Would your bootleggers have made lemonade if your government had asked them to?"

I wanted to sympathise with him, but there wasn't time. "When did they take you off Briggs? Do you know where he is?"

"I have no idea, Mr. Tancred. I don't think the Sûreté is interested in him any more."

"What about the security police?"

"They didn't mention him. I don't think they are interested, also."

"They should be. Someone is going to kill him to-night."

His expression didn't change; his face was suddenly as wooden as that of Qassab and his colleague. "Who is going to kill him, Mr. Tancred?"

"I don't know. The Syrians, the Palestinians, even the Kurds—it could be anyone. I just got the word on what they're going to do to him——"

He didn't ask me where I'd got my information. He seemed to shrink into his Sunday best suit, all at once cautious and uninvolved. "Stay out of it, Mr. Tancred. It would be best. The whole business—Briggs, Zaid, M'amselle Zaid. Stay out of it."

And that seemed to be all the advice anyone had for me. Non-involvement was the only recipe for survival; be neutral in love and war. Suddenly, now in the Ambassador's office, hearing Bredgar echo what Hacobian and, it seemed, everyone else had told me, I felt as I had felt when I discovered Ahmed's body. I wanted to vomit, but there was nothing in me any more; even anger, after a time, scalds you dry and empty. I stood up, marvelling that my legs had the strength to hold even the thin shell that was all that remained of me, and nodded to the Ambassador and Ben Criska. I had come back here to the embassy hoping, with no real optimism, that Tom Bredgar, the decent man who was doing his best to be a human being as well as an ambassador, would be able to do something to help me in my dilemma, to ask him what steps I should take to save both Briggs and Zaid. But the two roles, human being and ambassador, are not always compatible: governments long ago lost the weights by which to measure the human heart: there is no place in protocol for love or misery or grief. Bredgar was trapped by policy and the system. And by history, by the errors, omissions and lies that had got us, America and Britain, into a position where the Arabs no longer trusted us, where anything we might do was read as an act against them.

"I'll be at home, sir, if you want me. I mean, if you can do anything for Miss Zaid——"

"I'll do what I can, Paul." He put the two pieces of his glasses down on the desk in front of him, and stared at them as if expecting them, like magic spectacles, to give him a look into the future; then he looked up at me and blinked, as if I, too, were something he could not bring completely into focus. "I'm sorry, Paul. I wish there was something we could do. But there isn't."

"It will solve that problem we had about the planes and tanks," Ben Criska said, and had the grace not to sound pleased or triumphant. He didn't look at me, but gazed out at the darkening evening beyond the window. "That's the only way to look at it, Paul. The only way."

2

I walked home along the promenade. It was dark now and all the demonstrators had gone home for supper; they were not passionate enough yet to be able to sustain themselves on anger and hatred; that would come if war came. Hacobian had brought me in to the embassy in his own family car, a small Renault. "My wife has been waiting at home all day for me to take her and the children to her mother's. She has never liked me being a policeman. To-day, for the first time, I can see her point of view."

"Will you change to another job?"

"I am too old for that, Mr. Tancred. More than that, I don't think I should want to do anything else. All days are not as bad as this one. Sometimes I actually can *help* people. You don't always get that opportunity in other jobs. I am only sorry I could not help you, Mr. Tancred."

And now an hour later I was still in need of help and not getting it. I trudged home. I didn't think people trudged any more: it sounded like one of my father's words. Even walking is becoming an old-fashioned word in America; Detroit is making obsolescent more than just last year's model. But to-night I did trudge: despair can weigh down your feet as much as snow or mud. It was a beautiful evening, but I wasn't aware of it. There were still some strollers on the other side of the road, but they were only dark ghosts, shadows that I didn't really see. Cars went by, headlamps blazing and engines roaring, every driver a Stirling Mossadegh, but they made no impression on me. Only when one car drew up to the kerb and flashed its lights at me did I look up. The old prickling at the back of my neck hit me again and I straightened up, looking about for a gateway to duck into.

Then Grimsby-Orr said, "I say, old man——"

I laughed with relief and some sort of cockeyed amusement. Usually I find something almost inane about the English *I say, old man.* Anyone hearing it for the first time, whether an old man or not, waits expectantly for what is to be said. But the greeting is usually followed by a dead silence or something so inconsequential as to leave you still waiting expectantly. But now Grimsby-Orr's greeting had a reassuring sound to it, the sound of British unflappability. I crossed to the car and almost flung my arms about him.

"You old sonofabitch," I said.

He looked at me quizzically. "Thanks, old man." He seemed to recognise that I was under some sort of strain, but he made no comment on it. "Care to hop in? I'll drive you home."

He drove a right-hand Morris Oxford that he hurled around like a souped-up chariot. He did a U-turn in a gap in the strip that divided the road, causing three other cars to stand on their noses as they had to brake, almost tore the engine out of the car as he sped it down the avenue, swung it around in another U-turn on two wheels and jerked it to a stop in front of the Zaid house.

"Ever had an accident?" I asked.

"Lost count. Once down in Jordan I drove the old bus down a two-hundred-foot precipice. Very exhilarating."

"*This bus?*"

He laughed. "Relax, old man. It's been completely rebuilt, did it m'self. It's as good as it ever was."

"I'll bet." But the little exchange with him, almost as meaningless as the exchanges between Janet Ponder and me, had made me forget for the moment how I had been feeling when I had got into the car. Then I saw the black car parked up in front of us. "Who's that? Somebody waiting for me?"

"I don't think so. A couple of security chaps, they're up in the Zaid flat with your girl friend." He took a pipe out of the glove-compartment, lit it and filled the car with smoke. He waved a hand, clearing the air a little. "Sorry. Hardly ever smoke, but sometimes one——" He put the pipe back in his mouth, chopping off what he was going to say. He sucked on it for a while, gazing steadily at me all the time. Then: "It's a bad show that, isn't it? I mean, old Zaid turning out to be working for the Israelis."

"It soon gets around, doesn't it? Where did you get it—out at Shemlan?"

He ignored that one. "We always suspected there might be someone else here working for them. That chappie they fished out of the sea a fortnight ago was too small-time, not important enough to have been the only one operating here. But Zaid——!" He blew another cloud of smoke, out the window this time. "Just goes to show, doesn't it? I wonder why he would do it? Never struck me as the sort who would be a traitor for money."

"His wife was Jewish."

"Oh, really?" I felt a small glow of pleasure at his surprise; they didn't know everything out at Shemlan. "That could explain it, then. What about the girl?"

"No. She's as innocent as you or me."

I felt rather than saw him smile. "Who said we were innocent?" He looked up towards the house, then back at me. "You didn't get on the blower to me about what they're going to do to Briggs."

"Who did tell you?"

Another cloud of smoke went out the window. "We employ the same contact as Criska. Only he doesn't know it. We get a lower rate because he gives the information to Criska first. You chaps always throw your money around too much. I remember the good old days when you could get all the information you wanted for a couple of quid." He looked at up at the house again. "They'll do Zaid, too, you know."

"Do you know where Briggs and Zaid are meeting?"

"I was hoping you could tell me that. Thought Criska might have paid the contact a bit extra, got a bit more than we did."

"Criska doesn't know any more than you. Or if he does, he didn't tell me." For a moment I wondered if Ben Criska had known more than he had divulged. But there was no time now to entertain suspicion; if I went back to him he still wouldn't tell me. I had already been written off as *persona non grata* in our own embassy. But now I was suspicious of Grimsby-Orr; or anyway curious. "What were you going to do?"

He sat puffing on the pipe, then he opened the door of the car, knocked out the ash and with his back still to me said, "I'm a bloody fool for thinking so, but it seems wrong to me to let two chaps be knocked off like that. Something *should* be done."

I know it is a novelist's phrase, but I actually seemed to feel my heart leap. Something quickened in me, anyway; I leaned across, grabbed him by the shoulder and pulled him round. "For Christ's sake—I've been looking for someone for the last two or three hours to say *that*! Let's do something!"

"Yes," he said calmly. "But what?"

"We've got to find that meeting place. Just before those fellers came to the house, Lucille said something about Sidon. That mean anything to you?"

"Nothing in particular. But it's down south. It could mean perhaps that someone is sneaking over the border to-night. If Briggs is selling those planes and tanks to Israel, it's a big deal. Zaid may want someone more important than himself to okay it."

I looked up towards the house, to the lights showing in the top apartment. "I wonder if Lucille knows exactly where in Sidon?"

"If she does, how are you going to find out? Those two fellers aren't going to let you be alone with her."

"How good a conversationalist are you in Arabic? I mean, can you chatter on without any effort?"

"I once had a five-hour natter with a sultan down on the Trucial Coast and was never lost for a word. Talked about everything from falcons to women. That good enough?"

"Choose your own subject to-night, falcons, women, anything you like, and natter away like you've never nattered before. This is what I've got in mind——"

When we rang the doorbell of the Zaid apartment, Qassab opened the door. He nodded to Grimsby-Orr, whom he seemed to know, then looked at me. Slowing up my Arabic, as if I were still in the initial stages of learning the tongue, I said, "Miss Zaid has invited us to have a drink. May we come in?" I looked past him at Lucille who had come to the bottom of the three steps that led down from the living-room. In English I said, "Remember, you've invited me and Mr. Grimsby-Orr to cocktails? Is it still on?"

She still looked in a state of shock. Her face was pale and her eyes almost blank, and I wondered what they had done to her when they had taken her away. I thought she was not going to respond, not catch on that Grimsby-Orr and I had something planned that needed her co-operation. Then her eyes cleared and she smiled. "Of course." In Arabic she said to Qassab, "We all have to drink and eat something. Why cannot I have the servants prepare something for us? You may be waiting here hours for my father. He would never forgive me for not having offered you the hospitality of his house."

So they had got nothing out of her as to where her father was right now. Qassab bit his lip and looked at the second man, who for the first time showed some life in his wooden face: his eyes lit and he nodded eagerly. "All right," said Qassab. "But you are our guests, gentlemen, not M'amselle Zaid's. So you will let us entertain you while she arranges for the food and drink."

I had had a faint hope that I might be able to sneak out to the kitchen while Lucille was there, but Qassab wasn't as careless as all that. I was edgy with impatience: we had no idea what time the assassination was planned for: it was already almost eight and Sidon was more than half an hour's drive from Beirut. If Briggs and Zaid were meeting down there, they would not leave it too late, not if they wanted to get back to Beirut and catch a plane out to-night. Sunday night was a poor night for scheduled flights; no one from the embassy ever travelled on a Sunday night if it could be avoided. Whatever flight they intended to catch, Briggs and Zaid would not spend too long hanging around in Sidon. They must know that with the exodus now going on out of Beirut, it would be too risky to turn up at the last minute to take your seat on a plane.

Lucille had gone out to the kitchen to tell the servants

to prepare drinks and something to eat. "Nothing fancy, make it as quick as you can," I called after her, then grinned idiotically at Qassab and the other man, who had been introduced to Grimsby-Orr as Abdurrahim. I said in stumbling Arabic, "I ask for simple food."

Abdurrahim looked disappointed, but Qassab just nodded and continued to look at me as if trying to make up his mind about me. Then Grimsby-Orr picked up the conversation as he might have a squash ball, began to bang it back and forth, drawing Qassab and Abdurrahim into the verbal rallies without their knowing they were being trapped. It was a beautiful performance by Grimsby-Orr, a virtuoso effort in multiloquence: he tossed them rhetoric, spun them circumlocution, even recited them a poem. I just sat and nodded my head at appropriate moments, now and again sneaking a look at my watch and feeling myself beginning to sweat.

Lucille came back into the room, passed around a tray of *mezzeh*, the traditional Lebanese hors-d'oeuvre, looking covertly at me as she passed behind Qassab and Abdurrahim. She came to me with the tray. I looked over the selection, pointed to a bowl of chick-pea purée and said, "That place you mentioned to me, down south. Is that where your father is going?"

Grimsby-Orr, waving his empty pipe as if it were a baton, was still talking flat out, rhapsodising in Arabic about the joys of cricket: I caught references to Sheik Trueman and Sheik Benaud, two caliphs I had never heard of. Qassab was still watching me, but he did not appear particularly suspicious of what I had just said to Lucille.

She pointed to some stuffed eggs. "He has gone there."

"Do you know the address?" I examined some rollmops, wondering if this was an ironic joke on Lucille's part, serving a Jewish favourite to a couple of Arabs. I wondered how much enthusiasm Qassab and Abdurrahim had for their job. Were they like me, involved against their will in a cause that confused them? Then I remembered they were security men. You are not drafted into the security police: you are there because you have produced your own evidence of commitment.

Abdurrahim, a round of Arab bread in each hand, had got up and come to stand beside Lucille. I smiled up at him and said in my halting Arabic, "They are good, yes?" He nodded enthusiastically, and I looked at Lucille and said, "Don't say the address in front of these guys."

She pointed to some olives. "How shall I tell you, then?"

"Write it on a paper napkin. Give it to me with a drink."

But the houseman had already come in with a tray. He passed the drinks around, Martinis for Grimsby-Orr and me, arak for Qassab and Abdurrahim. As the houseman handed each of us our drink, he gave us a paper napkin each. I took mine, raised my glass to Qassab and Abdurrahim and managed to pour half the Martini down the front of my shirt. As I dabbed hastily at myself, Lucille was already on her way out to the kitchen. Grimsby-Orr covered beautifully with a lamentation on the sad waste of good liquor, an elegy that seemed in turn wasted on two such obviously strict Muslims as our two companions. Lucille came back with a fresh napkin, I took it from her and handed her the wet one. I put the fresh napkin up to my face, pretending to wipe my mouth, and saw the pencilled scribbling on it. It was time to go.

I looked at my watch. We had been here twenty minutes: would it look suspicious if we left so soon? But we had to risk it. I raised my glass to Grimsby-Orr this time and said, "Time we were going."

He nodded, put down his pipe, looked at his watch and shot to his feet. "Oh, my God! Church!" He deluged Lucille, Qassab and Abdurrahim with apologies; but he had forgotten it was Sunday evening! He should have been at church an hour ago, God forgive him for his sin! Qassab and Abdurrahim, religious men as they were, would understand and forgive him his unforgivable rudeness, but God must come first with all good men who hoped to attain Heaven . . .

We went out with a chorus of pleas for forgiveness, promising to pray for Qassab, Abdurrahim and Lucille; were out of the house and half-way down the steps to the car before we heard Qassab coming after us. "Oh, God!" Grimsby-Orr said, and we pulled up and waited for him to demand that we come back.

But all he did was to hold out Grimsby-Orr's pipe. "You forgot this. And may God reward you for your devotion. You will forgive me for saying so, but there are not enough truly religious men among Englishmen to-day."

"You speak the truth," said Grimsby-Orr, and when Qassab had gone back up the steps he added, "Including this one. Last time I was in church was to get married. Do you believe in God?"

"Yes."

"So do I. Just lost faith in the chaps who speak for him. Well, where do we go?"

I opened the paper napkin and Grimsby-Orr switched on the light in the car. He peered at the scrawled address, then switched the light off. "I know the street. It's an alley in the *suq*."

He put the key in the ignition, but I put my hand on his. "Look—do you really want to come? You don't have to, you know."

"I've always admired the Arabs, you know. They believe in the grand gesture, doing something heroic, sacrificing more than just one's time and a few words. I don't see myself as a bloody hero, but I feel it's time I made a gesture as a man instead of as a bloody government puppet. I'm not doing it for the Arabs—matter of fact, it will be against them, won't it?—but it's time I did something. Good Christ, there's little else left for me to do here now!" His voice almost broke, but he recovered in time. He started up the engine, threw it savagely into gear. "Just pray we're in time, old man."

3

"Have you got CD plates on your car?"

"Never use them, more nuisance than they're worth. Get you nothing but abuse from other drivers." We were on the Khaldeh motorway and Grimsby-Orr was doing his best to blow the engine right out of the car. "In any case, we certainly don't want CD plates to-night. We're being anything but *diplomatique*."

The Morris Oxford was rocketing along the road, every part of it protesting at what it was being asked to do; Grimsby-Orr crouched over the wheel, his ears laid back, and strove to push his foot through the floor. We passed the Radio Orient transmitter, the red light at the top of the mast blinking in the dark sky like a lost and angry star; then we had swung off the motorway and were on the narrower Sidon road, every bump in the macadam coming up like a small explosion through the frame of the car. The whistle of the wind was deafening and I tried to wind up the window on my side.

"Wouldn't bother!" Grimsby-Orr yelled. "Hasn't worked since I put the old bus over the precipice. Don't you like British air-conditioning?"

Oh Christ, I thought, *is everything going to finish up as a tragic farce? Is the car going to break down before we even get to Sidon, are we going to end up sitting beside the road miles from anywhere while Briggs and Zaid are murdered according to plan?* But the car was holding together despite Grimsby-Orr's efforts to wreck it. We swept through Damour, over the bridge and round the curve of the hill; Grimsby-Orr drove in the middle of the road all the way, like the Arabs, and I wondered if he, like them, trusted in Allah. But there was very little traffic on the road and our luck held.

We tore through a tiny hamlet, a collection of houses like square white rocks scattered beside the road. "Nebi Yunes!" Grimsby-Orr shouted. "Where Jonah was supposed to have been coughed up by the whale!"

"I'll bet he had a better trip than I'm having!"

He laughed out loud, shaking his head in delight. Now that he had committed himself he was like a schoolboy: this was an adventure, something to be enjoyed. I felt a flash of annoyance at him, but it quickly went. He was not callously careless of the end result of the adventure of what happened to Briggs and Zaid; he was working off steam, enjoying himself while he still could. When the chips were at last down, I knew he wouldn't be laughing.

He was already thinking about what lay ahead of us: "Puzzles me, why pick Sidon to meet? Nearest big town to border and it's always a good thing to meet in a big town, less conspicuous. But there are fifteen thousand Palestine refugees in Sidon, one-third of the town! Rather like having a picnic in the lions' den, eh?"

I had forgotten the Palestine refugees. Not all of them cared passionately about returning to what they still called Palestine; nationalism may be a stimulant for the poor, but they can't feed on it. But there were sure to be some cells of the Palestine Liberation Army in the town, and suddenly it struck me that they would probably be the assassins. It was hardly likely that any of the other extremist organisations would move in to do such a job in PLA territory. Extremists are as jealous of each other as they are of the common enemy. If the PLA were the intending assassins, it was not going to be easy to get Briggs and Zaid out of Sidon. We were rushing headlong in the old Morris Oxford into a mine-field. Doubt and fear suddenly assailed me: somehow I hadn't counted on having to be any sort of hero. Up till now I had thought of myself as no more than a messenger bringing a warning; my biggest concern had been my ignoring of my official neutrality. But now all at once everything had another, frightening perspective: Briggs and Zaid might not be the only ones to die to-night.

We swept around a promontory and there was Sidon up ahead. The street lights were blacked out, but scattered lights showed among the houses; would they be the houses of some of the Palestinians, who had seen so much misery they had become careless and fatalistic? The night had lightened a little, the stars breaking through, and I could see the Castle of the Sea, seven centuries old and built by the Crusaders, standing like a defiant fist at the end of the long arm that connected it to the town. Beyond it was the small harbour, some fishing boats, their sails furled, riding there like sleeping seabirds.

Grimsby-Orr slowed the car as we approached the outskirts of the town. Then he swung it off the road and we bumped down a lane between low stone walls. He pulled up, switched off the engine and we got out. At once I smelled the heavy perfume of fruit and saw the trees stretching away on either side of us.

"Orchards." Grimsby-Orr's voice was low. "Oranges, apricots, bananas. We'll cut through here, come out in the back of town. Watch out for irrigation channels. I'm wearing new suède shoes, dammit."

We clambered over the stone wall, one so old that all the rocks in it seemed to have merged into each other, congealed with time. Sidon was the farthest point north that Christ had come and he might have sat on this very wall and told the Canaanite woman to go home, that her daughter had been cured. I touched the wall for luck, suddenly reduced, like all men who are afraid, to superstition, and stumbled on after Grimsby-Orr through the dark orchards. We came up behind some houses and a dog growled at us; a voice called out, but we had already moved on into the darkness. I heard a splash and a curse; Grimsby-Orr had put one of his new suède shoes into an irrigation channel. We climbed over another wall and then we were among the houses of the town.

We moved down a long narrow street, keeping in the shadow of a high wall on our left. Two men passed on, grunted "*Saideh*," but showed no interest in us; in the darkness we must have passed for townsfolk. It was not going to be so easy when we came to the *suq*. Bazaar people, chained to their small stores, hardly ever moving out of them, are naturally curious about outsiders, especially Europeans who intrude at night.

Sidon, fortunately, was not Beirut: it didn't have much to offer the townsfolk after dark and most of them stayed home. A bus clattered by: it had only two passengers, two men staring gloomily out from its dimly lit cage like prisoners on their way to a life sentence. On the opposite side of the road, some men sat in a coffee shop, staring at an old movie on a television set on the counter: Claude Rains said, "Round up the usual suspects," and the men in the coffee shop all laughed: it was hard to tell whether their amusement was simple or sardonic. Then we crossed the road, turned down an alley and were in the maze of the *suq*.

There were more people about here. The tiny narrow shops were still open. The storekeepers lived in their shops, stayed open till it was time to fall into bed: you never knew when you might earn just a few more lire from some last-minute customer. A man, thin as a wire doll, grabbed at me as I went past; a claw tried to drag me into his carpet store. I shook myself free, trying not to antagonise him, not to create any commotion, and hurried on after Grimsby-Orr. The *suq* had lost its daytime noise and bustle, but the occasional radio still chopped at the ear as we passed a doorway: *Be on guard against the infidel*, warned a demagogic announcer. People stared out at us from the caves of their shops, curious but not antagonistic: these were more used to tourists than the Kurds in their colony. But several of them came to the doors of their shops and gazed hard after us; one man

193

called to another and the two of them began to follow us down the alley. Grimsby-Orr swung abruptly round a corner, quickening his pace, then round another corner. I followed him, stumbling over a heap of baskets as I rounded the second corner and having abuse shouted at me by the storekeeper hidden somewhere in his shop.

Then we were outside a bakery, a store larger than any of the others in this narrow street.

"This must be it," Grimsby-Orr said, looking up at the number on the blue enamel plate above the door.

We brushed through the curtain of beads hanging in the doorway. A small boy, grey with flour, appeared like a wraith around an outcrop of sacks of flour. Grimsby-Orr told him we wanted the man who owned the bakery and just as silently the boy disappeared. We stood there among the sacks of flour and to-day's left-over loaves; the poor would come in to-morrow and buy them at half-price. From somewhere at the back there came the smell of newly-baked bread. Then the baker himself appeared, a grey muscled ghost who held a lump of dough in one hand like a rock. He stared silently at us, his dark eyes the only life in the grey deadness of his face. Grimsby-Orr looked at me: it was my game from now on.

"We are friends of Naami Zaid and the Englishman." I kept my voice low; there was no way of knowing if someone was listening out in the alley; the beaded curtain shut out the alley completely, and I wondered where the two men were who followed us. "Are they here?"

"Who are you?" The baker's voice was a soft husky growl, as if his throat were lined with flour. I told him our names and he continued to stare at us, making up his mind what to do next. Then abruptly he jerked his head, turned and went back into the bakery itself. We followed him.

It was a large room, the rear wall lined with ovens that stood open, the grates beneath them cold and black. A second wall was stacked high with sacks of flour; the other two walls had racks on which were scattered some thick loaves, like rounded stones, and a stack of the flat Arab bread. In the far corner was an old-style Arab oven, a beehive shape with a small fire glowing inside its base; this was evidently the source of the smell of newly-baked bread. The room was lit by a single electric bulb hanging from the centre of the rough ceiling, its glow only seeming to emphasise the shadows around the walls.

Briggs, Zaid and a third man stood watching us from behind a barricade of flour sacks.

CHAPTER 13

It is disconcerting, to say the least, to look at two men whom you think you have come to save and find them hating you. Briggs and Zaid stared at us as if we were enemies; and I felt myself crumble inside. *We shouldn't have come,* I thought. *They won't understand why and they will label me with their prejudiced, stereotyped image of an American: the interfering, do-good Yank who can't mind his own business.* Then something in me rebelled. Grimsby-Orr was here, too; and he was not here because he was an interfering do-gooder. He had come for the same reason as I had, because we could not see two men sacrificed in the interests of expediency. If I had also come because I owed an old debt to Briggs, that was something between just him and me and did not concern Zaid and Grimsby-Orr.

Zaid said predictably, "You shouldn't have come, Paul."

"You've been a bit of a stupid bugger, chum." The word came out as *booger*; I remembered that in Korea, whenever Briggs got angry, the Mancunian vowels got thicker. He looked at Grimsby-Orr. "You couldn't stay out of it, either, could you?"

The stranger stood just behind Briggs and Zaid, but somehow you knew he was not the low man on this particular totem pole; he was not saying anything now, but till we had arrived he had been running this show. It was difficult to tell whether he was Jew or Arab; you could only say he was a Semite; all at once I remembered the photo of Madame Zaid, that she too had had these same features. Semite to-day has come to be associated almost exclusively with Jews; to be anti-Semitic is to be anti-Jewish and nothing else. But Shem had fathered both the Arabs and the Jews, and this stranger could pass for either one. He could be a traitor or a patriot; he had the ideal natural disguise for either.

Grimsby-Orr said, "I think you'd better listen to what Tancred has to say."

"They're going to kill you. I don't know whether it's planned for here or somewhere else, but they're going to get you to-night."

"Who are?" Briggs looked first at Zaid and the stranger, then at me.

"I don't know."

"You don't know who's going to kill us or where they're going to do it? Come on, Paul, make your story better than that. Why did you really come? Are you still trying to bugger up my business?"

"I don't care a damn about your deals now! I tell you it's true—they're going to get rid of you to-night!" What I was saying suddenly sounded ridiculous, melodramatic: it was not the dialogue of a diplomat. I looked at Zaid, glad to be able to tell him some facts, to sound credible: "The police know about you, too. They're at the apartment now, holding Lucille. Don't tell me I shouldn't have come. Should I have sent her?"

Zaid suddenly looked as if he was about to weep; the mention of Lucille and the police had turned him from agent back into father: he loved her, I knew that, and I had cut him down savagely. But there was no time to show any mercy: the killers might already be in the alley outside.

"Doc, you've got to believe me! Get out of here, get back to Beirut and grab a plane! Or——" I looked at the stranger "—if he's from over the border, go with him. But for Christ's sake, don't hang around here!"

The baker and the boy watched us, not understanding a word but understanding perfectly the atmosphere: fear is a universal language. And there was fear in the big room now: my own, Zaid's, it was beginning to show, too, in Briggs' and the stranger's faces. Only Grimsby-Orr showed no concern, but that didn't mean he was unafraid: that freckled, reddish face had been used as a mask too often to give away anything as personal as fear.

The baker went on working, like an automaton. He took dough out of a great wooden vat, slapped it on a curved plank, jabbed at it with a big wooden comb, sprinkled water on it, then with a long-handled spatula flipped the flattened dough off the plank and slapped it on the inside of the beehive-shaped oven. It would stick there, occasionally popping as a bubble of dough burst, then after a few seconds he would whip out the pancake of bread with a long fork, drop it on a bench and turn back to the vat of dough to repeat the process. The boy was stacking the bread that had cooled, neither he nor the baker taking their eyes off us as they worked. A cat came out of the shadows, curled itself round the boy's bare foot, but he was unaware of it; his skinny leg remained stiff like a thin stake and the cat gave up and slunk back into the shadows. Then we heard the swish of the beaded curtain in the shop.

Everyone stood still, even the baker. He glanced at the stranger and after a moment the latter nodded. The baker went out, in his hand another lump of dough: he carried it like a weapon, ready to throw. We all stood without moving, seemingly without breathing. We heard a murmur of voices, nothing distinguishable, then the swish of the curtain again. The baker came back into the bakery, nodded at us all, and went back to his oven. One of the pancake loaves had burned while he was out of the room and he flipped out the charred oval and dropped it on the floor. The smell of the burned bread hung heavy in the air.

"Well?" I said. "Do you get out of here?"

"We haven't finished our deal——" Briggs turned to the stranger. "What about it?"

The man spoke for the first time, a quiet hard voice, a voice used to authority and decisions, some of them, I suspected, decisions of expediency. "There isn't time, Mr. Briggs. I am not going to authorise such a large transfer of money without more information than you have given me. I can have a man in any port you care to name to-morrow, to look over some of the planes and tanks. If they are satisfactory, the money will be paid at once."

"Okay then." Briggs was disappointed, but I knew he was not a man who let disappointment slow up his momentum. "Have a man in Famagusta to-morrow. I'll be at the Grecian Hotel."

"How do you get to Famagusta to-night?" I said.

"I'll go to-morrow morning. There'll be a plane out then."

"Where do you stay to-night? They'll still be looking for you."

He grinned, but there didn't seem to be much amusement in him. He had been living on his nerves these past few days, despite all his show of boisterous unconcern, and now the effort was catching up with him. "Don't worry, chum. I shan't embarrass you by loading myself on you. You took the trouble to shove your neck out, come all the way down here——" He waved a hand, a gesture of thanks. "That's enough, Paul."

I didn't reply. I felt I should ask him to come home with me, but I knew how dangerous it would be. "We'll find you a place," Grimsby-Orr said. "In the meantime, I think you'd better get the finger out. The longer we stay here——"

Zaid said to the stranger, "I'll go with you. I can't go back to Beirut, not if the police are waiting for me." He looked at me pleadingly. "Paul, look after Lucille. Get her out of the country. Tell them she had nothing to do with what I've been doing——"

"I think they know that. They'll let her go, maybe even to-morrow. Or anyway soon. They aren't extremists here——" Then I remembered the extremists somewhere outside in the alleys of the town, waiting to kill him and Briggs. "I mean, the government. She'll be all right."

He nodded, worried but unable to do anything but rely on me. But he knew he could trust me; I loved her at least as much as he did. "Tell her I'll meet her in Paris." He looked at the stranger, said apologetically: "She wouldn't come to Tel Aviv. She wants to be neutral ——"

The word had a hollow ring in this room where everyone was so committed, even Grimsby-Orr and myself; even the baker and the boy were not neutral, not neutral enough to save them if the assassins burst in now.

"Come on!" I said impatiently, and turned towards the door leading out to the shop. And heard the bead curtains rustle.

The stranger and Grimsby-Orr, the two most experienced at this sort of thing, were the first to act. Grimsby-Orr slammed shut the door, grabbed a sack of flour; the stranger jumped to help him and between them they dumped it against the door. Then the baker came alive; he was a big man, accustomed to handling the sacks, and he flung them against the door in a fury of desperation. Someone was thumping against the door, but it was old and solid: for all I knew it might have once kept out both Saracens and Crusaders. The stranger took a quick look at the stack of sacks, like a tumble of grey boulders, nodded appreciatively, then led the way out through a door at the back of the room. As we went out, jostling each other in the narrow doorway, I smelled bread burning again in the beehive oven.

We were in a long narrow yard. There was no moon, but the high stone walls of the yard had a luminosity of their own, as if they had been coated with some sort of phosphorescent flour. A shed stood in one corner and I caught a glimpse of an old truck parked there. I stopped, trying to get my bearings in a place where I could expect no recognisable landmarks; even when Briggs and I had broken out of the prison camp we had known, from careful study of it at long range, the lay-out of the surrounding countryside. But I was lost here and abruptly I felt a sense of hopelessness. I might just as well turn back into the bakery and wait for the assassins. After all, they weren't after *me*.

Then sanity returned as quickly as it had left me: the killers, whoever they were, were not going to be selective about whom they killed in the next few minutes. "Paul!"

It was Briggs calling hoarsely to me. He had swung up on to the roof of the shed, crouched there waiting for me to follow him. I didn't even look to see where the others had gone. Briggs was the reason I was here; I had to stick close to him, otherwise my coming here was meaningless. I clambered up on to the hood of the truck, reached up, grabbed Briggs' hand and swung up on to the roof of the shed. I looked back for a moment and saw Grimsby-Orr and Zaid going out a gate at the far end of the yard. Then I followed Briggs off the shed roof, over a wall and on to the roof of the house next door. How we did not crash to the ground in the next few minutes is something I'll never know: there must be some Providence that guides the feet of infants, drunks and fools, especially diplomatic fools.

One roof led to another, some flat and smooth, some angled and slippery and uneven with tiles. We ran the length of an alley, slipping, sliding, jumping; once I fell to my knees, slid half-way down a tiled roof, saved myself only by grabbing at a television aerial. I patted the aerial, forgiving television for all the boredom it had given me, scrambled to my feet and went on running after Briggs. I dimly saw him hurdle a low parapet, then instantly a dark cloud exploded about him. I couldn't pull up; I went over the parapet and was hit in the face by a bird. They were pigeons: they rose up around us in a whirr of wings: it was like being caught in a cloud of smoke that had suddenly turned softly solid. For a second it was terrifying: wings beat against my face and I thought I was going to suffocate. Then the cloud had cleared, Briggs was picking himself up out of the wire netting cage he had demolished, and we were scrambling over the opposite parapet on to the next roof. Then we had come to the end of the alley.

Five men stood below us. None of them appeared to be armed, but they were not neutral bystanders. One of them suddenly pointed at us, rushed to the corner of the building and yelled back up the alley. The other men began to shout and a moment later stones began to whizz up over the edge of the roof.

But by then we had dropped down off the back edge of the roof and were in a garden. A fountain played somewhere; I could hear its tinkling even above the shouting out in the alley. This garden was, like the bakery yard, surrounded by a high wall; it was one of the surprises you occasionally find in an old *suq*, an oasis left over from better times. This house might be that of one of the bigger merchants; the garden was his retreat, maybe even his status symbol. The night was hot and I could now feel the sweat soaking me; but this dark, almost invisible garden was a haven of coolness. But there was no time to savour it.

Briggs had found a gate at the back of the garden. He wrenched it open and we were out in another alley, a lane so narrow that two men could barely pass abreast. We ran up it, stumbling now and again on the rough ground, hitting a wall and bounding off it, but never losing our feet. I was glad of all the ski-ing I had done in the mountains in the winter with Lucille, of all the tennis I had played with some of the teachers up at the university: what I had done for pleasure might now help to save my life. I was not exhausted, not yet, and I felt I could keep on running for as long as was necessary or till the assassins caught up with us.

But Briggs was gasping for breath, running flat-footed now. Once he stumbled and I thought he was going to go down; but he pulled himself up in time and kept running. We had almost reached the end of the narrow alley when the first man came around the corner. Briggs hit him on the run, his fist going ahead of him like a battering-ram. The man went down, grunting as Briggs trod on him and went over him. A second man came around the corner and Briggs hit him, too; but this man didn't go down at once. He grappled with Briggs, but he might have done better to have fallen over. Briggs hit him again and again, thumping at him savagely; the man let go, slid down, made a weak effort to hold Briggs by the legs, then let go. Briggs walked right over him and I followed.

We were in another alley, a short wide one. We turned left, ran up past some stores, through a tall arch and found ourselves in a broad courtyard. We were in a *khan*, one of the old inns built to house the caravans that used to follow the trade routes out of the desert and the mountains down to this seaport town. Covered galleries ran right around the courtyard, dark as tunnels. We followed one of them, heading for the open arch we could see at the other end of the courtyard. We had almost reached the end of the gallery when the men, half a dozen of them, came through the arch out of the *suq* behind us. They couldn't have seen us in the darkness of the gallery, but the sound of our running feet must have been amplified by the half-enclosed corridor. A shot rang out, then another and another. I stopped dead behind a pillar, pressing myself close against the cold rough stone. I had half-expected the hunters to show us no mercy when they caught us, but it had been a supposition: there was no proof they were going to kill us. But the bullets hitting the stonework were a reality: they were all the proof I needed.

Briggs was flattened against the pillar up ahead of me. I could only see the vague outline of him, but he looked ready to drop. "Look, Paul——" His breath was coming out of him in yelps, like a dog in pain. "Get out of here. I'll stay—I'm the one they want——"

"Balls." It wasn't diplomatic language, except perhaps in the naked upcountry of New Guinea. But I was feeling better; the resignation of a few minutes ago had disappeared. I was still scared, but now that something was happening the frustration of the past few days was rapidly wearing off. To try to survive is something constructive; to try and make someone else survive is even more so. I sprinted across the open space between the two pillars, flattened myself against him as two more shots ricocheted off the pillar I had just left. "We're getting out of this together. Nobody's going back this time—not like in Korea——"

Another shot rang out; a bullet hit the pillar behind us. We were pressed against each other like lovers; I felt rather than saw him turn his head. "Is that why you came down here?"

There was no way I could answer that; I am embarrassed by even honest sentiment. I just jerked his arm and took off at a run along the rest of the gallery; he hesitated a moment, then I heard his heavy footsteps pounding after me. There was a fusillade of shots, but we got safely through the far archway, swung right down a wide street, crossed it on the run and plunged into a dark cobbled lane.

Five minutes later we were out in the orange groves. We slowed down to a quick walk, gulping air into our aching lungs. I was distressed enough myself, but Briggs was much worse: his breathing was a series of loud whistling gasps, punctuated now and again by something like a moan. Once we came to a low wall and he could hardly lift his legs over it; I had to turn back and help him. Finally he stopped, leaned against a tree and gestured weakly at me.

"I'm buggered." Again it was *boogered*: Manchester was thick on his tongue. "Do what you like—I've got to take a breather——"

I was glad of the rest; and I wanted a chance to find out

where we were. These were not the orchards through which Grimsby-Orr and I had entered the town; they had been on the north side of town. But how far east or even south we were, I had no way of knowing. I was facing east and up on my right I could see the outline of some ruins; if that was the Castle of St. Louis, then we had to turn left to find Grimsby-Orr's car. Then I remembered: "You must have come down here by car. Where is it?"

"It's down on the quay by the harbour."

That was on the other side of town: we could forget it. "All we've got to do," I said, trying to sound confident, "is keep walking through these orchards till we hit the Beirut road. Then I'll know where we are."

"Then we'd better get cracking." Briggs took a huge breath, trying to get his lungs working properly again. "The buggers have got dogs out for us."

I heard them coming out of the alleys of the town, fierce baying that put an instant chill on the warm night air. "What the hell——?"

"Just like Pyongyang, eh? Remember the gooks and their dogs?"

"But that wouldn't have been the police chasing us just then—or the army. They would be the only ones with dogs——"

We had begun to move through the groves, moving fast but not running yet; Briggs had got his breath back, but not all his energy. "That was the PLA, I'll bet. That's who are after us—or after me. They sound like they've got a whole bloody company out after us. They're organised, they've got guns, dogs, the lot. They do a lot of their raiding down into Israel from here. It's supposed to come from Syria, but just as often they start out from here."

"What do the Lebanese do about it?"

"What can they do? They don't encourage them, like the Syrians do, but it's pretty bloody hard to stop them unless they catch them in the act."

"They're doing nothing to stop them now."

"They might be, for all we know. But by the time they do stop them, it might be too late——" The dogs were in the far end of the orchards now. "We'd better come to that Beirut road pretty bloody quick!"

We started running again, stumbling through the long grass between the trees, once or twice hearing fallen oranges pulp with a soft squish beneath our feet as we trod on them. I was wondering where Zaid, Grimsby-Orr and the stranger were; but there was no time to worry about them. Then I heard the burst of fire way over on our left; then a second and a third burst. I felt nothing, not even a stab of sickening despair for whoever had been caught in the firing. I was too intent on my own escape, running hard to avoid the bullets meant for me. To be afraid is to know the depth of your own selfishness; charity isn't a natural feeling when you're running for your life. If Zaid, Grimsby-Orr or the stranger had died then, I would only regret their deaths if I should survive myself.

The dogs didn't seem to be gaining on us, but neither were we gaining on them. The orchards seemed to stretch for miles; I began to wonder if we would ever run out from between the orange trees. The sweet smell seemed to thicken as I gasped air into my lungs; I was going to choke on the perfume of oranges. Sweat was pouring out of me now and I was becoming conscious of pain: aching ribs, skin torn off my shin, an ankle that had been twisted as we had run over the cobbles of an alley. And I was afraid, too: I was as conscious of that as much as of anything.

Suddenly I missed my footing, fell headlong into water. Panic swept through me as I went down; my face hit the water and I went under. I struggled frantically, afraid now of drowning; then abruptly sanity came back, I almost burst out laughing. I was on my knees in no more than three feet of water; Briggs was floundering beside me. We were in a shallow canal, a long straight channel about eight feet wide off which the narrow irrigation channels ran into the orange groves. We picked ourselves up, turned right and began to run through the water, following the canal. The bottom was rocky but somehow we kept our feet; it was hard work lifting our legs through the water but we kept going. Then we heard the men and dogs coming through the trees on our right.

We dropped flat, crawled to the far side of the canal, lay there with our heads just below the bank. The lower half of my face was below the water, my cheek pressed against the cold mud of the bank, a tuft of coarse grass hanging down like a bizarre wig over my head. I stared across the dark mirror of water, saw the five men, all carrying automatic weapons, come through the trees, one of them holding an Alsatian dog on a leash. The water was not cold, but I could feel a chill taking hold of me; and suddenly I had lived through all of this before. *The gooks were coming down the hill from the prison camp, the dogs sniffing and growling, and the chill of the Korean night had got into my bones, making them brittle and useless.* I felt Briggs move in the water beside me and I put out my hand and clutched his leg. Neither of us was going to go back this time.

The men stopped on the bank of the canal, no more than twenty feet from us. I could not see them clearly, but I didn't need to see their faces: their guns were enough identification, enough statement of their intention. They said nothing, their silence adding to the tense stillness of the night. An insect crawled out of the tuft of grass over my head, began to move, like a shifting, aggravating itch, through my hair. I tried to tighten my scalp, but already the skin was stretched tight over all my body. The insect crawled on, down the back of my neck, slid mercifully off me into the water.

The dog growled, sniffed along the edge of the bank; I waited for him to lift his head and bark at us. Something disturbed the water farther up the canal; an eddy swirled by, the water covering my nose. I held my breath, trying to keep the water from going up my nostrils; I could feel Briggs' leg trembling beneath my hand, as if he too was trying to hold back a sneeze or a gasp. The men stood there like statues, their silhouetted featureless heads turned straight towards us. I saw one man move slowly, the barrel of his gun coming round in an arc; it stopped, pointing straight at me, then moved on. Suddenly there was a burst of fire; I almost jumped out of the water. The bullets hit the water upstream, where the eddy had started; there was a scrambling sound, then some animal went yelping off through the groves. One of the men said something, the dog barked excitedly, then the group moved off up the canal. I raised my head and sucked in air, laying my head back against the cold, foul-smelling mud of the bank as against a soft welcome pillow.

Briggs stood up, reached down and pressed my shoulder. He whispered, "We're going to make it."

Ten minutes later we came out on to the Beirut road. We waited in the shadow of a medlar tree till a car passed, then we crossed the road and headed away from town. I knew where we were now. Five minutes later we came to the lane down which Grimsby-Orr had driven his car. We turned down it, moving cautiously now: the Palestinians might have discovered the car, be waiting there for us. The lane was silent but for the clicking of a cricket; Briggs and I moved noiselessly through the thick grass at the side of the dirt track. Then I saw the car up ahead, a man standing by it, a gun in his hand. I stopped, feeling every nerve in me open at its end. There was no going back; it was too late to make a dive for cover. The man turned round, the gun came up.

Then the man said, "I say, old man——"

I stumbled forward, laughing weakly. Grimsby-Orr dropped the stick that I had thought was a gun, swung open the door and pushed me and Briggs into the back of the car. Then he jumped into the front seat, started up the engine, somehow or other turned the car around in the narrow lane between the bordering stone walls, bounded it up the track and out on to the main road.

We turned north, heading for Beirut and safety.

2

"What happened to Zaid and the other guy?"

"Afraid they copped it. They died at once, that's the only comfort. Damned lucky I didn't get it myself. I got down below a wall a bit quicker than they did. Zaid fell on top of me, that's how I know he died right away. The baker and his boy got away, but I hope the poor devils have got somewhere to go. I should think he's finished in the bakery business in Sidon." He was driving fast, but not as furiously as when we had come down from Beirut. The adventure was over and now he was subdued, driving with what for him was sedate care. He said over his shoulder without looking around, "Why did you pick Sidon, Briggs?"

Briggs was lying back in the seat, a boneless heap. He

had been exhausted when he had got into the car, but that had been only physical; now he was stunned by emotional exhaustion, seemed drained of all those reserves that had kept him going in the past. Perhaps with the death of Zaid and the stranger he was at last looking at himself with no disguise; pain is an acid that can dissolve everything but the core of ourselves. The poets could no longer help him, nor all the lies. I felt a sudden deep pity for him, but pity wouldn't help him, either.

His voice was dead; even the Mancunian vowels seemed gone. "That was Perlmutter's idea——" So that was the stranger's name: a comic name for a man whose whole life had probably been one of drama and had ended on the predestined note of tragedy. "The baker was a Palestinian. Perlmutter had been coming backwards and forwards for years. But they must have got on to him, him and the baker, too. Or was it me they'd got on to?" He looked at me for an answer, but I had none. "I mean, was it just me they'd intended to get to-night or the whole lot of us?"

"Probably all of you," said Grimsby-Orr comfortingly, but his voice held no conviction.

I stared out at the night stretching away like a vast empty room on the seaward side of the road. The stars were out now, tiny holes in the ceiling of the room that hinted, but only hinted, of another world beyond the darkness. I thought of Lucille and wondered how I would tell her of her father's death.

"Why did you do it?" I said. "You and Zaid? Why the deal?"

Briggs didn't turn his head, still sat slumped in the seat. "I talked to him on the way down. Funnily enough, I don't think he was the usual sort of traitor. He didn't want either side to win. He told me that all he wanted was peace. He wasn't even acting for Israel because his wife had been a Jew—though maybe that started him off. All he was on was the side of peace."

"Buying planes and tanks?" I didn't mean to sound cynical, but I couldn't help it.

He looked sideways at me. "You blokes claim to be all for peace. But you've got the biggest army, navy and air force in the world."

"No bigger than the Russians."

"Another crowd that's always barracking for peace." He heaved himself up in the seat; some of the old energy began to move in him again. "Don't blame Zaid. He was as honest as anyone else here in the Middle East. He carried too big a handicap, that was all. He was an Arab who tried to be rational."

"And you? What made you switch?"

He grinned at me; he was recovering. "You're using the old needle a bit, aren't you?"

"I'd like to know, too," said Grimsby-Orr up front; I felt the car slow a little as his foot eased off the pedal. "You see, I happen to think the Arabs aren't the villains in this situation."

Briggs said cautiously, "You think the Israelis are?"

"No."

"Who, then?" But Grimsby-Orr didn't answer, and then Briggs went on: "No, I don't think they are, either. The Jews *or* the Arabs. I don't know if Israel should ever have been started in the first place, but now it's here it's a fact and it's got to be faced. And it's entitled to live. You don't kill an unwanted kid once it's been born, not if you have any claim to be civilised. I was on the Wogs' side to begin with——"

"Don't call them Wogs," said Grimsby-Orr coldly. "Some of my best friends are Arabs."

"Some of my best friends are Jews, but I still call them Yids. Names don't worry me." He grinned at me again. "I even have some Yank friends."

"Sometimes I wonder," I said.

He said nothing for a while, then he sighed and went on: "Well, as I said, I was on the Arabs' side to begin with. That is, if a bloke like me should be on *anyone's* side. But the more I dealt with them, the more I got fed up with them. They're all suspicious of each other, some of them even hate each other more than they hate the Jews. There was a joker from Damascus who'd sooner shoot King Hussein than take a potshot at Eshkol down in Tel Aviv." He looked at me again. "You met him, Colonel Marik. By the time I met him, I was just about to give up. Everyone wanted to buy for the Arab cause, but everyone wanted to be sure he was the one who got the planes and tanks, not some Arab neighbour. Then Zaid came good with an offer——"

"Did you know he was an Israeli agent?"

"He told me Friday night, when he took me around to that doctor's."

"He took a risk trusting you, didn't he?"

"The diamond game and the arms game are run the same way. On trust. He knew that."

Then we were coming into Beirut, up past the Pigeons' Grotto. The big hotels loomed up on our right; one or two of them had washed their windows with blue dye, ready for the black-out if it should be enforced. The cafés and bars were still lit, the tables crowded with men sitting over their *arak*, coffee, mineral water, their heads roped together by coils of smoke. From the outside, as we sped by in the old Morris Oxford, everything looked peaceful, routine, just as it had ever been. Perhaps this was all Zaid had been working for, the *status quo* of living in a rut.

"Where are you going after this?" I said.

"Famagusta," Briggs said.

"You'd still sell to the Israelis?"

"Why not? If this war scare dies down, how long do you think you or the Russians will keep up this moratorium on arms? Don't judge me now, Paul. Wait another twelve months, see how guilty I am then."

We swung down on to the curve of the Corniche. Grimsby-Orr said, "Where are you going to spend the night?"

"Anywhere. I'll find one of the small hotels, book in there."

"No, you won't," I said. "You'll come home with me."

Grimsby-Orr turned his head. "You think that's wise, Paul? Those fellers might still be upstairs with your girl, waiting for Zaid to come home."

"They won't hear me going into my apartment. And they'll be gone by morning." I glanced at Briggs. "I want your signature on that cheque you left me. You forgot to sign it."

He laughed, shaking his head. "Don't I beat the band? If ever I make my million, I'll never be able to hang on to it. I'll leave it lying around somewhere——" He pressed my arm. "Okay, Paul. I'll come home with you. And——" The car pulled up short of the Zaid house, Grimsby-Orr switched off the lights and engine at once. Briggs looked at Grimsby-Orr as the latter turned around, then he looked at me. "And thanks to both of you. I'm not such an ungrateful bugger I don't appreciate what you two did to-night. I hope I can do as much for you some day."

"You could forget all about selling those planes and tanks," Grimsby-Orr said.

I had already got out of the car. Briggs started to follow me, but stopped, looking from one to the other of us. Then he said, "I'll think about it."

"Will you let us know before you leave in the morning?"

"Yes."

"Can we trust you?"

"That's up to you. How much capacity for trust do you have?"

Grimsby-Orr considered a moment, then nodded. "Goodnight, Briggs. I'll see you at the airport to-morrow. Sleep well."

He started up the car and drove off, switching on his lights only when he had gone past the Zaid house. Briggs stared after the car. "Why didn't Whitehall ever trust blokes like him?"

I didn't answer. We walked along the sidewalk, past the garage and turned up the steps. The security men's car was still parked by the kerb. I looked up at the house and saw the lights still on in the upstairs apartment. In my mind I saw Lucille sitting there with Qassab and Abdurrahim, waiting in anguish for news of her father, waiting with equal anguish for my return. I couldn't go straight to bed. I had to go upstairs, tell her that I was home and that her father would never be home again. Qassab and Abdurrahim would take me up to the Ministry for questioning, but I could claim diplomatic immunity. I would be declared *persona non grata* first thing to-morrow, but I was already that. The Ambassador would just have another reason for getting me on a plane as quickly as possible.

"Take it easy," I said to Briggs.

We went up the steps between the dark oleanders. We reached the patio and I took my key from my pocket. Then I heard the hissed "That's him!" in Arabic; and the two men hurtled out of the shrubbery. For the second time that night I had the impression of *déjà vu*. I went down as the first man hit me; out of the corner of my eye I saw the second man drive the knife into Briggs. Then my head cracked against the ground and everything went black. I could not have been out for more than a few seconds, but when I sat up the two men were already plunging down the steps. I staggered to my feet, stumbled to the top of the steps, then pulled up. It was no use going after them. The light-coloured Volkswagen, the one I had seen two nights ago, had already pulled up and the two men were tumbling into it. Then it roared away along the sea-front, in the same direction it had taken the other night.

I turned back, crossed quickly to Briggs and knelt down beside him. His jacket was wide open and the front of his shirt was dark with blood. He lay on his back, staring up at me with eyes that were already beginning to lose their focus.

"Why?" His voice was just a rumble in his throat.

"Why what?"

"Why didn't you let them kill me down at Sidon? Why bring me all the way back here?"

"Doc, I didn't plan this! Christ Almighty, why would I do a thing like that to you?"

"Where did all your trust go, Paul?"

"Doc, I tell you I didn't know anything about this——"

But he just shook his head and died before I could tell him that the assassins, whoever they were, had mistaken him for Zaid, that it was Zaid they had meant to kill the other night.

CHAPTER 14

"I still can't believe it," Janet Ponder said. "I've been expecting it, but I still can't believe it. I've never been so close to a war before. Do you think the Israelis will bomb Beirut?"

When the phone had rung in my apartment this morning and Bill Lebow had said, "Get down here right away, Paul. The war's on. The Israelis have started bombing Egyptian airfields," I couldn't at first comprehend what he was saying. I hadn't really been asleep, yet neither was I fully awake. I lay in a stupor till Lebow's insistent, agitated voice made me sit up and mumble, "What's started?"

"The war, for God's sake! There's a meeting in fifteen minutes—move your ass!" When Bill Lebow started getting crude, it was time to move your ass. I fell out of bed on to legs that seemed like those of an old man, straightened up, shook my head to clear it and then everything came back with a sickening jolt.

I turned around as Lucille said, "What's the matter?"

We had spent the night together for the first time, but her dead father could not have objected. I had loved her throughout the night, but there had been no sex: it had been love compounded of comfort and pity. To love is partly to pity and last night we had been more united by pain than we ever had been by pleasure.

I had still been on my knees beside Briggs' body when she, Qassab and Abdurrahim had come downstairs, switching on the light in the patio. They must have heard the commotion of the attack, brief though it had been, or maybe Qassab had been watching for my return; I never bothered to find out. Lucille dropped down beside me, clutching at me, asking frantically if I was all right.

It had been an effort to get to my feet, to pull her up with me. At first I could say nothing to her, just hold her close to me. With a man, a friend, dead at my feet, how did I begin to tell her that her father was also dead, was lying somewhere in an orange grove outside Sidon with God knew how many bullets in him?

Then Qassab said, "Who is this man?"

"Briggs." I was shocked at how normal my voice sounded: it answered automatically, like one of those voices that tell you the time, the weather or that the number you have dialled has been changed: Briggs had died at 10.27 in fine weather at the wrong place. "He is English."

"Briggs?" Qassab looked down at the body with new interest. "Oh yes, we have heard of him. Who did this, Mr. Tancred?"

"I don't know."

"Were they robbers? Why did they kill him?"

Why complicate things still more? I thought. Qassab and Abdurrahim had come here to-night looking for Zaid because he was an Israeli agent, but someone must have had that information three nights ago. If they had not mistaken Briggs for Zaid, Briggs would still be alive and Qassab and Abdurrahim would be out now looking for Zaid's murderers. Or would they? Would they have closed the file on the traitor, glad to have let "Persons Unknown" dispose of the problem for them? Would they have wanted to go searching among all the Arab groups in Beirut? The Lebanese had their own diplomatic problems, their own dilemma of what constituted neutrality.

"I have no idea," I said, and Qassab nodded his head as if satisfied.

"I shall call the police," Abdurrahim said, and went back upstairs to the Zaid apartment.

"Did you go to church, Mr. Tancred?" Qassab said.

He was gazing steadily at me, and I realised he was much sharper and brighter than I had given him credit for. "No, I went down to Sidon. To bring back Zaid."

"Where is he?" Qassab said, and I felt Lucille's fingers clutch at me.

I felt the sobs starting in her even before I said, "He is dead. He and another man, one from over the border, were shot by the Palestinians."

"Are you sure it was the Palestinians, Mr. Tancred?"

I caught the warning in his voice: the case was closed, he was already retreating to a neutral position. "No," I said. "I'm not sure. It could have been anyone——"

Lucille was weeping silently, her face buried against my chest. I could only express my comfort through my hands and arms: I had no words for her. I held her tightly and looked at Qassab. "Will you want M'amselle Zaid again to-night?"

He hesitated, then shook his head. "I am taking your word for what you have said, Mr. Tancred. If it is true that Zaid is dead——"

"It is true."

"I shall talk to my superior, then. Perhaps he will think it best if no more questions are asked." He was still speaking slowly, doubly careful now that I should understand not only his Arabic but what he was also not putting into words. "But you must come to the Ministry if we send for you. We shall want a statement, just for the record. You understand, Mr. Tancred?"

Only too well, I thought; but just nodded.

Then I took Lucille inside, into my apartment, and five minutes later the police arrived with an ambulance. Hacobian was not with them, and I was glad of that: at least he was saved from involvement in the masque that now went on. I left Lucille in the apartment, went out to the patio and answered the questions put to me by the young officer in charge. They were questions that already had answers I was only expected to confirm.

"You were attacked by two robbers?"

"Yes."

"You would not recognise the men again if you saw them?"

"No."

"The dead man was just paying you a visit?"

"Yes."

"He was a visitor to this country with no relatives here?"

"Yes. No."

"Thank you, Mr. Tancred. We shall inform the British Embassy and they can contact his relatives in England. You don't have to worry about him any more."

They put Briggs on a stretcher and threw a blanket over him. I wanted to weep for him, but the tears wouldn't come. *You don't have to worry about him any more*, the police officer had said; but grief and regret are just as hard to bear as worry. What would be hardest to bear would be the memory of the hurt, bewildered look on his face as he had died. You can't plead your innocence to a dead man; he is beyond argument. It was no consolation to argue that a dead man can't take with him the pain he knew when he was alive, not even the pain of the last moment of living. Till I died myself, I would not know how much instant hell a man takes into eternity with him.

The small party went down the steps, the three policemen and the two ambulance men carrying the stretcher. A few people had gathered at the bottom of the steps, but these were not demonstrators, only the morbidly curious who have to look at the dead to enjoy their own existence. I watched them slide the stretcher into the ambulance; Briggs went out of my life as an anonymous blanket-covered heap; and then the tears came. I turned around and Qassab was standing behind me.

"I am sorry, Mr. Tancred." The toothbrush moustache quivered like a small mouse on the long blank face. Qassab was full of surprises: he was more than just sharp and clever, he could understand another man's tears. "To lose a friend is to lose a limb. May God comfort you."

Then he and Abdurrahim left and I went into my apartment. Lucille sat in a chair staring at the wall opposite. She looked up as I came in and said, "Have they all gone?"

It was as if I had just seen off the last of an evening's crowd of guests. "Yes," I said carefully, waiting for her to break down again.

"Then I'll go to bed." She stood up, smoothing out the creases in her skirt.

"Stay here." Then I added hastily, still careful not to crack the shell of her: "You can sleep in my bed. I'll stay out here."

She even managed to smile. "You don't have to be circumspect any more, *chéri*. Papa would understand." Then she came to me, put her arms round my neck. "It's as bad for you, isn't it? You'll miss Caradoc as much as I'll miss Papa."

"Yes." I kissed her softly; and that was all that was needed. She suddenly began to sob, the keening sobs that I had heard from Arab women, the harshest sound of grief I know. I held her to me, led her to the bedroom and we lay down fully clothed. The rest of the night seemed to take for ever to pass. Then it was morning and the phone had rung.

"What's the matter?" she said.

"The war has started. Israel is bombing Egypt. I've got to go down to the embassy." I went into the bathroom, splashed water in my face, combed my hair and came back into the bedroom. "Finish your packing. I'll see you're on a plane this morning."

She sat up, all at once tense. "I'm not ging, Paul—not if you're not——"

"I'll be going, too." I kissed her cheek. "In a matter of

days, as soon as I can get away. We'll talk about it on the way out to the airport. I'll call you from the office as soon as I know what plane you're on."

"What if the police won't let me go?"

"I think they'll let you go. They'd rather you went than stayed."

The Ambassador had exactly the same sentiments about me. "I've been given an advance hint, Paul. They have to make a gesture of some sort, so it looks as if the embassy is going to be downgraded to a legation. I'll be asked to leave and so will some of the staff. That relieves me of having to ask Washington to recall you." He took off his glasses, a spare pair, and put them on the desk in front of him. He looked tired but relieved, as if he would welcome the enforced vacation from being an Ambassador. "Why did you go down to Sidon, Paul? Why, for Pete's sake?"

We had had the meeting, a short busy one, then everyone had gone back to his office. Bredgar had nodded at me and I had stayed behind. He knew of Briggs' and Zaid's death; Ben Criska's contact must have been on the job early this morning. Nothing had been said at the meeting, but as soon as we were alone Bredgar had given me the facts as they had been given to him. They were true enough as facts; now he was asking for an interpretation of them. But that was more than I was prepared to give.

I said simply, "Briggs was a friend of mine, sir. He once saved my life in Korea. I owed him something."

He peered across at me short-sightedly, the look of a man trying to puzzle out what he had just been told. *He doesn't want to understand*, I thought, *he wants to be as neutral and uninvolved as all the rest of them*. But I had misjudged him. He put his glasses back on, said, "Where would you like to be posted, Paul? Sometimes they'll listen to an Ambassador's recommendation."

"Thank you, sir," I said, careful that my voice didn't break. "I think I'd like somewhere quiet, somewhere with no problems."

"I don't think that place exists for us Americans, Paul."

"Iceland, sir?"

He smiled. "I think that would be too cold for your girl-friend. Think of somewhere else. Ask her."

216

I stood up. "I'm only sorry I botched it here. It's going to be a long tough job for us, trying to get the Arabs to understand us. I just wish I knew what was the right way."

"Don't we all?" he said.

Then I went down to my office and Janet asked me if the Israelis would bomb Beirut.

"I don't think so, Janet. I think it's the Arabs we have to worry about from now on, not the Israelis." I looked out at the street below, thick with demonstrators. They had not been there when I arrived, but it hadn't taken long for them to gather. With no Israeli embassy to storm, they had to find another enemy; I wondered how large the crowd would be outside the British embassy. Our full Marines detachment was on duty, posted around the entrance and out in the compound in back. I could see the riot police, wearing helmets now, stationed outside the front gates. An armoured car stood at the corner, its young commander doing his best to hide the anxiety that must be tearing at him: he was not like the police, trained to use force against his own countrymen. "Are you going to leave us, Janet?"

"No, Mr. Tancred. Karl rang me this morning, said he could get me on a plane, but I said no. I think I ought to stay, don't you, Mr. Tancred? What would you do in my place?"

"I'm not in your place, Janet. I wish I were." She looked at me puzzled, but I didn't give her time to ask me any more awkward questions. I said, "Could Karl get someone on a plane for me?"

"Why, yes, I guess so. I could ask him." She picked up the phone, and asked for the Swissair number. "Who's it for, Mr. Tancred?"

"Miss Zaid. Miss Lucille Zaid."

I could feel Ruth Hacker gazing at me, but I didn't turn to face her: I had done all the answering I was going to do, I had had enough of trying to justify everything I did. Then Janet hung up, said, "The plane leaves in forty minutes. Karl will have the ticket for Miss Zaid out at the airport for her. The plane is going to Paris."

"Fine. Couldn't be better." That was to have been her destination if she and her father had made it out last night.

Then Ruth said, "When will *you* be going, Mr. Tancred?"

"Who said I was going?"

"Aren't you?"

She sat there in her invisible plastic bag, already beginning to enjoy the war. She would stay on, gaining in importance as the staff was reduced: duty is as much a vanity as anything else with some people and I could see now she had been waiting years for an opportunity like this. She despised all of us career men; we came and went, but it was the people like her who stayed on, kept the continuity, bore the ups and downs.

"That's up to the Lebanese." It was the best answer I could give her, but it was enough. She stared at me a moment longer, then began to put paper in her typewriter, careful to have the exact number of copies that Washington called for. The war must not be lost for lack of documentation.

"You better hurry, Mr. Tancred, otherwise Miss Zaid will miss the plane." Janet, too, began to fit paper into her typewriter, but she crumpled the carbon. She snatched the paper out of the roller and dropped it into her wastebasket. I had the feeling that somehow I had let her down, too.

2

The airport was a glass madhouse. I hustled Lucille through the thick swirl of people, found Janet's Karl, a tall good-looking blond who took charge with Swiss efficiency, working calmly as if this were no more than a holiday crowd of tourists; then Lucille and I retreated to a corner, stood there and tried to find words for our farewell. I saw Sandra Holden and waved, and she came across to us. I introduced her to Lucille and they nodded to each other, bleakly but not unsympathetically, each of them reminded again of her own loss by that of the other.

"I am sorry about Caradoc," Lucille said; I had told her about what I guessed Sandra felt for Briggs. "He was a nice man."

Sandra nodded. She was wearing dark glasses, but they didn't hide the fact that she had been weeping: the strain was there around her mouth. "I waited for him last night, didn't go out on the flight he'd booked for me. Then this morning Mr. Grimsby-Orr came to tell me. I suppose it was on the cards for him—Doc, I mean——" She stopped, and behind her glasses she must have blinked. Then she shook her head, made a gesture of resignation. "He once said he never wanted to grow old. Perhaps he wouldn't be so unhappy—I mean, if you can be anything after you're dead——"

"I don't think he would have minded growing old," I said. "Not if he could have been somewhere where all the world was green."

The dark glasses looked at me blankly, then the public address system called her name impatiently. She shook our hands, turned quickly and disappeared into the crowd; I had the impression that she had begun to weep again as she had turned away. I wondered where she was going, where she would finish up; not, I hoped, back at Aberystwyth or somewhere like it, among the second-rate comedians; she deserved better than that.

Lucille looked after her, then turned and looked up at me. "Where is the world all green?"

I bent and kissed her cheek. "Wherever you are." It was not much, but it was right for that moment: the words of farewell are so often trite. The public address system crackled again: passengers for Paris were to report at once. I took her arm and we moved through the frantic press of people to the gate. I held her tight, felt her teeth against my lips as I kissed her. Then she was going through the gate, looking back at me and saying something. All I caught in the noise was "—Paris," but it was enough. Where we should go after Paris was something for the future and the State Department to decide. Right now it was enough to know we had a rendezvous.

I went out of the terminal to the cab rank. I was blind, still only seeing Lucille, beautiful and sad, as she had disappeared through the gate. I bumped into a man and he turned round. It was Captain Hacobian.

"Just the man I want to see! You heard about Briggs, of course?"

He nodded. He was in uniform this morning, out of his Sunday best and back to his work clothes, his face stiff and blank under the peaked cap.

"Hacobian——" I felt in my pocket, took out Briggs' unsigned cheque. "I've taken your advice. I don't think it would be a good idea to take Ahmed's body out to his parents. Not to-day, especially." I had a spasm of guilt; I couldn't even keep faith with a simple boy who had done me no harm. "Mr. Briggs left some money and I'll give them some, too. Would you do me a favour? See they get the boy's body so they can bury it and tell them I'll have the money out to them by lunchtime." I would find someone to deliver it, perhaps Danny Nahmad. "I'd appreciate it, Hacobian."

He stared at me and for the first I saw the strain in his face, the muscles working beneath the smooth tanned skin. I also became aware of those around us, the silently watching cab drivers, one or two policemen, some soldiers. I felt the antagonism, even the hate, and suddenly I knew they were waiting for some gesture from Hacobian, the Armenian. *Oh, Christ*, I thought, *help him*; and waited in horror for the spittle in my face. But I had forgotten the dignity, the strength of the man. He leaned forward, said without moving his lips, "Forgive me, but I have to live here——" Then he turned on his heel and walked away.

The onlookers were disappointed, but he had made some gesture and they would have to accept it. Some of them sniggered and one man shouted in triumph, as if he had just seen his football team score a goal. I looked about for a way out of here. But none of these cab drivers would take me back to town, not even for a million lire tip: they had to make *their* gesture.

Then a voice said, "I say, old man——"; and there was Grimsby-Orr in the old Morris Oxford pulled up beside the rank of cabs. I pushed past the drivers, wrenched open the door of the Morris and scrambled in beside him. I was trembling with anger, shame and impotence; and with something else, nationalism. If they were going to make me a target because I was an American, then I wasn't going to hide myself. I turned to look back at the sullen, hate-filled faces, ready to shout defiance at them if only I could find the words.

Then I felt Grimsby-Orr's hand on my arm. "Simmer down, Paul."

He let in the gears, jerked the car away from the cab rank, rescued me from committing another blunder. He sped down the road out of the airport, swung into the wide road that led back towards Beirut. "They are as bewildered as you are, Paul. Give them time. They've been waiting years for this war and now they're not quite sure what they're expected to do. The Lebanese aren't like the other Arabs. They are practical, and that's the biggest handicap you can have in a holy war. Even the Crusaders discovered that."

I sat back, slowly regaining control of myself. "What about the other Arabs? Do we give them time, too, the impractical ones?"

"We have to. They've lived all their lives in a land of mirages. You can't blame a man if he's reluctant to give up the illusion for reality. America is for real, as you say, isn't it? Aren't there some people there who long for illusion?"

I thought of my mother and father, still looking back at the mirage of the past. "Yes, I guess so."

"Give the Arabs time, Paul. As your friend Briggs said, it depends on our capacity for trust. Ours and theirs." His foot eased on the accelerator; the car slowed. He drove in silence for a while, then he took his hand off the wheel, looked at it with that puzzled look of his, and said, "I'm sorry he died, Paul. I'm beginning to think he wasn't such a rogue, after all."

"No more than the rest of us," I said.

Helen MacInnes

'The queen of spy writers.' *Sunday Express*

ABOVE SUSPICION
ASSIGNMENT IN BRITTANY
THE UNCONQUERABLE
HORIZON
FRIENDS AND LOVERS
REST AND BE THANKFUL
NEITHER FIVE NOR THREE
I AND MY TRUE LOVE
PRAY FOR A BRAVE HEART
NORTH FROM ROME
DECISION AT DELPHI
THE VENETIAN AFFAIR
THE DOUBLE IMAGE
THE SALZBURG CONNECTION
MESSAGE FROM MALAGA
THE SNARE OF THE HUNTER
AGENT IN PLACE
PRELUDE TO TERROR
THE HIDDEN TARGET
CLOAK OF DARKNESS
RIDE A PALE HORSE

'Helen MacInnes is totally original. No one creates more realistic, more credible characters than she does.'
Alistair Maclean

'The hallmarks of a MacInnes novel of suspense are as individual and clearly stamped as a Hitchcock thriller.'
New York Times

'Helen MacInnes can hang her cloak and dagger right up there with Eric Ambler and Graham Greene.' *Newsweek*

FONTANA PAPERBACKS

Eric Ambler

The world of espionage and counter-espionage, of sudden violence and treacherous calm; of blackmailers, murderers, gun-runners – and none too virtuous heroes. This is the world of Eric Ambler.

'Unquestionably our best thriller writer.'
Graham Greene

'He is incapable of writing a dull paragraph.'
Sunday Times

'Eric Ambler is a master of his craft.'
Sunday Telegraph

THE MASK OF DIMITRIOS
THE SCHIRMER INHERITANCE
THE NIGHT-COMERS
THE CARE OF TIME
THE DARK FRONTIER
THE LEVANTER
SEND NO MORE ROSES
UNCOMMON DANGER
THE INTERCOM CONSPIRACY
UNCOMMON DANGER
DIRTY STORY
DR FRIGO
JUDGMENT ON DELTCHEV
PASSAGE OF ARMS

and others

FONTANA PAPERBACKS

Fontana Paperbacks: Fiction

Fontana is a leading paperback publisher of fiction. Below are some recent titles.

- ☐ ULTIMATE PRIZES Susan Howarth £3.99
- ☐ THE CLONING OF JOANNA MAY Fay Weldon £3.50
- ☐ HOME RUN Gerald Seymour £3.99
- ☐ HOT TYPE Kristy Daniels £3.99
- ☐ BLACK RAIN Masuji Ibuse £3.99
- ☐ HOSTAGE TOWER John Denis £2.99
- ☐ PHOTO FINISH Ngaio Marsh £2.99

You can buy Fontana paperbacks at your local bookshop or newsagent. Or you can order them from Fontana Paperbacks, Cash Sales Department, Box 29, Douglas, Isle of Man. Please send a cheque, postal or money order (not currency) worth the purchase price plus 22p per book for postage (maximum postage required is £3.00 for orders within the UK).

NAME (Block letters)_____

ADDRESS_____

_____

While every effort is made to keep prices low, it is sometimes necessary to increase them at short notice. Fontana Paperbacks reserve the right to show new retail prices on covers which may differ from those previously advertised in the text or elsewhere.